Re:ZeRo

-Starting Life in Another World-

"Sorry. Wait up for me until we're finished talking." Subaru stroked Rem's head to put her at ease.

Crusch

Anastasia

Emilia

Re:ZERO -Starting Life in Another World-

The only ability Subaru Natsuki gets when he's summoned to another world is
time travel via his own death. But to save her, he'll die as many times as it takes.

CONTENTS

Re:ZeRo

-Starting Life in Another World-

VOLUME 6

TAPPEI NAGATSUKI
ILLUSTRATION: SHINICHIROU OTSUKA

YEN
ON

NEW YORK

RE:ZERO Vol. 6
TAPPEI NAGATSUKI

Translation by Jeremiah Bourque
Cover art by Shinichirou Otsuka

This book is a work of fiction. Names, characters, places, and incidents are the product of
the author's imagination or are used fictitiously. Any resemblance to actual events, locales,
or persons, living or dead, is coincidental.

RE:ZERO KARA HAJIMERU ISEKAI SEIKATSU
© TAPPEI NAGATSUKI / Shinichirou Otsuka 2015
First published in Japan in 2015 by KADOKAWA CORPORATION, Tokyo.
English translation rights reserved by YEN PRESS, LLC under the license from
KADOKAWA CORPORATION, Tokyo, through Tuttle-Mori Agency, Inc., Tokyo.

English translation © 2018 by Yen Press, LLC

Yen On
1290 Avenue of the Americas
New York, NY 10104

Visit us at yenpress.com
facebook.com/yenpress
twitter.com/yenpress
yenpress.tumblr.com
instagram.com/yenpress

First Yen On Edition: February 2018

Yen On is an imprint of Yen Press, LLC.
The Yen On name and logo are trademarks of Yen Press, LLC.

The publisher is not responsible for websites (or their content) that are not owned
by the publisher.

Library of Congress Cataloging-in-Publication Data
Names: Nagatsuki, Tappei, 1987– author. | Otsuka, Shinichirou, illustrator. |
ZephyrRz, translator. | Bourque, Jeremiah, translator.
Title: Re:ZERO starting life in another world / Tappei Nagatsuki ; illustration by
Shinichirou Otsuka ; translation by ZephyrRz ; translation by Bourque, Jeremiah
Other titles: Re:ZERO kara hajimeru isekai seikatsu. English
Description: First Yen On edition. | New York, NY : Yen On, 2016– |
Audience: Ages 13 & up.
Identifiers: LCCN 2016031562 | ISBN 9780316315302 (v. 1 : pbk.) |
ISBN 9780316398374 (v. 2 : pbk.) | ISBN 9780316398404 (v. 3 : pbk.) |
ISBN 9780316398428 (v. 4 : pbk.) | ISBN 9780316398459 (v. 5 : pbk.) |
ISBN 9780316398473 (v. 6 : pbk.)
Subjects: | CYAC: Science fiction. | Time travel—Fiction.
Classification: LCC PZ7.1.N34 Re 2016 | DDC [Fic]—dc23
LC record available at https://lccn.loc.gov/2016031562

ISBNs: 978-0-316-39847-3 (paperback)
978-0-316-39848-0 (ebook)

1 3 5 7 9 10 8 6 4 2

LSC-C

Printed in the United States of America

CHAPTER 1
IMMATURE NEGOTIATIONS

1

Right now, the Return by Death phenomenon was on the third series of loops from Subaru's point of view.

The first set concerned the loops related to the badge-theft incident on the day of his summoning.

The second was centered around the demon beast attack on Roswaal Manor.

"This is the third one… I've died twice already, and what do I have to show for it?!"

In the previous loops, Subaru had pieced things together from information gleaned over several run-throughs of Return by Death, managing to break out of seemingly impossible situations. Yet this time, Subaru had blundered to his "death" not once but twice; he didn't even have the full picture of what had happened in each loop that led to his death.

But even with such paltry gains from Return by Death, he'd gained one, and only one, solid piece of information.

"Petelgeuse Romanée-Conti…!"

He, the commander of the oddballs in the Witch Cult, was the root cause of the entire tragedy that had befallen the village and mansion. Eradicating that abominable madman was now the driving force behind all of Subaru's actions.

To escape from the loop, he needed to cast a very wide net and dredge the depths of his memory.

—The hatred that Subaru had accrued from his first and second deaths stoked the flames of his bloodlust.

"First, I need to figure out how much time I actually have."

The Witch Cult raid on the mansion and village had taken place in the preceding half a day before Subaru had reached the village. Pathetic details of his second death aside, Subaru had arrived in the village at more or less the same time.

"Working backward from that, I have at most five d… No, four and a half days?"

Upon voicing the words, Subaru ground his teeth at just how little time it was. When considering how long it took to travel from the royal capital to the mansion, that didn't leave him more than two days. In that limited interval, he had to stop the Witch Cult—by wringing Petelgeuse's neck.

"I can cry about it later… Next is figuring out the victory condition for breaking out of these loops."

An absolutely unavoidable tragedy would unfold at the mansion and the village, and the Witch Cult was responsible. The only answer that Subaru could come up with in response to his current fate—

"I'm going to butcher Petelgeuse."

By putting an end to that crafty murderer, that madman, the root of all evil, everything could be saved.

And clearing that simple condition required an equally simple solution—in other words, power.

Subaru needed a group of his own to face the Witch Cult under Petelgeuse's command. When he considered that, the military might of the Emilia faction was actually quite meager. In the first place, Subaru had never seen a hint of private troops under the command of Roswaal.

Perhaps Roswaal himself was so powerful that he didn't need an army to defend his territory.

"Come to think of it, where the hell was Roswaal during the attack…?"

Subaru hadn't caught sight of him during his first or second time through the current series of loops. The magic user was gaudy in both appearance and fighting methods; if he'd fought seriously, there would have been clear evidence around the mansion. But no such signs were apparent.

"The Witch Cult attacks right when Roswaal's away? Or maybe Roswaal couldn't fight because he was assassinated out of the blue?"

If it was the latter, then the Witch Cult had been meticulous, and if it was the former, Roswaal had truly dropped the ball. Subaru could only sigh either way.

"…Besides, I still don't know anything about that monster that wrecked the mansion at the end of my second time around."

He recalled the sight of the four-legged beast he had caught a glimpse of right before his death, so massive that the creature could have been mistaken for a mansion itself. Its breath froze everything around it; no doubt Subaru had died from the freezing cold. If that monster was part of the Witch Cult's arsenal…

"I really don't have enough strength to put up a fight."

Barring his way were the Witch's disciples, Petelgeuse, and quite possibly that snow-breathing monster as well. The balance of power simply put Subaru at an overwhelming disadvantage. He needed a way to bolster his side.

—And Subaru knew just the place for that.

2

After dropping by the shops and stalls along Merchant's Street, running through the middle strata of the royal capital, Subaru and Rem arrived back at Crusch's mansion right on the cusp of evening. Holding each other's hands under a sky gradually becoming scarlet, they were greeted by Wilhelm at the front gate.

"I see you have returned."

The aged gentleman, dressed in long-sleeve, formal black clothing, narrowed his blue eyes as he saw the two of them nestled so close.

"Sir Subaru, I believe it is the nature of a boy to have a fickle heart, but as an individual, I cannot approve."

"What are you talkin' about, Wilhelm? I'm just holding Rem's hand so I don't get lost. Isn't that right, Rem?"

"Yes, of course it is. Subaru's sense of caution is rather lacking, so I would be too worried about what might happen were I to take my eyes and hands off him. Even when we were at the mansion, I couldn't let my guard down."

"Er, I think that might be overstating it just a little…"

Subaru and Rem lightheartedly responded to Wilhelm's remark. Subaru smiled weakly after hearing Rem's seemingly earnest reply as he shifted his gaze to the area in front of the mansion's entrance.

"Seems like someone's meeting with Crusch again?"

He was looking at the dragon carriage outside the iron-barred front gate as he posed the question.

The carriage lacked showy ornamentation but was still somewhat refined, no doubt to display the owner's status. Subaru saw that the red land dragon drawing it along had a very glossy-scaled hide. The driver, wearing formal clothes of his own, did not engage in pleasantries beyond a simple acknowledgment with his eyes.

"Correct. Now that she is participating in the royal selection, Lady Crusch cannot refuse those who request an audience with her. Of course, she invited some of them herself."

"Guess all sorts come out of the woodwork to meet with a potential future king. Well, I guess even people like that have their own problems…"

Wilhelm broke into a wan smile as Subaru briskly stated the facts. But then, the old man's face twitched. His blue eyes peered into Subaru's, seemingly searching for something.

"Sir Subaru. Have you had some change of heart while you were away?"

"Ehh? What is it all of a sudden? Did I become a lady-killer in the two or three hours I was gone?"

"You wear the visage of a man haunted by an ordeal…and one of no small consequence."

Subaru responded to the words with nonchalance, but his expression changed. It shifted from a vague smile to a "real" one.

"Oh, Wilhelm, you big kidder. What, you think I went through some kind of weird transformation?"

"It is difficult for me to call it a minor change. There must be a reason why there is now such a dark glint in your eyes— I understand better than most."

As the man nodded, Subaru realized that he had never taken a good look at Wilhelm's eyes. Wilhelm was an individual seething with hatred against someone for some unforgivable sin, which was no doubt why he had noticed the flames of hatred burning within Subaru.

"Are you…going to kick me out?"

"No. It is no doubt best to let you do what you wish, Sir Subaru. I much prefer you as you are now, rather than how you were but a short time ago."

The two exchanged dark smiles. Though neither shared what tormented him on the inside, they understood each other at least on the surface.

"Subaru. You are making a bad face."

"Hee-hee-hee… Er, ow, ow, ow! Hey, Rem! You'll tear it off…!"

The pair's excessively dark exchange was interrupted when Rem painfully pulled on Subaru's ear.

"Please do not give me reasons to worry."

"Hey, it's super rare for you to ask for something, but you're being way too vague. In any case, you can relax. I'll deal with everything from here on out, somehow."

Rem, unable to keep track of the conversation, had grown concerned. Subaru poured as much affection as he could into a smile.

Now that he knew what he needed to do, Subaru didn't feel apprehensive at all.

* * *

—After all, it was reassuring to know that the only thing he had to do was murder someone.

So Subaru wondered why Rem's face seemed even more concerned than before. Her eyes showed her hesitation, but just before she said something...

"It would appear that the guest will be taking his leave."

As Wilhelm murmured, a man exited the mansion's entry hall and began striding toward them. He was a tall man with long blond hair, clad in formal clothing with sophisticated trimmings. He was probably thirty years old, give or take. He had an air of capability about him.

The man casually acknowledged their gazes as he reached the front of the gate, touching the well-groomed beard on his chin.

"My, my. What unusual people."

The visitor's smile was warm, his manner of speaking was gentle, and he had a low, beautiful voice that seemed to naturally filter into people's minds. He gave them a friendly look, but Subaru did not recognize him. Naturally, this brought furrows to the young man's brow.

"Ahh, pardon my rudeness. I am called Russel Fellow. I hope we can see more of each other in the future...Subaru Natsuki."

"...Thank you kindly. Incidentally, how do you know my name? Someone give it to you? Anonymity is more my speed, so if my name gets around, I'll be too embarrassed to go about my business."

"Just a little something I heard through the grapevine. After all, you are a famous man who declared himself the knight of Lady Emilia, candidate at the royal selection conference. That being said, few are aware that this very person is currently staying at Lady Crusch's residence."

Subaru was guarded, but Russel displayed no ill will on his face. Even so, Subaru was cautious of what might be hidden in the reply. The man seemed to be intentionally engaging him in a verbal joust, which made it hard for Subaru to like him.

The atmosphere was steadily worsening when Wilhelm briskly interrupted with an aside.

"Mr. Russel. Did your meeting with Lady Crusch go well?"

Russel shrugged and shook his head.

"Unfortunately, no. Lady Crusch is a remarkably strict person. She turns rather sharp eyes toward us, as she is quite strict in her views. Judging from events to date, swaying her will not be easy."

"Is that so? How unfortunate. If you have not yielded, it will be difficult to make others agree."

"With a noble title and you on her side, I think it is the other candidates I should pity, Mr. Wilhelm... You call yourself Wilhelm Trias now, yes?"

Wilhelm nodded in response to Russel's words, lowering his deeply wrinkled face. "As I am now, nothing good will come from invoking the name of my wife's family."

"You are very strict as well, so much so that I am mightily impressed as someone who cannot live in the same fashion. That being said, allow me to cheer on your side."

The conversation, which was inscrutable from the outside, came to an end, and Russel walked to the dragon carriage in front of the gate. Then, just before climbing in, he looked back and said, "Should Lady Crusch succeed in her current endeavors, we would feel nothing but delight. It would help achieve your great ambition as well, Mr. Wilhelm. I have high hopes."

With that, Russel climbed aboard the dragon carriage. Wordlessly, the driver saluted and spurred the land dragon to a run. Like the man holding the reins, the land dragon was very unsociable and surprisingly silent as it galloped away.

Subaru watched the dragon carriage fade into the distance as he asked Wilhelm about the visitor.

"Wilhelm, who was that guy?"

"Russel Fellow, treasurer for the Merchant's Guild operating here in the royal capital. In name, he is a merchant like any other, but he is a crafty manipulator of both legitimate and unscrupulous movements of goods in the capital. It would be wise to assume he knows more about you than simply your name, Sir Subaru."

"Eww. It's downright creepy to have an older man interested in me instead of a girl."

"Mm, I share that sentiment. Now, then—"

After his response to Subaru's casual banter, Wilhelm turned to face them once more.

"Mr. Russel was the last visitor for today. I had thought to finally head in, but…did you have something you wished to discuss, Sir Subaru?"

Subaru scratched his face, feeling awkward about throwing off Wilhelm's plans. That said, beating around the bush wasn't going to help anything.

"Sorry, but I'm the last visitor for today. I want to have a talk with Crusch—the topic is…whether she could lend me a hand with something."

3

"That you are my final visitor for today is an amusing turn of events."

Heedless of the fact that her schedule had gone awry, Crusch responded with a good-humored smile.

Dressed in male attire, Crusch was sitting heavily in a chair in the reception room with her legs elegantly crossed. She stroked her deep-green hair, her amber eyes narrowing as her gaze pierced his chest.

Subaru thought her sharp look would have bowled over his old self in an instant. Now, with Rem at his side, he didn't feel nervous at all facing her like this.

In the meantime, Ferris stood behind Crusch, his feline ears twitching as he glared at Subaru in obvious dismay.

"Fortunately, there is a break in my schedule between now and supper. I am able to humor you without any issues until then."

"Since mew asked out of the blue, this is the only time she has available, *meow*. The depth of Lady Crusch's indulgence should make mew bow your head to the ground in gratitude, Subawuuu."

"Do not be concerned. I need no thanks nor groveling."

"Oh my, Lady Crusch. Your gallantry and generosity are making me fall for you even more… I'm in love!"

Ferris and Crusch engaged in their usual game where the master rebuked her servant for his attitude.

"Beating around the bush won't solve anything, and I don't think you like that stuff, anyway."

Subaru needed to be careful how he broached the topic, but a roundabout discussion would only draw Crusch's ire.

"You sought this audience. I shall let you start— What is it you want?"

She really did get right to the point.

Subaru licked his dry lips to moisten them, took a deep breath, and dived in.

"The Witch Cult or whatever it's called is planning to attack Roswaal's territory. I want you to lend me your strength so we can crush them."

Subaru cut right to the issue at hand: These were the conditions necessary for fulfilling his goal. He needed raw fighting power to oppose the Witch Cult. Without Roswaal to rely on, he had to go elsewhere, and Crusch was a good fit.

"I see. The Witch Cult, is it?"

Subaru's request garnered various reactions from the others in the reception room, but Crusch nodded. When her glossy lips turned up in a wry smile, Subaru was startled by this side of her he hadn't seen before. Her response had betrayed all of Subaru's expectations. But the fuse had already been lit. Subaru's heart beat hard and fast as he waited for Crusch's next action, when…

"What is the matter? I told you, this is your time to speak."

While Subaru hesitated, the thin smile remained on Crusch's face as she inclined her head. The unexpected remark threw him off somewhat.

"Er, I mean… It's as I said just now."

"Surely you do not intend to conclude with that request alone? What is your reason for asking this of me? What will come about as a result? What advantage would I gain from accepting your call for aid? One cannot dub this a negotiation when those things are not yet clear."

Urk. Subaru's voice caught. Crusch seemed turned off as she closed one of her eyes. From that gesture alone, Subaru knew just how impudent he had been.

"I suppose you're right about that. Sorry, that was rude of me. I mean, er, bear with me a little; I don't really have any experience with negotiations like this."

"It's only natural to acknowledge personal shortcomings. Do not worry. But this conversation lasts only until supper—keep this in mind."

Mentioning the time limit directly after a display of generosity plainly showed that she was employing both the carrot and the stick.

"First, the reason I'm asking for your help... Put simply, we don't have enough manpower, way too little to stand up against the number of Witch Cult attackers. As a result, we can't fend off the assault."

"A simple story. But is Lord Mathers not sufficient by himself? He may well be the strongest fighter out of anyone in Lugunica. The Witch Cult should be no match when relying on numbers alone."

"If they all gathered in one place, that might be the case, but it's not. There's only one of Roswaal, and they'll be attacking at least two places at once."

If nothing else, the village and the mansion were already two targets for certain.

He remembered hearing "sweeping clean" and the like multiple times. It was possible they'd assault even passing dragon carriages and traveling merchants.

"I see. I understand your position. However, is this not Lord Mathers neglecting his domain? The duty of a lord is to maintain his martial might to keep the peace. If his overconfidence has led him to be lax in these duties, his reputation as marquis will inevitably suffer."

"I can't disagree with a single word you said. Anyway, for those reasons, we don't have enough to deal with the Witch Cult. I want something to fight with, the power of numbers."

For the purpose of negotiations, Subaru concealed that Roswaal and the power he brought to the table might not even be present.

He glanced sideways at Wilhelm. If his request was accepted, Wilhelm was of course a part of Crusch's forces that he hoped to borrow. Perhaps understanding the meaning behind Subaru's gaze, Crusch exhaled as she seemed to sink into deep thought.

"The Witch Cult… They are finally making a move, I see…"

"Mm-hmm. Well, we figured as much when Lady Emilia, a half-elf, rose onto the stage…"

As Crusch murmured and Ferris agreed, master and servant nodding to each other, Subaru furrowed his brows. But before he could ask anything, Subaru shifted his focus to his side—where Rem, seated there, silently pursed her lips as fierce emotion poured out of her. The expression on her profile was intentionally blank, but her internal turmoil was obvious.

The Witch Cult, the object of Rem's hatred, was now Subaru's greatest enemy. He probably had the same look in his eyes as she did.

"Your circumstances are clear now. Next, I'll hear the reason for choosing to ask my house for aid…and your logic in doing so."

"I picked you and your people because you have the best chance of turning this thing around. Besides, you've given Rem and me your hospitality, and I think it's easier to work with you than the other candidates."

Subaru had expected this line of questioning, so he had an answer prepared.

Deep down, he believed there were others who were easier to deal with than Crusch. But Subaru's own sentiments, and the ease of contacting her at the moment, had led him to the current meeting.

"Easier to work with, you say."

"Yeah, that's right. That's why I wanted to come speak to you about th—"

"Subaru Natsuki, allow me to correct you about one thing."

As she received Subaru's reply, Crusch gave him a beaming smile, rich in meaning, as she raised a single finger.

"My hospitality for you as a host has engendered a misunderstanding. For this, I apologize."

"…What do you mean, a misunderstanding?"

"I am not treating you like an enemy. However, Emilia and I are already political rivals. Do you see? Emilia stands in opposition to me."

"Er, but you took us under your roof…"

"Because a contract had been formed. Your treatment is part of that agreement. Regardless of how I treat you in this mansion, it does not change our position as rivals beyond these doors."

Even the first time around, Crusch had declared that Subaru would be her enemy the moment the contract was over. It was both a sincere statement of fact and a declaration that it was useless to seek anything from her.

"In other words, there's no chance of joining forces with you?"

"That is a different matter altogether. As I said before, Subaru Natsuki, if there are to be negotiations, there must be acceptable benefits for both sides. Everything until now, including your motivations, have served only to clarify your premises. I merely wish to ask from your point of view what I stand to gain from lending you military strength. After all…"

At that point, Crusch's words trailed off. She put down an elbow, resting her chin against her palm.

"It could be said that no explanation was really necessary. Now that Emilia's lineage is common knowledge, we have been expecting the Witch Cult to make a move. Regardless of the circumstances, we were already sure of this."

Apparently, Crusch had never questioned that the Witch Cult would try something. Perhaps it could be called common knowledge peculiar to her world. Either way, it was working in Subaru's favor.

"That being the case, this negotiation hinges on mutual benefit. In your case, you would be able to borrow my house's might to eliminate the menace of the Witch Cult. What of my house, then? This is what I ask you."

"S-simply saving people isn't—"

"It would be ideal, in a sense, if that were reason enough for us to mobilize."

The gaze Crusch turned upon Subaru was like a blade, cutting apart the illusion in his reply as it aimed to inflict a mortal wound. Subaru desperately grasped for a comeback before he was shut down altogether.

"Ahh, right. For example, lending a hand in this time of crisis would mean that our camp would owe you a pretty big favor..."

"—Am I to take that to mean you understand that if I accept your proposal, it would entail Emilia's forfeiture in the royal selection?"

"Eh?"

The sharp thrust of her comment left Subaru's mouth hanging open.

"It is natural, yes? Throwing yourself at the mercy of another lord when your own territory is in danger is an issue of fitness for the throne. If someone cannot protect their subjects through the rule of law and strength of arms, how can they be expected to shoulder the burden of an entire kingdom? Subaru Natsuki. I shall correct you about one more thing."

Crusch pointed the tip of her finger toward Subaru, cowed into silence, as if ready to drive it through him.

"By conducting these negotiations, you bear Emilia's fate on your shoulders. Naturally, everything you say affects her, and it carries the same weight as Emilia's words. This is not a decision you should make lightly, nor are the words you say easily taken back."

"...Ah, uh..."

"Moreover, I ask again—should you owe me in this matter, it will mean the defeat of the Emilia camp. Are you truly fine with this?"

It was only at this moment that Subaru began to genuinely understand his position. They were not participating in a lighthearted after-school debate club where Subaru had no real responsibility to bear. Theirs was a great stage where a single statement could alter the fates of many people or even decide the direction the entire kingdom would take.

"But even so…"

Too late, he realized what a heavy burden he carried on his shoulders. But Subaru ground his teeth.

Just as Crusch said, borrowing her strength under the present terms meant that Emilia would lose her place in the royal selection—a failure from which there was no turning back. But if he didn't lean on Crusch's strength, all that awaited was the rampage of the Witch Cult's fanatics and tragedy.

Subaru's brain painfully creaked from the ceaseless back-and-forth of the scales in his head.

"—Still, I want you to help us."

"…Even if it means losing the royal selection?"

"It's better to be alive than not. If you die, that's the end of everything."

Subaru's shoulders fell as he replied, unable to conceal his dejection and despair at his own powerlessness.

If you die, then it's over.

The terrible spectacle of the ruined village, of Rem, who was sitting right beside him, meeting a cruel death—Subaru didn't have the courage to witness it again.

He lowered his head and swallowed the humiliation. It was necessary so he could at least save their lives.

"Understood. In that case, the House of Karsten shall not lend you any assistance whatsoever."

4

For an instant, Subaru froze, unable to process what had just been said to him.

"—Huh?"

It was less a word and more a sound of doubt that was also a simple indication of incomprehension. But Crusch brushed it off, crossing her slender legs.

"I repeat. Your request for my house to send aid to the Mathers domain—to lend military forces to Emilia—is hereby rejected."

Subaru gritted his teeth as Crusch spelled it out in terms he could understand. Feeling belittled by her composed statement, Subaru flew into a rage.

"Don't f—! Why are you…?!"

"First, the advantage to my side that you so bitterly conceded—Emilia's defeat in the royal selection—has no weight as a bargaining chip of use in these negotiations. Do you understand why?"

"Wh-what the hell? Kissing one of your rivals good-bye should be plenty worth it for you…"

"Do you realize what you have said? As far as Emilia's defeat is concerned, it will come about without any intervention on my part whatsoever."

"What are…"

…*you saying?* Subaru would have said, but then he realized it for himself.

"As you have stated, without aid, Emilia cannot protect the Mathers domain. Meaning, at this rate, and completely without my involvement, Emilia will be defeated in the royal selection."

"—"

"Indeed, were I to recklessly lend assistance, the knowledge I was involved in Emilia's defeat would itself become a problem with the other candidates. As you are aware, my house is currently the favorite to win this royal selection. If it became known that I booted another candidate from the contest, I could not fail to attract the enmity of all the others."

In other words, as long as she quietly watched, Crusch would gain the benefit Subaru had indicated with no harm to herself. There was no reason for her to court danger unnecessarily; it would be akin to snatching chestnuts out of a fire.

But that meant—

"You're going to let the people in Roswaal's…in that village be slaughtered by the Witch Cult's attack?!"

Subaru had shouted, but Crusch's icy gaze gave him pause.

"I shall correct your misunderstanding. And I am changing the subject, Subaru Natsuki."

"Ugh…!"

"It is Emilia's lack of power to protect her domain and Emilia's lack of ability that has invited disaster upon her populace, not mine."

Lack of power…lack of ability—the weight of those words shocked him.

Subaru felt a need to rail against Crusch's claims. And yet, the childish, emotional retorts welling up within him did not grant him the strength to refute Crusch's sound argument.

"It would seem you have said your piece."

Crusch checked the time, as indicated by the amber light of the magic time crystal above the reception room's door.

"It shall soon be Earth Time. Time for supper. All according to schedule, apparently."

Seeing Crusch about to rise from her seat, Subaru was suddenly stricken by nervousness as he called out, "W-wait!"

He raised his hand to stop Crusch from breaking off the conversation, desperately searching inside his head for some way to keep negotiations going.

"Y-you'll really abandon them? The folks in the village haven't done anything wrong! There's no reason for them to die!"

But the words that came out of Subaru's mouth were little more than a feeble attempt to appeal to another's charity. A faint look of disappointment entered Crusch's eyes as she listened to his immature reasoning.

"I told you. I am not the one whose strength is insufficient…"

"Don't you feel bad knowing and abandoning them anyway?! If you have the power to save them, why won't you?! What's wrong with helping people?! Because it's someone else's land, it's not your problem?!"

"Would you just shut up and listen a little—"

"It's fine, Ferris."

"But Lady Crusch! This time he's gone too far, *meow*!"

"He has bared his spirit. It does not sit well with my beliefs to withhold an answer."

Though Ferris howled in dismay, he quietly bowed to Crusch's command. Watching him from the corner of her eye, Crusch sat straighter in her chair. After taking a deep breath, she mulled over Subaru's statement.

"You ask is it wrong of me to overlook this, to allow them to die?"

"That's right! You're aiming to be king, right?! Carry the whole country on your back? What kind of king overlooks a whole village?!"

"I shall correct one misconception of yours."

Crusch raised a finger. Her gaze shot right through Subaru, seemingly reproaching him for his frivolousness.

"When I rejected your proposal, I stated one reason. I shall elucidate the other chief reason for my doubts."

Crusch had another reason for not being open to Subaru's proposal—the reason she was abandoning Emilia. And that was—

"And that is because I do not trust your story enough to order my house into action."

Her statement threw the premise of the entire meeting back at Subaru, stunning him.

"Wh…aa?"

"The Witch Cult? Yes, it's possible that they would make a move at this juncture. It would be consistent with their creed and their activities to date. I can make a deduction based on those factors. However, the problem lies elsewhere."

"Elsewhere…?"

"It is a simple matter. How is it that you can determine the exact place, date, and time of where they will strike next?"

Pointing her finger toward Subaru, Crusch's eyes and voice were like daggers.

"The Cult is absolutely inscrutable, to the point that its true nature is completely unknown. It's telling that their organization has survived for hundreds of years while evading destruction, causing immense damage in the meantime. So how exactly have you learned of their next vile act?"

"That's… But you never said a word of that before…!"

"I did not feel the need to be that explicit. Since you could not accept it, I pointed out the heart of the matter for you. If you still cannot, there is but one possibility."

In place of Subaru, cowed into silence, Crusch slowly spelled it out for him.

"Naturally, wouldn't you know about the Witch Cult if you were part of it?"

"Don't mess with—!"

This time, fierce, irrepressible emotion rushed to his throat to turn into a scream. But it stopped just on the verge of that, though not because of Subaru's self-control.

"—"

That reason was the increasingly ghastly aura rising from Rem as she silently watched the exchange between Crusch and Subaru.

"Lady Crusch, surely you jest."

Crusch tilted her head at the modesty of Rem's tone, no different from before.

"There is no way that Subaru could be part of the Witch Cult."

"Is that so? Judging by Subaru Natsuki's statement, if he cannot voice the reason he has such knowledge, I can reach no other conclusion. Have you not sensed for yourself why I say this?"

"—I have not."

No doubt Crusch detected the slight hesitation in her statement. Rem, who could sense the Witch's scent coming from Subaru, had been tripped up by Crusch's casual, leading question.

"At any rate. For both of these reasons, my house cannot lend Emilia aid due to insufficient trust. Moreover, you have not been granted the right to act as a negotiator in the first place, have you?"

"Ugh…"

"Earlier, I threatened you by stating that Emilia's advance or retreat rested upon your shoulders, but in truth, the problem precedes even that. At this juncture, you have no responsibility at all."

—He'd charged ahead alone, tried to protect things alone, and failed alone.

Crusch's words calmly tore into Subaru's bared heart.

"…As you are now, meekly remaining here under my protection, you possess no power that can move me."

"—!!"

Over and over again, her words crashed into him, exposing Subaru's helplessness, pressing onto him his ignorance, driving home his spinelessness, and mocking him for being senseless, rash, indiscreet, and ugly, with backhanded sympathy thrown in for good measure.

Subaru was overwhelmed by the realization that absolutely nothing had gone the way he wanted.

Had he made a mistake somewhere? He was only trying to do the right thing. Thinking himself correct, he believed someone would help him, and so he had searched, beseeched, and begged. Wasn't that what you were supposed to do?

"The Witch Cult is coming! They're going to slaughter everyone in the village…!"

Subaru pleaded with so much anger and sadness that he felt like his throat was about to burst.

He'd seen it. He'd felt each and every one of their deaths. All the precious people he cared about had turned to white crystal as everything in the world froze over.

If nothing was done, the heartless reality of the situation meant that it was certain. That tragedy would happen again.

Why can't anyone understand that?

Why won't people get out of my way and let me prevent such a terrible fate?

"Kill them…just kill them already! Don't you get it?! You can't let people like that live! Kill them! Help me, damn it…!!"

Subaru fell to his knees, prostrating himself as he earnestly implored her for assistance.

If he needed to put his forehead to the floor and beg, he would happily play the clown. As long as Crusch would lend her strength, he didn't mind being looked down upon or insulted. He'd even bark like a dog or cluck like a chicken. As long as his bloodlust could be sated, then—

"—So that is the true motive for your actions?"

But in the face of Subaru's sincere, unwavering, humiliating plea...

"You hate the Witch Cult. That's the reason you approached Emilia, is it not?"

—This woman of influence, who never made decisions based on her emotions, held not the slightest shred of pity.

5

Torn apart by her cold voice and gaze, Subaru was speechless, his shoulders trembling. Engulfed by a torrent of emotions, Subaru no longer knew whether he was feeling anger, sadness, or some strange mixture of the two.

"No... I—I just want to save everyone..."

Crusch's conclusion was off the mark.

The idea that he acted solely because of hatred for the Witch Cult was nothing more than a misunderstanding from an incomplete perspective.

Subaru's feelings were always rooted in trying to help others, weren't they?

And yet, he could not raise a single word in rebuttal.

"You cannot deceive others with the lies you tell yourself. Right now, the glint in your eyes can only be called bloodlust or madness. Have you not noticed, Subaru Natsuki?"

Crusch's gaze was both harsh and yet filled with something that resembled pity.

"They have been like that ever since the moment you returned to the mansion."

Her dry observation elicited a dramatic reaction from Subaru.

Unwittingly, he covered his eyes, as if to find out for himself that which he could not see, even though it only further proved that he could not refute Crusch's accusation.

"I do not know why you are so obsessed with the Witch Cult. The Cult has perverted the lives of many. Perhaps you are one among them. Perhaps your anger and hatred are entirely just. However, that is irrelevant in these negotiations."

"Even if—even if I hate the Witch Cult, so what? Th-they're the blight of this world. It'd be better if you just killed every last one of 'em. It's true, that's what I think, but it isn't a reason to break off negotiations and abandon people…!"

"Do not change the subject again, Subaru Natsuki. It's true; my suspicion that hatred is the reason for your conduct is unrelated to negotiations. More precisely, the fact that you are unfit to negotiate with me is of great import, for it brings into question the propriety of what you seek to discuss."

"What do you mean…unfit?"

Subaru, clenching his teeth to the point that they seeped blood, kept lobbing questions in an attempt to cling to something. The end of this conversation meant the end of negotiations. That was his pressing fear.

"If my hypothesis is correct, and the motivation for your actions is an unbridled loathing for the Witch Cult, then I can only wonder if you approached Emilia purely to use her as a stepping-stone in the first place."

"I…approach her…stepping-stone…?"

"It was clear that if Emilia participated in the royal selection and the circumstances of her birth were made public, the Witch Cult would predictably move according to its beliefs. If someone was hoping to catch the cultists under their thumb despite the fact that it was normally impossible to find even a trace of their activities, no other plan could have greater odds of success."

"You're saying I'm using Emilia as a pretense to get revenge?!"

Subaru pounded his fist into the table before him, raising a shout at the unbelievable accusation.

"Do you think your display just now and simply yelling 'no' can convince me…? Hatred shows clearly in your eyes, and bloodlust oozes from your every word, the sort that clings to a person so thickly and grows so hard, it can never be scraped away, let alone forgotten."

—*No! No, no, no, no!*

Crusch's statement did not capture Subaru's true character in the slightest.

"They're evil whether I hate them or not! You can't let people like that live! That's why we should kill them all! That'll save everyone! It'll help everybody! No one has to suffer—those bastards just need to die!!"

"I have told you already, Subaru Natsuki. If you do not even believe the lies you tell yourself, there is no chance they will deceive anyone else."

While Subaru breathed raggedly, his eyes bloodshot, Crusch refuted him in a hard voice. As Subaru's shoulders heaved, she looked up at him with narrowed eyes from her seat and spoke.

"Bereft of hatred, bloodlust, and bile toward the Witch Cult, your statements are unconvincing."

"Wh-why…?"

When Subaru spoke with a broken voice, Crusch looked at him with sympathy and pity in her eyes.

"Do you really not understand?"

However, Subaru's brows furrowed with perplexity at what Crusch was getting at. She lowered her eyes, unable to conceal her disappointment and dismay at his reaction.

"—You have not said, 'I want to save Emilia,' even once."

"…Huh?"

"You claim to want to save people, to protect people, smoothing things over on the surface while darker emotions boil up inside you. At the very least, it is inconsistent with what I saw of you in the throne room."

Unable to understand the meaning of Crusch's words, Subaru wavered, his gaze hollow.

—I wasn't thinking about saving Emilia?
"—"

It couldn't be true. Ever since he had been transported to this new world, from the first time she had saved his life, Subaru had lived for Emilia. His feelings were no different in the throne room, during the incident at the parade ground, or even during his negotiation with Crusch. If the situation was left to play out as it was, he'd lose her and the village. His actions were for the sake of saving them.

And absolutely, absolutely, absolutely not because hatred had seized his heart—

Abruptly, a voice struck Subaru, breaking the silence.

"I cannot permit you to advance any farther."

Subaru's mind was instantly jolted back to reality. In front of him was Wilhelm, standing straight. The elderly man had placed himself beside the table separating Subaru and Crusch with compassion on his deeply wrinkled face.

For some reason, that downward, tender gaze was really rubbing Subaru the wrong way.

Abruptly, something tugged on his sleeve.

"—Subaru."

Rem was grasping Subaru's sleeve, her eyes filled with sadness.

"Please calm down. Nothing will come of losing control here. And if you do, I won't be able to fight off Master Wilhelm."

"…Control? What are you talking about? I'd never do anything viole—"

"Wait, wait, wait. Then what do mew intend to do with that tablespoon you're squeezing so hard? Maybe your parents raised you badly, but that's not how you hold one, *meow*."

When Ferris pointed it out, Subaru realized for the first time that he was holding a tablespoon in his right hand—and that he was crudely gripping it backward, like he was going to stab someone with it.

—How… When did I…?

"Just like Rem pointed out, violence will get you nothing, *meow*. If you fly into a rage here, I'll just keep Rem occupied while Old Man Wil slices you in half."

"Moreover, I do not want to issue such a command. To do so after you have stayed here for several days would cause political problems, and I would rather not stain the carpet that my father sent me as a present."

In the face of Subaru's insolence, Crusch still behaved reservedly. This was at once a display of the greatness of her character and scorn for the powerlessness of Subaru, who had nothing to wield in anger save a tiny utensil.

All of it really rubbed him the wrong way.

But instead of an apology, dogged insistence came out of his mouth.

"...So you're not going to lend a hand, no matter what, then?"

"Correct. Your statements are not credible, nor does cooperating with you hold any attractiveness for my side. Accordingly, I shall observe from a distance."

"The Witch Cult...is coming. When they get here, they're going to kill all the people in that village. Knowing but not doing anything means it'll be your 'Sloth' that kills the village."

Subaru glared at Crusch, invoking the title of a certain despicable madman.

"Quite arrogantly put. Consequently, there is one more thing for me to add."

While Subaru gave her a filthy look, Crusch stood up, staring straight back into his eyes.

"I am able to largely discern whether a person is lying. I can boast that, since far back, I have never once been cheated in negotiations."

Suddenly, Crusch began to speak on a different topic. She continued to peer into Subaru's eyes as they clouded with doubt.

"If my experience is anything to judge by, what you speak are not lies."

"Th-then...!"

"You wholly believe that your assertions are the truth, and therefore, they are not lies to you. Those in such a state are called madmen, Subaru Natsuki."

It was then and there that Subaru clearly understood that negotiations had failed.

"—!"

Continuous clenching of his teeth had cut the edge of his lip, sending blood dribbling down his jaw. Crusch narrowed her eyes as she watched the painful image.

"Ferris, go ahead and heal him."

"I don't need it!"

Before Ferris could move a muscle, Subaru rejected the offer and stood, practically leaping from his chair.

"Suppertime is here. Will you not be joining us?"

"You wouldn't want to eat at the same table as a madman, would you? No matter how eccentric your taste or style might be, that'd be a bit too far even for you."

Subaru replied to sarcasm with sarcasm as he reached for the reception room door. Following suit, Rem stood at attention and politely bowed to Crusch.

"It has been a short time, but thank you for the hospitality. On behalf of my master, I offer my thanks."

"So this is your…no, Marquis Mathers's reply?"

"Yes. He instructed me to respect Subaru's wishes in all things."

Subaru couldn't see Crusch's expression during the incomprehensible exchange, but Crusch's voice seemed to bear no small amount of regret as Rem stated her farewells.

Whatever she felt, it was clearly not the coldness she'd shown to Subaru, and it was infuriating him.

"Rem, let's go."

Picking up the pace, Subaru called out to Rem and opened the door.

"Have you anywhere else to turn to?"

"Make sure you become a good king, okay? The despotic type that tosses aside the weak."

Spitting out his reply without turning around, Subaru slammed the door shut.

And thus, in pathetic fashion, the curtain lowered on the negotiations.

6

It was well into the evening when Subaru bolted out into the Nobles' District after negotiations had broken down.

The sun had already dipped low in the west. The aura of night was slowly creeping over the world. With the light of the crystal lamps lining the road shining down upon him, Subaru leaned back against an iron fence, spitting out curses.

"Shit. One thing after another..."

The exchange with Crusch rose in the back of his mind—and with it, the humiliation he had suffered.

"Those know-nothings... Why don't they understand I'm doing the right thing...?!"

The swirling vortex inside his chest was emotion close to hatred toward the woman who had impeded his path.

Things had turned out this way because she hadn't seen for herself that tragedy or the laughter of that cruel, conniving madman. It was because she had not heard it. She hadn't experienced it for herself, so she didn't understand: They were beasts and could not be suffered to live.

"Fine. Fine already. My messing up, people with no feelings, gotta forget all that. Right now I need to focus more on what's in front of me...!"

Rather than stand still and mope, the right choice was to move forward, one small step at a time. After all, to Subaru, with so few cards to play, time was a precious thing.

"Sorry to keep you waiting, Subaru."

While Subaru tapped a foot in annoyance, Rem passed through the gate, returning to her spot beside him. She was carrying the luggage they had brought with them to the Crusch residence, neatly packed up and ready to go. After Subaru's caustic outburst and furious exit, he had been waiting while Rem went to gather their things.

"...Sorry. Gimme the luggage; I'll haul it."

"It is fine. The bags are not heavy, and you are still recovering, Subaru."

Rem politely declined Subaru's offer and hefted the luggage in her arms. Normally, Subaru would have insisted, but with his mental resources otherwise occupied, he did not dwell on the matter.

"Come to think of it, you weren't opposed to leaving, were you, Rem?"

"Correct. It was your choice, Subaru."

"Well, after all that, I can't exactly come crawling back for more healing. Whatever Emilia bargained for it, I feel bad for her."

Emilia had tendered something to pave the way for Subaru's medical treatments. Subaru had distinct feelings of guilt on multiple levels for wasting her kindness again.

But Subaru was sure it'd be all right. Once he rescued her from this crisis, they'd be able to make up, so she'd probably forgive this, too.

To that end, among other things, Petelgeuse had to die.

"Subaru. About the…negotiations with Lady Crusch…"

"She made a big deal about trustworthiness, benefits, and other pointless crap. No shred of human decency in her. How can anyone put up with that high-and-mighty attitude—?"

Subaru interrupted Rem with his curses, cutting off her attempt to raise the subject. Perhaps she sensed his desire to not revisit the matter, because she brought up something else.

"What will we do now, Subaru? If what you say is true, there is not a single moment to lose."

"If?"

"…There is not a single moment to lose. Will we be returning to Master Roswaal's mansion?"

Subaru interjected about a part of her line that bugged him, but Rem didn't bite. Subaru shook his head in response to her latter question.

"Nah. Right now, if it's just us heading back, there's not a whole lot we can do. We've gotta go with a big enough crew to put up a decent fight. And if we can't do that, we need to find another way somehow."

If only Subaru and Rem showed up to help, it would result in a repeat of what had come before. Yes, if they departed sooner than previous times, there was a chance they could make it back to the mansion safely without encountering the Witch Cult. But it would probably be very difficult repelling the Cult with nothing but the resources the mansion had on hand.

"We just don't have the numbers. What the hell has Roswaal been up to...?"

By himself, Roswaal was powerful enough that they might be able to send the Cult packing. So what was that court magician doing at the very moment they needed him most...?

"Subaru. Actually, in regards to Master Roswaal... There is a very high chance he will be absent from the mansion for several days."

"—?! You knew? So Roswaal not being at the mansion was preplanned?"

"Master Roswaal was to visit Garfiel's... Er, the place of an important individual within the dominion, and he planned to stay there for several days."

"Shit, his timing sucks! So that's why they can't repel the attack!"

Rem's answer bolstered Subaru's concerns, and he clawed at his head as he spat his frustrations like a curse. Now that Roswaal, their greatest weapon, could not be relied on, his earlier estimate rang true: They were at an overwhelming disadvantage. Subaru and Rem turning back early wouldn't make any difference.

"Looks like I was right. I've gotta bring the cavalry with me somehow..."

Subaru, revisiting his first conclusion with renewed confidence, nodded to Rem, who watched him all the while. The objective was set, but time was short. If he wanted to at least do better than the previous two loops, he had to leave the royal capital the following day. Considering that night was falling, this left him with about half a day to work with.

"Anyway, we've got no choice but to look for help from someone else. Rem, how well do you know the layout of the capital?"

"Fairly well, since I have come here several times before and spent quite a bit of time looking around with you over the past few days... But who?"

"First, let's find an inn. The rest comes after that. At the latest, we need to leave the capital tomorrow or we won't make it in time. Anyway...I'll think about everything after that."

Subaru bluntly told Rem that they had to prepare to the greatest extent possible. Seeing out of the corner of his eye that Rem had quietly accepted his plan, Subaru looked up at the sky without another word.

From the other side, darkness was creeping across the sky above the capital. It felt like it was an ill omen.

The shadow moved eerily and sluggishly, as if implying storm clouds were gathering along Subaru's path...

CHAPTER 2
A PIG'S GREED

1

"—I may not look it, but I am a surprisingly avid reader."

The girl who spoke was sitting in an extravagant chair, resting one elbow upon it. She was flipping through an exquisitely bound book in her other arm, already perusing the latter half, and the sight made her seem different from the girl Subaru remembered.

She wore a long-sleeve red nightgown similar to a negligee with an identically colored cape draped over her shoulders. Her voluptuous body was plain to see in her outfit, but the girl showed no outward sign of concern that a man was present.

The girl was so natural, completely immersed in her book, that it was easy to forget she was in the middle of receiving a guest.

"—"

Subaru felt himself unintentionally taken in by the solemnity of her gestures. Her graceful white fingertip traced the characters as her eyes passed over them. The young man felt like he could watch her all day. Perhaps it was because this unknown side of the girl before him had enchanted him.

"—"

As Subaru stepped on the carpeted floor in his sneakers, he felt unsure of what to do now that he'd been ignored. He was wondering if he was permitted to enter, but the lady of the household was not paying him any attention. When he'd tried to forcefully begin a conversation, she'd rebuffed him at the first word.

Surely she wasn't telling him to wait until she finished reading her book...

"That's excessive no matter how you cut it..."

Though he tried to deny his unease, seeing her leisurely turn the pages made that difficult. In point of fact, Subaru knew that the girl's personality was not incompatible with such irrationality.

Her hair was orange, reminiscent of the sun; her eyes were crimson, like a fire that would scorch away everything it touched. She had glossy white skin and a striking feminine figure. The thick perfume wafting around her was like poison. It was difficult for the word *beautiful* to sufficiently capture the sight of her as she silently examined her book.

How much favor must the heavens have shown her for her to be loved by all?

—Her name was Priscilla Bariel.

She was one of the candidates for the royal selection, as well as the next prospective cooperator Subaru sought an audience with.

2

Subaru's shoulders sank when he learned Reinhard was absent from the royal capital—a fact he'd confirmed after departing from the Crusch compound and while Rem was securing an inn. Reinhard was the last one Subaru had hoped to rely on.

An elderly couple inhabited the villa in the capital set aside for the Astrea family and had been charged with its care. When Subaru arrived without any forewarning, the two had welcomed him in and lent an ear to his request, but...

"The young master returned to the main household with his liege, Lady Felt, and her family some two days ago. We can offer contact with him from our side, but..."

Just as he'd mentioned during his visit to the Crusch residence,

Reinhard had left. Even though he remembered what Reinhard had said, Subaru had still clung to a slender thread of hope, but his pleas went unanswered.

Even if he could reach Reinhard somehow, the distance from the royal capital to the main household of the Astrea family, and from there, the distance to the Mathers lands, was fatal. The odds of him joining their forces in time were despairingly low.

Subaru said his farewells to the elderly couple. Then, once he was out of sight of the mansion, he clutched his head.

"Roswaal and Reinhard are seriously useless, and right when I really need 'em, too…!"

This time, everything was going wrong. One prospective collaborator fell through after another, leaving Subaru truly at the end of his rope.

If only his Return by Death restore point brought him back to the night when he'd parted ways with Reinhard—

"If you don't have it, you don't have it… Think, think, think, think. I don't have strength, numbers, time—anything. Racking my brain is the only thing I can do."

Desperately turning the gears in his head, Subaru earnestly fought to come up with the next best plan of action.

Now that he'd scratched Crusch and Reinhard off the list, Subaru had scant few cards left in his hand to pick from. Considering the circumstances, pleading with the Knights of the kingdom would no doubt produce the same results as his negotiation with Crusch. Besides, Subaru felt nothing but mistrust toward them.

—At the very least, now that Crusch, someone he thought he had a good relationship with, had abandoned him, a storm of paranoia toward others brewed inside Subaru.

Not even realizing how this was narrowing his already limited options, Subaru could think of only two other people. However, one meant bowing his head to "The Finest of Knights," someone he hated more than the Knights in general, which was unthinkable.

That left Subaru with a single candidate.

Rem caught up finally. Seeing Subaru deep in thought, she called out to him.

"Subaru, what should we do now? I—"

"It's all right. Leave it to me. You don't have to do anything. Don't...do anything. Just stay right behind me. That's enough."

After that interruption, Rem turned a frail smile toward Subaru as he continued thinking to himself.

—*I absolutely have to stop Rem from bearing the brunt of everything.*

Subaru knew that if it was to save him, Rem wouldn't hesitate to hurl herself at danger and cast her life away. He had to protect her, no matter what.

Subaru was certain that she was emotionally dependent on him, and it was his duty to save her.

Whatever might happen, he had to avoid losing her. There was no other option. If he couldn't protect Rem, saving Emilia and the villagers would lose all meaning. Even indulging his hatred of Petelgeuse would be—

"Wait, that's..."

Subaru touched his temple as an exceedingly violent thought instantly came to mind.

Just then, it had almost seemed as if eliminating Petelgeuse was a higher priority than saving Emilia and the others. Wasn't that exactly the thing Crusch had pointed out earlier...?

"It's all right. Everything's all right. I'll...get this right. I'm gonna do it. I...gotta do it."

Subaru reassured himself, seemingly speaking for his own benefit. He ruminated on those words and pretended he had noticed nothing, as if he were putting a lid on top of a bottomless pit.

This was the only way Subaru Natsuki could maintain his own sanity.

3

The next morning, as dawn broke, the two returned to the Nobles' District to follow the slender thread that bore Subaru's remaining hopes.

*   *   *

The Nobles' District on the upper section of the royal capital was lined with dazzling buildings. The showy facade of the stately mansion Subaru and Rem arrived at did not betray their expectations.

No, it was more appropriate to say that it was showier and more extravagant than they had imagined.

"No need to ask around for who this belongs to. I can't imagine anyone would have a hard time figuring out the owner of this place…"

Subaru was nonplussed. The sight of the luxurious mansion was not one he'd soon forget, even from afar. The roof was painted over with gold that cast the light of the morning sun in all directions, while a number of intricate images had been engraved into the walls. As far as he could see, there were even reliefs adorning the windows, and a number of statues he could only call avant-garde art dotted the courtyard.

The home was an acute reflection of the tastes of a big spender. Subaru couldn't help a dry smile when he considered how the spectacle so aggressively asserted the owner's will.

As Subaru was rooted to the spot in front of the gates, Rem stood beside him with a dumbfounded expression on her face for once. If the point of the building's outward appearance was to give guests a shock, it had accomplished its goal ten times over.

"You're not gonna tell me this was the previous owner's style, are you? I feel sorry for him."

"Ahhhh, well actually this is the Princess's tastes at work. It was a pretty extreme makeover, you know? I sympathize with the folks who worked straight through the night, but she slapped their cheeks with sacks of gold coins so they couldn't complain."

"Hey, that's completely different from slapping people around with a wad of bills. Whacking people with a bag of coins would totally count as actual violence."

The man standing on the other side of the gate laughed at Subaru's joke. The man slid his thick fingers into the gap between his black helmet and his neck and scratched.

Below his pitch-black full helm, the gateman was dressed roughly, like some kind of bandit. Though he made for an odd sight in general, what stood out most had to be the fact that he was missing his left arm from the shoulder down.

This casual one-armed man who concealed his face named Al served as the retainer of the woman Subaru had come to see. Calling himself a mercenary, he was similar to Subaru, summoned from the same world. That was the basis for the strange rapport between them, as well as the reason for Al's friendliness upon their early morning visit.

"So what are you doing out here at a time like this? As you can see, I have low blood pressure, so I'm seriously not a morning person. If you're inviting me to go hunting for a bite or something, I might not be completely up for it."

"Nothing so tame as a family restaurant. Today, I'm here to speak with your Princess."

"Princess…?"

Unable to see the expression behind the helmet, he had no idea how Al was looking at him at that moment. An unpleasant pause followed as the one-armed man seemed to mull it over.

"Well, I did get to recharge my supply of maid energy, so I guess I can take a message."

"That was more meaningless than I expected. Besides, it's not like you don't have any maids in this mansion, right?"

"Hey now, you don't understand Princess. You think we can have maids waltzing around when Princess thinks she's the cutest in the whole world? The only thing we have in the mansion is a cute young butler."

"My fault for asking… It might lower the value some, but yeah, can you pass on a message for starters?"

"Sure thing," answered Al in a casual voice, leisurely vanishing back inside the mansion.

Rem, standing to the side and a single step behind him, maintained her silence as her neutral expression tightened. But through her fingertips, lightly grasping his sleeve, he could sense the worry she couldn't hide. Subaru wanted to wipe away her concerns, but that wasn't possible when he harbored the same ones.

"Well, it is ridiculously early in the morning… In that girl's case, I'd expect her to say something like, 'You are interfering with my precious time for slee—'"

"Hey, you can come in and meet her!"

Al poked his head out from the mansion's entrance, his laid-back voice interrupting Subaru's barb.

For a moment, Subaru was taken aback at the unexpected speed of the reply.

"I-isn't it insanely early, though?"

"You wouldn't expect it, but Princess is one hell of a morning person. The flip side is that she goes to bed really early at night. Either way, come on in."

Al laughed at Subaru's hesitation and invited them inside with a carefree demeanor. As they followed behind him, it soon became clear that the building's interior was similarly intense to the exterior.

Even an untrained eye could tell. Expensive-looking fixtures and pieces of art were on display in the corridor, almost to the point of impeding movement. The apparently compulsive need to adorn even lamps and picture frames with gold felt like a form of insanity.

"I suppose it's all a little blinding at first, but you get used to it. It's not as bad in the morning like this, but the halls are seriously scary at night."

"I'm not a little kid, so you don't have to tell me the halls are scary at night. What kind of adult are you?"

"The eyes of the statues glow."

"Your master's messed up in the head."

When Subaru examined the statues lining the hallway more closely, he noticed they had something like gemstones embedded in their eye sockets. They probably would glow when it got dark. Both purchaser and designer had a screw loose.

Rem followed behind both of them, and he could hear noises coming from her nose every so often. Rem had a keen sense of smell, and she'd apparently picked up some kind of unsavory scent, staring at the back of the iron helm as they walked along.

The trek of the mismatched trio soon came to an end.

"Princess is in the top room up there. The whole floor's one really decked-out room."

"Sounds kinda like a hotel suite. Can we go in?"

"Well, *you* can, bro."

Al's reply contained a clear implication when he approached the stairs and indicated the floor above with his thumb. At the unsettling undertone, Subaru shifted a guarded look his way.

"Hey now, I'm not saying it to be mean. Princess said she'd only meet with you. The young lady'll be escorted to the guest room."

"You think I'll just hand her over when you were talking about recharging your maid energy earlier…?"

"You got me there, but don't worry, I'll be waiting right here in front of Princess's room. It's a pity, but I'll leave escorting the young lady to my senior, Schult."

Anticipating Subaru's concerns, Al's voice suggested he was barely restraining his laughter when he snapped his fingers. Immediately, a young man with curly pink hair and red eyes appeared. The only words Subaru could think of to capture the youth's essence were *pretty boy*. His small frame was dressed in a butler's outfit, while his face showed a stern, fervent devotion to his duties, but somehow, he gave off the impression of a pervert.

"Take good care of our guest, now."

"Yes, leave it to me."

When Al gave the youth a pat on the shoulder, the pretty-boy butler offered a formal reply and proceeded to escort Rem. Instantly, she glanced back at Subaru, seemingly at a loss.

"Sorry. Wait up for me until we're finished talking. All the dangerous people in this mansion, Helmet Guy included, are gonna be on the top floor, so just relax and wait up."

"That's harsh, bro, making me out to be some suspicious guy. Though intruders do say that about me pretty often."

Subaru ignored Al's peevish reply and stroked Rem's head to put her at ease. Rem almost closed her eyes like she was ticklish, bowing her head as she resigned herself to the inevitable.

Afterward, she gently drew close to him and whispered an additional word of caution.

"Understood—please be especially wary of that person."

Rem's eyes looked at Al for only a single moment. Apparently, he'd really set off her alarms.

"Mm, got it."

Though Subaru truly wanted to believe in his amiable compatriot, Rem's appraisal of his trustworthiness was more natural. Considering the back-and-forth at the Crusch residence, it was best to regard Priscilla's people as opponents as well.

Subaru nodded and smiled. The pretty-boy butler led Rem along, vanishing down a corridor.

"Phew. Not bad, bro. I see she's really sweet on you."

"If you're gonna do that, just do a proper whistle. Not that I can whistle with you."

It wasn't as though the weather was cold enough that it physically prevented anyone from whistling. For the most part, Subaru had bitter memories of how he'd tried and failed to learn to whistle since way back.

"Ah, no can do. Lips aren't intact. I can't manage a real whistle."

"Th-that so. Sorry 'bout that."

The answer was heavier than Subaru had expected, so he abandoned any thought of pursuing the matter.

"Well, it's a pity to keep the young lady waiting like this, and Princess gets annoyed and scary if you make her sit around too long. Better head upstairs, pronto."

"Short and sweet. Big help… Incidentally, what's Priscilla's mood like today?"

Since he was dealing with Priscilla, her current disposition would affect the results of any discussion to a rather frightening degree.

"Mm, I don't think it's particularly good or bad, so that means you really can't go in expecting anything. Princess's moods can change before, after, or during a conversation, and they can go up, down, left, right, or bounce all around the place. What she likes to talk about isn't set in stone. You need to be good at ad-libbing to get by."

"So a no-prep match… The worst kind for me."

He climbed upstairs, slipped past a dancing hall, and came to a door—an exceedingly ornamented one.

"This is Princess's way-too-big private room. She never calls me inside, so I'll wait here while you go ahead."

Ever relaxed, Al sat on the stairs leading up to the door. As he did so, he drew his curved broadsword from his back-of-the-hip sheath and laid it over his lap.

"She's not in that bad a mood, is she? I don't wanna get sliced to ribbons, and I'm tired of dealing with her when she's unreasonable and in a temper."

"…Sorry, but she's dumped a lot of her unreasonable demands on me, too."

After Al gave his petition a blunt reply, Subaru took a deep breath and pushed open the door.

4

—And so, we return to the beginning of Subaru's standoff with Priscilla.

After he entered, Subaru spotted Priscilla waiting for him at the far end. She sat in a chair positioned above some stairs, elegantly continuing to read, not acknowledging Subaru at all.

Without an opening line to get things started, Subaru's bewilderment and nervousness only grew as time steadily pressed onward. That's why when the sound of Priscilla's book suddenly closing shut reverberated through the room, Subaru's shoulders jumped in surprise.

"—Now, then."

Subaru gritted his teeth a little, feeling like his weakness had been blatantly exposed. Priscilla, not looking like she cared one bit, stroked the cover of the closed volume as she made her remarks.

"'Twas a boring tale."

"…You sure looked like you were into it, though."

"When reading any book, it is proper to become immersed in the world between the pages and be able to state what was gained after finishing a tale. Only a fool would declare something boring without completing it."

It seemed she was as avid a reader as the claims said. After declaring the foolishness of appraising unfinished books, Priscilla took the volume she had read in full and tossed it into the air without warning.

"—Ahh."

Subaru watched, lost in bewilderment, as the soaring tome suddenly burst into flames. Scorched by the incredibly powerful fire, only black ashes remained dancing in the air.

"Now then, this is robbing me of my precious morning reading time. At the very least, have you brought me a tale to pique my interest more than that book?"

With a devious, crafty smile, Priscilla recrossed her lithe legs and pointed a white finger at Subaru. He felt as if the heat of her fingertip were pressing against his forehead when he willed his parched tongue to move.

"—It's about Emilia, a royal selection candidate, same as you. I want you to lend me your strength so I can break her out of a tricky situation she's in right now."

"—"

Closing a single eye, Priscilla silently prodded Subaru to continue. Under her red gaze, completely unmoved, Subaru earnestly concentrated on the words he'd rehearsed.

And so, he laid out everything over the course of several minutes before reaching his conclusion.

"The Witch Cult…is it? …Hmph."

Propping herself up on her elbow, Priscilla supported her head with her hand as her other hand slapped her knee. Having listened to the very end of the modified version of what he'd said at the Crusch mansion, she had murmured to herself with some deep-seated emotion before she closed her eyes.

"Yes, the Witch Cult. If no one does anything, they're going to hurt an awful lot of people. Emilia won't be the only casualty. I want to take them down before that happens. That's why I need—"

"Hee-hee. Heh."

"—?"

Abruptly, Priscilla leaned forward, her shoulders slightly trembling. Subaru's brows rose at the small sound from her mouth, and Priscilla's head snapped up.

"Ha-ha-ha-ha! Amusing! You are very amusing. I see, you've certainly swayed my heart more than that book. You must be incredibly talented to come up with a farce like this!"

Priscilla laughed and laughed, mocking Subaru. It was the howl of a fiendish, carnivorous beast. He instinctively understood that this was the kind of smile that a cat might wear while tormenting a mouse to death with its claw.

"…! What's so funny?"

"That you do not understand makes it a true masterpiece. Tell me, do you actually fail to comprehend just how illogical your actions have been?"

Priscilla ran a finger through her orange hair, twirling it around as she giggled in amusement. Subaru remembered this manner of speaking, proclaiming the speaker had seen right through him. It was the same tone that Subaru had heard a number of times at the Crusch mansion. It was saying, *You just don't understand.*

"I do not know if you simply have no one to rely upon, but going around informing the opposition of your own side's weakness serves only your enemies' interests. For us, seeing you lower your head and say, 'We're too weak and desperate, please help us,' is a matter for celebration."

Priscilla tapped her temple with a finger as she ridiculed Subaru's desperate plea.

He'd considered the possibility that she would brush him off. But he hadn't expected she would tear into him like this.

"Not caring about appearances is fine, but you have considered this too little—far too little. Aiding the enemy to help your own camp when it falls into crisis… Your behavior is that of a talentless employee. You are hopeless. Death would be far preferable."

Priscilla rose from her chair while hurling insults without

restraint, going down the stairs until arriving right in front of Subaru.

"Indeed—'twould be better if I severed your head myself."

The next instant, Priscilla pulled a fan out from her cleavage, resting it upon the carotid artery on the right side of Subaru's neck. He had seen neither her step nor the swing of her arm; only a master could pull off this move.

Even though the fan was not a bladed weapon, Subaru felt like it could lop off his head the instant it moved.

"You couldn't even see it?"

Priscilla moved aside her fan, speaking as if Subaru's unwitting gulp bored her.

"Not just foolish but slow as well. There's no saving you… Though, to bear with such terrible treatment and still be thinking of your master—I admit such devotion is admirable. And so…"

Priscilla narrowed her eyes, audibly opening her fan and using it like a red curtain to conceal her own lips.

"Even I would have a bad taste in my mouth if I dismissed you with nothing but a laugh. Thus, I shall grant you an opportunity."

"…A-an opportunity?"

"Yes, an opportunity. 'This is your big shot,' in other words."

Priscilla's pronunciation of the modern phrase was strange; perhaps she'd learned it from Al. Priscilla folded her fan once more and extended it toward Subaru. For some reason, Subaru could not evade its straight, silent motion as the end of the fan pressed into his forehead, sending him tumbling onto his backside. Then…

"Lick it."

Priscilla offered her bare foot before his eyes.

"—"

Not understanding what she meant, Subaru felt his gaze wander between Priscilla's face and leg.

With Subaru seemingly lost, Priscilla spoke to him gently, as if explaining for the benefit of a poor student—or to torment her slave.

"Crawl across the floor, ruminate on your humiliation like a pathetic wild stray, and lick my foot like a babe suckling its mother's teat. If you can do this, I shall consider your proposal."

"Wha—?!"

"If you don't want to, that's perfectly fine. If your meager personal pride comes first, wave your tail and your master shall abandon you to the wilds. Either way should provide amusement."

Priscilla concealed her lips and smiled, as if to say she would enjoy his fall regardless of his choice.

Subaru felt his guts boiling over in anger at the pure malice of Priscilla's behavior. But though he was on the brink of crying out something in a coarse voice guided by emotions, he restrained himself. If he gave in to his feelings and charged ahead, these negotiations, too, would end in failure.

"—"

He looked between the foot still hanging before him and Priscilla's mocking smile. When he closed his eyes, he saw their faces one after another: Emilia, Ram, Beatrice, and the children and adults of the village. Little by little, he cooled the magma seething inside his belly.

In anguish and consternation, he came to the conclusion that—

"I...got...it."

Enduring the humiliation, Subaru kneeled and took Priscilla's foot in his hand.

When he thought of the agony-filled deaths Emilia and the villagers had to endure, how could the humiliation Subaru would taste in their place even compare? To avoid that hopeless future, to find the world he needed to reach, he didn't mind being a dog or worse.

His trembling lips neared the top of her white foot, about to press against her fair skin—when—

"Ahh, it seems you truly are—nothing but a very, very boring man."

The kick, from right before his nose, sent Subaru flying, as if he weighed hardly anything.

"—"

He flipped head over heels, losing track of which way was up.

Subaru couldn't comprehend what had happened.

An incredible blow slammed into his head and, after a few moments in the air, his entire body crashed into something. At that point, he stopped feeling anything.

It took his intermittent conscious thoughts an ill-defined amount of time to catch up and realize he was lying on the floor, limbs splayed.

A large volume of some kind of viscous liquid poured out from his nose.

"What you have is neither loyalty nor faithfulness. It is filthier than that. It is a dog's existence and a pig's greed. A lazy pig that wants, wants, wants. A swine's greed is the most unsightly of all."

Neither the ringing in his ears nor his nausea would stop. The inside of his skull was spinning. He heard Priscilla's voice from somewhere, but the details weren't sinking into his head.

"Even if you drive off the Witch Cult, I shall destroy your camp by my own hand for harboring such a beast. I have reached this decision based on your thoughtless actions."

As he lay down, she gripped his collar and violently lifted up his body.

When his torso was raised, more blood flowed out of Subaru's nose. Subaru coughed, finding it hard to breathe as she insulted him mercilessly at close range.

"—Take pride in this. It is you who has invited that woman's—Emilia's—destruction."

She thrust him away at full force, and Subaru's body rolled and slid all the way to the entrance.

"—Aldebaran!"

When she yelled in a sharp voice, the sole door to the outside opened from the other side. Al poked his face in and looked at Subaru, who was covered in blood by the door.

"What in the world happened here...?"

"Throw out this repulsive fool. Or cut him in half, I care not."

"Well, I sure care... Hey, c'mon, bro."

Without a single word of rebuttal to his enraged master, Al easily hoisted up the fallen Subaru and passed through the door. But on his way out, he gently turned his face toward Priscilla in the center of the room.

"Don't be so angry, Princess. Violence ruins your pretty face, y'know?"

"If you do not wish me to break your broken visage even further, take him and go. I will not say it again, Aldebaran."

"Like I said, don't call me that."

Quick on his feet, Al descended the stairs with Subaru over his shoulder and spoke in a considerate voice.

"Anyway, it's best if you get out while the going's good. It's Princess. If she changes her mind, it's not unthinkable for her to tell me to cut you down. Get out of here while she still thinks it's all right to not kill you."

"A-huu…?"

"This…is bad. I'll call the young lady you brought with you. Just get outside, okay?"

Al shrugged at the barely conscious Subaru, a deft feat under the circumstances. After that, he picked up his pace even more, leaping his way down the stairs.

5

"—Subaru?!"

When she saw Subaru sitting slumped against the mansion's gate, Rem's face went pale as she ran over.

Subaru was slack-jawed as Rem touched him. She checked the state of his injuries as she chanted a healing spell. A pale light enveloped the wound on Subaru's face.

"What happened upstairs?"

"Ahh, that. Looks like our Princess's mood turned sour. I told him to be careful, but… Well, you have about as much chance trying to perfectly predict the moods of a cat."

Al's reply was rather awkward but his statement did not carry a single shred of guilt or apology. Rem, aghast at his demeanor, was about to raise her voice in protest.

"...You don't...need to say anything."

"—! Subaru, can you think clearly?"

In accordance with his healing concussion, his fuzzy mind had begun to clear. Rem's face brightened at the sound of Subaru's voice, but she closed her eyes, focusing on his treatment.

"I really cannot let you out of my sight, Subaru. You were away not even an hour, and yet you return with such grave injuries."

"Hey, it's not like I'm trying to get hu—"

Now that his circulation had returned to normal, blood poured freely from his nose once more. Rem immediately caught the trickle with a hand she had held over him, drawing a handkerchief from her side and placing it against his head.

"Please hold this on your nose. The bleeding will stop on its own. I will continue treatment."

"......ight"

Subaru held his nose as Rem had told him while he received gradual treatment via mana. Meanwhile, Al watched, nodding as if to say, *Looks like you'll be okay.*

"There's no point just standing around, so I'll head back inside. I don't know what you were talking about, but from the looks of things, it didn't go well. If you take too long leaving, Princess'll seriously tell me to cut you down, bro."

"Cut Subaru down...?!"

"Hey, don't make that scary face, young lady! I'm saying she will! So get outta here before she gives me any orders. It's not like I wanna do something like that."

After his dramatic reply to Rem's overreaction, Al's shoulders sank as he shook his head.

"Well, take care of yourself, bro. And young lady... Ah, that's right, you're Ram. Take good care of bro here."

"—Ram is the name of my older sister. My name is Rem, Master Al."

When Al gave his flippant parting words and turned his back, Rem formally introduced herself. That instant, Al's feet stopped.

"…Rem?"

The one-armed man stopped before he looked up, then slowly turned around.

"Don't be silly. You're Ram, right?"

"I am Rem… Forgive my rudeness, but where have you met Sister, Master Al?"

Rem explained how he'd mistaken her for her nearly identical older sister as she posed the question. However, Al made no reply. He raised up his one arm and touched his helm, busily poking the metal.

"What the hell's goin' on here…?"

Al sounded nervous, seemingly unable to process the information. The increasingly rapid tapping offered further proof.

"So you're Rem…and your sister is Ram?"

"Yes, that is correct."

"This might be a weird thing to ask but…is your older sister alive?"

"…? I do not understand the meaning of your question. Sister is alive, as she should be."

The instant Rem gave that answer, Subaru, who had been listening to the conversation in silence, felt goose bumps all over his flesh.

"—This ain't funny."

A low, cold voice accompanied by a grave echo reached his ears.

Al was leaning forward, his hand over the forehead of his helm, murmuring as if wringing the words out of his throat.

It was only then that Subaru understood that Al was the source of the dreadful chill he was feeling.

An instinctive alarm went off, telling him that he could not stay here. Rem, sensing the same thing, gently pulled close to Subaru. She suspended the treatment, still bent over as she asked a question in an audibly guarded voice.

"Subaru. If I lend you my shoulder, can you stand?"

At those words, Subaru dipped his head in a nod, doing his best to match his movements to Rem's.

"Hey, relax. I'm not gonna do anything."

With a shake of his head, Al reeled in his ghastly aura and acted like they were needlessly concerned.

Subaru's shoulders subconsciously eased as the tension in the air dissipated. Even Rem's neutral expression softened as she, too, felt a sense of relief.

"Sorry to say this when the bad atmosphere just lightened up, but you'd better get going. Feels like I'm not in a great mood myself."

"...Understood. Please tell her thank you for her time."

"Roger that. Take care, now."

Concluding the proper social pleasantries with Al, Rem lent Subaru her shoulder. They walked off together, her petite frame supporting his weight as they put Bariel Manor far behind them.

They descended the hill, growing more and more distant from the mansion, as all the while Al continued to stare at their backs.

"You gotta be joking me. So that's what it was... Makes me wanna puke."

6

Now that negotiations with Priscilla Bariel had broken down, all paths were well and truly closed.

"My top priority was borrowing some muscle, but I guess I can't even manage that, huh...?"

Battered by despair and powerlessness, Subaru held his nose as the words poured out.

Priscilla had crushed him on that crucial day's morning, and already it was nearing noon. Only half a day remained until the time Subaru had set for them to depart from the royal capital—time-wise, he had even less margin for error. Yet in spite of that, he couldn't claim it was one step forward, one step back—every step had been backward.

"Setting that aside, that shitty, arrogant woman... She forgot all about the time I helped her...!"

Subaru was referring to having helped Priscilla escape the ruffians who had been surrounding her when they'd first met. The corner of his lips warped, and his tongue twisted in disgust.

The fact was, she'd behaved without the slightest shred of gratitude at the time, but even he hadn't expected her to be that heartless to someone desperately reaching out for aid.

And then there was Al, so uncaring that he didn't say a single thing about his master's violent act. They might be from the same world, but the man was useless to him.

"Damn every last one of those bastards. They don't know a thing. They don't understand… It's not like they're protecting anyone, but they still get in my way…!"

Subaru ground his molars in irritation. A cut on the edge of his lip dampened his tongue with blood, but the taste of iron didn't register—only that of anger and humiliation.

"—Switch gears, switch gears. This ain't the time to get sidetracked by those two idiots."

He had a lot to process.

Having sent Rem off in one final act of resistance, Subaru headed to their rendezvous point. His feet took him down the street, out of the Nobles' District and to the capital's central strata, the Commercial District. From there, he navigated the crowds, heading straight toward his destination.

"Wow! Hey you, mister! You look really hurt! Are you all right?"

"Huh?"

Subaru, surprised by the abrupt voice, shifted his gaze down, looking for its source. The person who hailed him was short in stature, not even reaching Subaru's hip. It was a beast-man child with an orange pelt, big round eyes, and an adorably joyful face, who was apparently stretching upward to get a better look at him.

"You're bleeding, aren't you? Sometimes I cut my mouth when I'm eating, so I know! That must really hurt! You look like you're ready to cry."

"I'm not bleeding for a little-kiddie reason like… Er, I'm busy so, later."

"Don't you want me to heal it? *Sniff-sniff, sniff-sniff.* Besides, the smell isn't just from your mouth, mister. You're bleeding from your nose, too, you know?"

The wound Priscilla had given him ought to have already closed, but the girl's sense of smell could apparently still pick it up. The unpleasant memory resurfaced as Subaru tried to brush the girl off. But before Subaru could do so, another girl found her first.

"Hey, Mimi. Don't be causing people trouble. You know you shouldn't make so much mischief."

At the sound of a soft voice, Mimi looked back, waving energetically with her short arms. The person who had found her approached, smiling at her enthusiasm.

"—!"

"I'm very sorry that my girl caused you trou... Mmmn?"

Subaru's breath caught. She immediately noticed his expression, which made her stop mid-apology.

The momentary surprise vanished. Instead, a look entered her eyes that seemed ready to welcome an unexpected event with open arms.

"You're... That's right, you're Subaru. Emilia's knight, Subaru Natsuki— So you're still in the capital, huh? What an unexpected surprise."

She was a small girl with soft pale-purple hair. Her narrowed light-blue eyes suggested she had gentle regard for others—but Subaru knew that the girl was avaricious deep down. Even if he was meeting her in a different place, there was no way he could mistake her aura.

"Anastasia Hoshin..."

"Mm, I see, you actually remembered me. I was right worried I didn't make much of an impression back there, so I'm kinda relieved... If you still recognize me after everythin' that's happened to you, everyone else should be able to, too."

Anastasia smiled as she spoke in a Kansai dia—a Kararagi dialect unfamiliar to his ears.

Subaru, shocked to have bumped into Anastasia, scanned the area. If Anastasia was there, that man had to be somewhere around—

"Relax, Julius is on other business. He's not comin'."

"...That so."

Subaru let his discomfort show in his reply once he realized that the reason for his unease was plain as day. Anastasia, putting a hand to her mouth in amusement, seemed to be under the impression he held little love for servant or master.

Subaru couldn't bring himself to think of the unexpected encounter as a golden opportunity. In the first place, there was Julius. Given the antagonism between them at the parade grounds, Subaru assumed joining forces with the Anastasia camp was utterly impossible.

"Well, you seem to be mostly healed up. I was just a teensy bit worried."

"...Thanks. You seem in pretty good health, yourself."

"I'm muddlin' through, I s'pose."

"Yeah! Muddlin' through!"

The Western-sounding reply to Subaru's sarcasm made the kitten laugh with amusement. Apparently, she was called Mimi, and she was accompanying Anastasia.

"Should one of the big players in the royal selection be walking around without an escort these days?"

"I am trying to travel incognito, after all. Is it not working?"

Anastasia looked around before showing off her outfit that she had created with the attire of local city girls in mind. Her clothes certainly fit in, but her trademark white fox muffler and huge purse didn't make for a convincing disguise. Apparently, Anastasia gathered as much from Subaru's look of disbelief and laughed.

"Well, how do you hide charm like mine? Besides, if anything happens, I have my very reliable, hard-working deputy captain, so no worries!"

"Reliable...deputy captain...?"

Anastasia stuck out her rather flat chest in pride as she spoke, but when he saw that she meant Mimi, Subaru adopted a dubious expression. Mimi, who was shooting the breeze at the different stalls, didn't look the part at all.

"I see you don't believe me, but it's true. She's the second-in-command of my private army. I think she'd hold her own against Julius a lot better'n you would."

"..."

"Ahh, did I make you mad? Sorry, sorry, my apologies. You just look like a fun person to tease. So, oops?"

Oops my ass. Subaru pursed his lips, making his displeasure clear.

"If this is just small talk, would you mind letting me be on my way? Unlike you, I have things to do."

"Well, you're no fun. Things to do like what?"

"I have to meet up with the girl who's traveling with me. After that, gotta get a dragon carriage and leave the capital. Stuff."

He was supposed to meet back up with Rem at one of the restaurants lining the royal capital's main street. Whether his pathetic attempts met failure or success, the two had planned to procure the dragon carriage they needed to leave the royal capital within the next few hours.

"Hmmm. Gettin' a dragon carriage. So you say, but can ya really? Right now, it's a lotta work findin' one here in the capital. I hear it's just one mess after another recently."

"Hard getting a dragon carriage? That shouldn't be a..."

Subaru would have continued to say *problem*, but the word caught in his throat.

In previous loops, he'd taken his dragon carriage for granted when he returned to the Mathers domain, but the vehicle from the first time around was a loan from Crusch. Considering that circumstances had been similar the second time around, he had assumed Crusch had lent them one then as well.

"Someone's buyin' up all the dragon carriages in the capital or somethin'. So if you wanna rent one right now, it's gonna take a lotta legwork."

"...Seriously?"

Anastasia suppressed a giggle while Subaru could only murmur in bewilderment.

She had no reason to lie. That would be an obstacle to even exiting the capital. Subaru clutched his head, almost unable to believe the difficulties besetting him.

"Miss, you shouldn't tease people!"

Mimi tugged on Anastasia's sleeve at the sight of Subaru bent over.

"Dragon carriages, you mean those lizard thingies? You can just lend him one, can't you, miss?"

"Wait, you have a dragon carriage I can borrow?!"

"I'm company president, so a dragon carriage or two is no big deal, see? But it seems you don't wanna talk with me very much, Natsuki…"

"Ugh… Sorry for…how I behaved earlier…"

When she pointed out how Subaru had tried to cut off their conversation, he replied with an awkward expression. Anastasia put a hand to her mouth and giggled when she saw it.

"It's fine, it's fine. I forgive ya. In exchange, would you stick with me for another chat? It's very important to maintain smooth relationships with others. How about the shop where you're meetin' the girl?"

Subaru couldn't summon the words to refuse the adorable merchant's smile.

7

"It's still a bit early for lunch, but it ain't good to sit down without orderin'."

Anastasia said this as she returned from the counter carrying a light meal—vegetables and meat sandwiched between two pieces of bread, kind of like an elongated hamburger. Mimi took it from Anastasia and happily buried her face in it.

It was a casual eatery along Main Street, right in front of the main gate of the royal capital. This gate had the most traffic in the entire city, where people ceaselessly entered and exited. The shop was packed; Subaru and the others had taken the last open seats.

"Natsuki, you should eat all ya want. Since you were plannin' to meet that girl here, you musta meant to eat, right?"

"I feel kinda bad making you treat me to lunch when I'm asking you for a favor. If I really wanna eat something, I'll take my meal with my friend later. Ana... Er."

There were many people around, but the establishment wasn't very large. He hesitated to call Anastasia by name in such cramped quarters.

"I don't really mind much, but if you're havin' trouble usin' my name, you could call me 'young lady'?"

"It'd be even harder to say that... Anyway, about the dragon carriage."

"Cuttin' right to the chase, hmm? You won't please your business partner if you prioritize only what you want. The core of negotiation is how much you can please the other party. You're not too good at that, Natsuki."

Chiding Subaru for being in such a hurry, Anastasia bit into her meal of vegetables and meat; the way she licked the sauce was charming somehow.

Though she differed from Crusch and Priscilla, Anastasia similarly possessed a unique charisma in each and every gesture that was nothing like ordinary people. Perhaps he ought to say that all the royal candidates had a special essence.

"It's a little awkward if you stare at me while I'm eatin'. I wasn't raised with very good manners, y'see. Am I doin' somethin' strange?"

"I haven't been educated in high culture enough to judge something like that... I don't think it's weird at all. You just don't, uh, often see a woman opening her mouth wide like that."

"...Are you tryin' to get into my good graces? If so, you gotta do way better'n that."

Anastasia snickered as she criticized Subaru's clumsy approach. Her heartless appraisal had quickly brought Subaru to his knees.

"Um, I'm not kidding around here. I'm really in a bind, that's why I wanna get to the point."

"If you wanna appeal to my sympathy, that's the worst plan possible when you're dealin' with a girl like me. But I applaud you for tryin'. You need a dragon carriage, right?"

Anastasia spoke while pulling a pen out of a pocket. From there, she spread open the paper wrapped around the pen, quickly jotted something down, and neatly folded the sheet.

"I've written down the location of a shop that should still have a dragon carriage and added my signature. This is all you need to accomplish your goal, Natsuki."

"Well, no need to act all high and mighty about it."

"I sure will—it's no fun if I just hand it over for free, is it?"

Speaking softly, Anastasia put the folded piece of paper down on the table. She gently rested her palm over it, hiding it from view, and grinned at Subaru when he winced.

The smile on her face looked different from the ones he had seen on her before.

"Don't tense up your shoulders like that; it'll be fine. I just want you to stick with me for a little chat. It's sad when you can't talk about anything except what you really need to. I don't think I'm being too greedy for wantin' to shoot the breeze with ya till that girl of yours shows up."

"Why? This is a lot of trouble just for some small talk with a guy like me. Not like you're gonna get anything out of it."

"I don't think there's a single thing in this world that's meaningless. You never know who might end up giving you insight. And out of everyone, I feel like you might have somethin' special for me, Natsuki."

"…I'm not really grateful if that's the impression you got from me at the royal selection assembly."

"It's not like I've met you anywhere else, Natsuki."

Subaru's desperate attempt at sarcasm was sliced down and cast aside by a sound argument. After evaluating Anastasia's request and goal, Subaru immediately resigned himself to his fate.

"Just to be clear, we're only going to talk until Rem gets here. And then I'll have you hand over that paper."

"I certainly lie and deceive people, but I assure you this is true. I can put that in writing if you'd like."

"You didn't even blink when you said that... What do you wanna talk about?"

"I told you when we started, didn't I? The core of negotiations is to get in good with the other party. If you wanna get better at talkin', you gotta get better at listenin'. A solid start would be findin' out what your partner's interested in."

Or more candidly, *Don't look like you're simply putting up with the conversation.* It would be bad for Subaru to stray from his commitment and sour her mood. He scratched his head and sank into thought.

"Hey, hey, miss, miss. I wanna eat more of what I just had. Pleaaaase?"

"Sure, eat all you like. Ah, don't make your mouth messy with the sauce. We don't want that adorable face gettin' dirty, do we? Well, that's kinda cute, too."

"Wipe it for me! Rub, rub! Yay! I'll be back!"

Once Anastasia cleaned up her face, Mimi flew over to a shop worker in very high spirits. Subaru did a double take as he watched the tiny girl.

"Earlier, you said that runt is second-in-command?"

"What? You're asking about Mimi and not me? You swing that way, Natsuki? Is it because you have a thing for kitty ears? That's why you're tryin' to get close to my girl?"

"I don't have any weird fetishes like that. In the first place, if I were into that..."

Subaru clenched his teeth as he recalled the image of a cat-haired knight at that mansion full of know-nothings.

"Anyway, no. It simply caught my interest. I think you said something about a private army?"

"For what it's worth, they're pretty famous in Kararagi. They're the

Hoshin Company's own mercenary band, the 'Iron Fangs.' I'm their sponsor, so of course I get the privilege of choosin' the members."

Anastasia spoke while shifting her gaze to Mimi, who looked absentminded all the while.

"She's suuuuper cute, isn't she? She's so much fun to hug and go to sleep with, you know?"

"It's my turn to ask if you 'swing that way,' geez. You're not telling me you twisted arms to get someone like that in as second-in-command, are you?"

"No need to worry; it's fine. I told ya, didn't I? That girl's the number two of the Iron Fangs all right, and she has skills worthy of deputy captain. That's why I can stroll around the capital with only her."

Sensing absolute trust in Anastasia's comments, Subaru observed Mimi's back once again. She really didn't look strong at all. But her master's words were convincing all the same. A candidate for the royal selection would never walk around with a lone bodyguard if that person wasn't capable.

"Ah, just to get this out, I won't talk in detail about the members, okay? I'm not generous enough to put all my cards on the table. In fact, I'm pretty confident it's a bad idea."

"Well, that doesn't make you sound as confident at all…"

Though she'd blunted any effort to poke deeper, Subaru engraved the name of the *Iron Fangs* into the back of his brain as one more potential threat. If he and Anastasia became overt enemies at some point, it would be yet one more wall to overcome.

"Natsuki, your brow is too wrinkled. You look like you're glaring."

"Hey, I was born with this face, okay? No need to go picking at a guy's complexes."

"Complex? Mm, that's fine. That said, you mentioned your birth, but where were you born, Natsuki? We don't see black hair very often around these parts, and your outfit stands out, too."

"I was born in Japan on Earth, and this is a tracksuit, probably the only one in the world."

It was a strange topic. His honest answer sounded like he was dodging the question entirely. Sure enough, it made Anastasia pout; her face clouded.

"Japan of Earth. Never heard of it. But…where is that?"

"Past the Grand Cascade. Far to the east, and then farther east past that is Zipang."

"The Grand Cascade…"

Subaru gave a flippant answer, expecting her to burst into laughter, but Anastasia sank into thought. Subaru raised an eyebrow at her completely unexpected reaction.

"You're not gonna laugh? Reinhard thought it was pretty stupid…"

"Mm. Well, you see, once in a very great while, you hear about people who hail from beyond the Grand Cascade. I never expected for you to claim your homeland is there, though."

"What, there's other jokers besides me? Famous people even?"

"If you want to know more, I think you should study up on 'Hoshin of the Wastes.'"

Anastasia still wasn't laughing when she offered him a piece of advice. Subaru cocked his head at the mention of "Hoshin of the Wastes." After all, that was Anastasia's family name. And Subaru recalled that "Hoshin of the Wastes" was also a heroic tale.

"You're not actually related to this Hoshin, are you? I thought I heard you saying you took up the name for yourself."

"It's the name of the founder of Kararagi. As a Kararagi native, I'm not completely unconnected, but there's no blood relationship. I just decided to call myself that. Fitting for someone who rose up to become a goddess of commerce, don't ya think?"

"Damn, you've got a lot of guts to come right out and say that."

She apparently rated her exploits high enough to warrant declaring herself a goddess without any hint of irony.

He recalled Anastasia's boast at the royal selection meeting that she wanted to get a kingdom for pure self-interest. That performance put her on a one-way train; there was no going back for her now.

"If I fail, people will point at me and laugh, though. But I've come this far. I'm not gonna talk too highly of myself when I'm still halfway to where I'm going."

Subaru had heard only a tiny bit about Anastasia's birthplace during her demonstration of conviction at the royal selection meeting. Apparently she'd been born in the slums of Kararagi and afterward rose to her present position on the merits of her genius alone. A great mercantile house, as famous as any nation, served her, and she had declared herself as a candidate for the royal throne. Not for the first time, Subaru felt like the person before his eyes was unlike any he had seen before.

"How can you do that much...? Aren't you afraid of failure?"

"Oh my, my, my. Natsuki, have you finally taken a proper interest in me?"

Subaru didn't have a plan; he'd simply voiced his honest doubts. Perhaps, just as Anastasia had taken it, he asked the question because he was finally looking straight at her: not a troublesome opponent, not someone connected to Julius, but Anastasia, the individual.

"Failure, huh? I'd say I'm afraid of that, too. I'm not exactly claimin' I've won every battle I've fought to get to where I am now. I've just kept winnin' the ones that really mattered."

"You never wonder if you've won enough of your bets? I mean, you have plenty as it is. You're a big-time merchant, you have lots of people around you, and..."

"—Can I really say I have plenty? I don't even know what would satisfy me."

Her low voice and piercing light-blue eyes made Subaru unwittingly stare at her. As Subaru fell silent, Anastasia finally softened her lips and suddenly changed the subject.

"I...have a dream."

Subaru said nothing as she tapped a finger against the counter, ignoring him.

"I've carried that dream with me since my time in the slums, never knowin' what the next day would bring, tryin' my hardest to live... I want everythin' I can get my hands on."

"Everything...you can get your hands on..."

"My dream is to see just who I can become, just how far I can go. But I won't compromise one bit until I'm satisfied I've done that. As long as I live, everything I can reach and take hold of will be mine. Will I die penniless? Or will I die fulfilled by the innumerable possessions around me? —My life is one big contest until I get one result or the other."

Subaru was overwhelmed.

He realized that the small-statured girl before him was an amazing person, someone he might even look up to.

Her fundamental character as a human being differed from Crusch's and Priscilla's. The power of her charisma was in no way inferior to theirs. No, to Subaru, in that moment, he had a much more favorable impression of her than the other two. With the division between him and the know-nothing Crusch, and considering Priscilla's arrogant dismissal, he thought that Anastasia might just be a heaven-sent final thread of hope that he might be able to count on.

For Subaru, unable to gather any reinforcements, this was one last possibility if he wanted to borrow strength from others.

"Hey, Anastasia. There's something I really wanna talk to you about..."

Subaru, who had initially treated Anastasia as a nuisance to be swept aside, was now meek toward her. *I can depend on her.* At that though, the image of Julius flickered in the back of his mind, stabbing Subaru's chest, but he suppressed that emotional wound with all his might as he tried to broach the topic.

"Hey, time-out. It's just been you askin' questions this whole time. I'm happy that you've taken an interest in me, but this isn't very fair, is it?"

Anastasia cried foul and brought his determined move to a halt.

"That's not really enough to call it unf— No, never mind. Talk to me."

"Yes, yes, compromise is real important. It's an issue of personal relations that comes even before negotiating... Natsuki, you look like you're leavin' the royal capital, but have you done enough sightseein'?"

"Don't call it something casual like sightseeing, geez. I'm not, and

I'm sure you aren't, either. Is this really the time for a trip just to feel better?"

Subaru shot down the topic interrupting his subject.

"I don't plan to just travel around, but don't turn up your nose at seein' the sights— People get something out of just explorin' a place with lots of people in it and takin' a look here and there."

Midway, Anastasia's strained smile vanished as she lowered her voice slightly. That change in her demeanor and expression stole Subaru's attention. She indicated the street with her chin.

"The atmosphere on this avenue's changed, like the shoppin' area before it. Did you notice, Subaru?"

"…Now that you mention it, it feels way more hostile somehow."

Subaru had known the sights of the royal capital for only a total of several days and hours, but even he could sense that the air of the royal capital felt different on his skin.

"The looks on people's faces have changed. The talk about the royal selection's brought all kinds of misers out of the woodwork."

"I think you're the pot calling the kettle black, especially when you're the one poking into their business…"

"Hey, when you compare the people goin' for tiny piles of coins to a gal who's after a whole kingdom, they're pretty pathetic. Besides, in business, speed is the name of the game… When you look at what people with a nose for money are doin', you see more of the big picture."

Anastasia thought about "the big picture" in a way Subaru could not fathom.

"When the ones at the top move, then the people start to move. When the people move, things move, too. So right now, traveling merchants are pouring into the royal capital from all over. If the people are there, things follow. So I can see this and that about what's to come."

"The things you see…are merchandise? Is there some special meaning to what they're selling in the capital right now?"

"You caught on fast. Incidentally, the prices of quite a few goods are in flux around here at the moment, but things made of metal have gotten especially expensive. Someone's snappin' up weapons like swords and spears inside the capital and out."

"Iron and weapons. I feel like I've heard about that before... Ahh, from Otto."

The conversation was from when he'd traveled with Otto during the first time going through the loop. Otto had been drowning in drink because he'd been carrying a large quantity of hard-to-sell goods; apparently, his bankruptcy really had been assured.

"Swords and armor... So not just iron itself but weapons and stuff? You don't think the people gathering up all that are planning to start a war, do you...?"

"Who's to say? It's possible the goal is more financial in nature. Workin' the market to favor you is more than enough reason. Merchants collude with one another quite a bit... If they think something's worth gettin', they'll grab it by the throat."

Subaru readily accepted Anastasia's reasoning. Certainly, merchants would be grateful toward another party creating a favorable business opportunity for them. A thriving industry was connected with a thriving city.

"From the way you're talking, is the person gathering up iron pretty well-known? Who is it, then...?"

"It's someone you know very well, Natsuki."

"Someone I know...?"

"—Duchess Crusch Karsten. She's been on an iron-buyin' spree here in the capital."

"Crusch is...?"

Subaru, who had been blithely following the conversation, was shocked to hear the name of someone that closely related to him. But when he thought about it, things added up. Crusch had been receiving guests day after day; maybe she wasn't just dealing with influential political figures but negotiating with merchants and bargaining for merchandise as well.

"I see, so that's why Russel showed up..."

"Russel Fellow? He's a big fish."

Quite naturally, Anastasia instantly recognized Russel's name. And thanks to Anastasia's information, scattered pieces of the puzzle were connecting inside Subaru.

"So all those people heading in and out, putting cargo in the courtyard even in the middle of the night, that was all a strategy to get merchants on her side?"

He remembered that on the night he'd exchanged wineglasses with Crusch, servants were busily working all around the place. But they seemed to move with a purpose greater than simply gathering metalwares. They seemed to be expecting something bigger than that—

"…Well, not like it has anything to do with me now."

Subaru initially felt the urge to pursue his doubt but gave up midway and cast it aside. Whatever Crusch was planning or whatever was disturbing the economy of the royal capital had nothing to do with him. All that mattered to Subaru now was finding a way to oppose the Witch Cult. There was nothing else. So why did he need to puzzle over unnecessary considerations like that?

While Subaru's thoughts ground to a halt, Anastasia murmured across from him.

"—My, my, I'll have to keep that in mind."

Subaru looked up, sensing a particularly weighty tone in her voice, when he saw she was gently holding out her palm. Without thinking, Subaru took the scribble that he would need to obtain a dragon carriage.

"Thank you, Natsuki. You've given me enough of what I wanted to hear."

The scribble and Anastasia's smile told Subaru that the conversation was over. But Rem still hadn't arrived at the establishment. And yet, she'd used the word *enough*—

When Subaru's thoughts reached that point, he realized—far too late—that something wasn't right.

"…Was this a coincidence?"

"—Well, Natsuki, what do you think?"

While Subaru gritted his teeth, Anastasia addressed him casually.

Her light-blue eyes seemed to see right through Subaru, as if they would never let the change in his expression slip past her.

—Just like a con artist watching someone who'd completely fallen for her act.

"So you set up that whole little 'chance meeting' in the street just to ask me about this."

"You got into a tiff with Crusch last night and went your separate ways, didn't ya? I figured you'd be easier to read now, in all kinds of ways. Your words, your eyes, and your expressions."

She'd tricked him. It made Subaru's blood boil, and his throat tightened.

"H-how can you be so satisfied with yourself?! Ambushing people like this…!"

"It pains my heart, too. But it's hard to smile and trade info smoothly with our relationship. It's natural to want some insurance when you're doin' business with someone you don't trust."

The way she looked straight at him and pegged him as untrustworthy needled his heart. Putting a hand on his chest, Subaru glared at Anastasia with resentment.

"So you misjudged me just because you don't like me, too…"

"Misjudged…?"

"I'm saying you're distracted by the stupid stuff right in front of you and missing what's important! Even though you'll regret your mistakes and missing the right path later…!"

"I wonder just what is right and what is mistaken here? Well, everyone's got their own opinions, but I'll give ya mine."

Anastasia cocked her head slightly while Subaru ground his teeth, her charming smile never faltering.

"If you want people to believe your path is just, you have to show them something concrete that backs up your claim. I don't see that in you, Natsuki. I can't help but value you less for the lack of it."

"—"

"Your worth is decided by what you've done… In other words, your past. No matter what you do, you can't change the past. So the worth of the Natsuki I know hasn't changed one whit."

Anastasia patted her own modest chest, looking at an enraged Subaru with upturned eyes.

"When you make a mistake, it never, ever goes away."

"—!!"

"Hey, mister, don't get any closer to Miss Anastasia. Mimi's super-strong, okay?"

When Subaru unwittingly took a step forward, Mimi thrust a large staff against his face. She'd wedged herself between Subaru and Anastasia, preempting Subaru's loss of control.

"Thank you, Mimi. But you don't need to do anything. I'm sure there's nothing Natsuki can do."

"...! How can you just...decide that I can't do anything like that...?!"

As Subaru spit and shouted, Anastasia put distance between them and crossed her hands behind her, tilting her head.

"Ahh, did I hit a sore spot there? Sorry if I did. But I won't apologize for using you. It's an ironclad rule among merchants to take anything that isn't bolted down. Besides, neither of us said anything that hurts us personally, did we? You asked me whatever you wanted, and you answered several of my questions, Natsuki."

"That's just because you led me into it! It's dirty... It's under-handed, damn it!"

"I told you at the start, I lie and deceive. And when I offered to put it in writing, you're the one who didn't want me to, aren't you, Natsuki?"

"I never said anything like tha...! You're the worst, master and servant alike! Eat shit!"

He should have remained true to his initial instinct, the distaste he'd had the instant he'd seen her face on Market Street. He should have known she was the worst of the worst from the simple fact that Julius served her. She'd manipulated him through the art of conversation into expecting that she might be trustworthy.

Truly, just how much disgrace did he have to endure before people were satisfied?

"...Haven't paid him back for Julius, either. Well, that was partly my fault, too."

Subaru gave no heed to Anastasia's words as he was about to rip up the paper in his hand and throw it away, but he hesitated right on the cusp of that impulsive action, knowing that he would then have truly gained nothing for all he'd endured.

"I'm relieved that you really aren't that stupid— Mimi."

"Riiight! Mister, turn this way!"

Subaru was breathing raggedly and clutching the paper in his hand when Mimi held her staff aloft. Subaru stood rooted to the spot while a pale light softly enveloped his face.

"Pain, pain, go away…!"

"—"

Using magic, she healed the cut on his lip that had been there before their initial encounter.

While Subaru was speechless, Mimi smiled at him, apparently without a single care in the world.

"Miss is high-maintenance, but she never means to do bad things, so forgive her, 'kay? This is why she doesn't have any friends."

"Mimi, you don't have to tell him that… Well, see you 'round, Natsuki."

Anastasia had thoroughly wrecked him to the point that even her follower had taken pity on him. Subaru's shoulders quivered as Anastasia turned her back on him.

"I'll add just one last lesson about the basics of negotiation, Natsuki."

Standing still, Anastasia's back remained turned to him as she raised a single finger and spoke.

"The secret is to prepare everything you can before you ever reach the bargaining table. Learnin' little tricks is all part of turnin' the situation in your favor. You have to know yourself and dangle what the other party wants in front of them. Where you come up short, Natsuki, is that you want and want, but you got nothin' to offer in return."

He didn't know Anastasia's real motive. Even if he listened to her, it was meaningless.

But he would understand the meaning of those words soon enough.

"—All right, let's go, everyone!"

Anastasia called out with a clap of her hands. Subaru raised his eyebrows at her gesture when the customers in the place rose from their seats all at once. Together, every last customer in the packed-to-the-brim establishment followed Anastasia out.

Every single person in the group was wearing a hood, concealing their true identity. However, when he looked more deeply, there were unnatural bulges under their hoods. From this, Subaru deduced they likely concealed animal ears.

Clear as a bell, the name of Anastasia's private army leaped out from the back of his mind—the Iron Fangs.

"What, you were all here? Ah, mister, see you later!"

Mimi smiled at her comrades as they filed out, giving Subaru a wave of her hand before she, too, darted away. The only ones left in the place were Subaru and the proprietor.

—That was what she'd meant by preparing everything you can before you sit at the table.

"Shit!!"

Unable to endure his own worthlessness, Subaru slammed his fist into the tabletop. With no customers remaining in the establishment, the proprietor quietly withdrew into the back. His face was as conflicted as Subaru's.

Subaru stayed like that, his shoulders shaking from humiliation, when a voice called out to him.

"—Subaru?"

It was Rem. She had arranged for them to meet at that place, and now she rushed over to Subaru.

"Subaru, what's wrong? Did something happ—"

"—It's nothing, Rem. How about on your end?"

Subaru interrupted Rem's concerned voice, covering up his current humiliation with all his might. Even if he told Rem about how Anastasia had gotten the better of him, it would change nothing.

Faced with Subaru's stiff demeanor, Rem closed her mouth, then she politely reported the results of her activities.

"I reported the covert maneuverings of the Witch Cult to the Knights' garrison. By invoking Master Roswaal's name, I was not dismissed immediately at the gate, but..."

The awkward wording and frail tone of her voice for the latter half pretty much told Subaru how that had gone down. Rem, Roswaal's servant, was more likely to be successful in spurring the Knights to action than Subaru, who had a grudge against them. Trying to exploit that was his final act of resistance, but...

"They didn't give you a good answer?"

"...It would seem that the Knights have a jumble of similar reports. Few concrete details are known about the Witch Cult's underpinnings, and apparently an endless stream of tips constantly flows in with no practical way to verify it."

"Ahh, I get it now. This is seriously like back when they had real witch trials... It ain't much of a joke if that's how the Witch Cult actually hides itself."

The sheer number of people afraid of the Witch Cult lurking nearby gave birth to imaginary phantoms in every corner of the land. Those fears took form as tips to the Knights, dragging down the value of any real leads as a result. That seemed backward somehow.

Both the arrogance of the Knights and the vileness of the Witch Cult were at fault. The Knights should have been rigorously checking out any and all potential leads related to the Witch Cult, considering how they were a blight to all.

With that, Subaru understood that all his plays had failed.

"If gathering reinforcements isn't possible... I hate it, but there's no avoiding it."

"What will you do?"

"Goes without saying. We head back to the mansion and get Emilia and Ram out of there. We'll bring them here to the capital or wherever Roswaal went off to—the destination doesn't matter. Anyway, where they are now is dangerous."

Petelgeuse's loud laughter came back to life in the back of his head. Subaru's fist trembled in frustration. Even if he wanted nothing more than to pulverize that bastard's skeletal face, he didn't have the means. Even if he did choose to take on the enemy with his current resources, it would invariably entail putting Rem at the tip of the spear.

—He would avoid that at all costs. Getting Rem hurt because of Subaru's thoughts and actions was unthinkable. He couldn't bear it.

If he couldn't drum up the strength to battle Petelgeuse, taking them on was unthinkable. Any option that meant losing Rem was out.

Even then, bloodlust made his insides seethe. The inexhaustible hatred was like a curse echoing over and over inside his skull.

"Excuse me, Subaru. Actually, about the dragon carriage needed to return to the mansion…"

"—It's tough to get one, you mean? In that case…"

While Subaru's blood boiled, Rem broached a topic that seemed difficult for her to bring up. He nodded at her concern and revealed the paper Anastasia had handed him. As promised, it had the name of the store and her signature. It was Subaru's consolation prize for his ignominious defeat during negotiations.

"If we go to this place and talk to them, they should treat us all right… I'm sure of that much."

"Really? Where in the world did you… Just as I'd expect of you, Subaru!"

"'As you'd expect.' Expect, huh… Ha-ha, you're funny, Rem."

"—?"

Rem, having no idea how he'd gotten a hold of it, couldn't have meant anything malicious or ironic by it. Even so, Subaru couldn't stop a dry laugh from coming out.

"There's no time. Let's get moving."

Pulling the bewildered Rem along behind him, Subaru walked out onto Main Street, heading for the indicated store. Annoyed by the jarring, disorganized noises, he clicked his tongue as he walked along.

"If we can get out of the capital within half a day, we can be back to the mansion by the third day. If we do that, we should have time to rescue Emilia and them."

Subaru had gone over his memories of the first time around again and again to make sure of that. The reason he couldn't state it with absolute certainty was because he couldn't rely on his memories from the second time around. Subaru Natsuki had frittered away the time that would have allowed him to compare and be on surer footing.

"The second time... Shit! How many days was I not in my right mind...?!"

He scratched at his head, berating his useless memories and his useless self as he continued to walk. Behind Subaru, Rem, whose strides were a different length from Subaru's, worked earnestly to match her speed to his.

But Subaru never noticed Rem doing that, for he had forgotten to look back.

CHAPTER 3
THE MAW OF THE WHITE WHALE

1

Anastasia's introduction had led him to borrow the largest dragon carriage he had yet seen.

Boasting a huge size, the land dragon's hind legs thudded along, making the ground shudder as it raced across the grassy plain.

"It's as fast as it is huge… That's great, but could it do something about kicking up all this dirt?"

The dust dancing upward clouded his field of vision, making Subaru squint in the driver's seat.

"This appears to be a land dragon normally used to haul freight. Therefore, its manner of running has no consideration for passengers, and since it is specialized for speedy travel, it has not been trained in running quietly…"

"It was the last one, and it's running without a break. Beggars can't be choosers, but…this is still kinda tough."

Fortunately, thanks to the land dragon's blessing—a special power belonging to particular individuals and species of that world—the dust did not directly affect them, though Subaru could not help but be annoyed at the poor visibility.

Subaru wound up looking at the sky, hoping for any change. The clouds flowed overhead as the sun gradually changed its angle. These signs meant the passage of time, and thus, Subaru's heart smoldered little by little.

—Surely they were moving far quicker than they had during the previous iterations of the loop.

They had not been able to gain reinforcements, but departing by dragon carriage on the second day was a major departure from before. They would be able to make it over the highway in half a day, arriving at the mansion on the dawn of the third day. They were gaining more than half a day over the first time around—surely enough time to get Emilia and the others out of the mansion and to flee from the Witch Cult.

"The problem is…the possibility of encountering the Witch Cult along the way like last time."

According to his vague memories of the second time around, he'd been inside a cave when he truly regained consciousness. If he had been en route back to the mansion, it was possible that the same thing could happen this time, too.

When he thought of how Rem had been killed, and how he had spent nearly an entire day pulling her along before they left the cave: "It means they must have infiltrated the area outside the mansion days in advance."

But he didn't know exactly which day that was. The tragedy would fall the morning of the fifth day. The second time around, Subaru's deduction that it had taken him a day's worth of time to get out of the cave put his encounter with the Witch Cult between the third and the fourth day.

"In other words, even if we arrive tomorrow morning, that doesn't mean that we're any less likely to bump into them…!"

Not knowing what they could expect made him grind his teeth hard enough that blood seeped into his mouth.

Subaru glanced to the side at Rem, who was holding the reins and concentrating on driving. Once again, were they to encounter the Witch Cult, he'd have no choice but to rely on Rem.

Subaru had thought of making clear beforehand that they might encounter the Witch Cult, but when he tried to speak the words, he realized that his voice simply wouldn't come out.

It was not fear of the penalty for divulging information gained via Return by Death.

Certainly, he was terrified of that pain. No sane person could endure the agony of that squeezing on the heart. He didn't even want to think about tasting it again.

But that pain was not the reason Subaru hesitated to speak of the Witch Cult. He had another reason, one he could not escape.

—Would Rem really believe what Subaru told her?

"—!"

Just thinking about it sent a chill running up Subaru's spine. Unable to endure it, he hugged his own shoulders.

His heart rate quickened to a stupid degree. The urge to vomit seized his innards. The stress of his extreme situation had kept him from getting a wink of sleep. The physical fatigue was rotting his mind and body alike.

At that moment, Rem was the person he could trust most in that entire world. Even Emilia had cast him aside. After Crusch, Priscilla, and Anastasia had rejected him one after another, Subaru had fallen into paranoia, doubting anything and everything.

In that moment, Rem was all Subaru had.

Rem was the only one he could call an ally beyond suspicion, someone in whom he could unwaveringly place all his trust.

If he revealed things about the Witch Cult to her, and her face became clouded with suspicion, what would it do to him? It frightened Subaru to even think of it.

"This isn't the time to get cold feet…!"

Venting in a hoarse voice was the only thing he could do to drive away his cowardly emotions. The land dragon drowned out his voice, fainter than a whisper and reaching only Subaru's ears.

Afraid as he was, he couldn't keep it to himself. Now that the possibility of encountering the Cult remained, keeping his silence was nothing less than a betrayal.

After all, Subaru had lost his life and returned to take hold of the best possible future.

"R-Rem… I need to talk to you ab—"

"Subaru—there is a gathering of people on the road ahead of us."

"Eh?"

As Rem glared to the front, Subaru followed her gaze to see a number of silhouettes hovering in the cloud of dust. He gaped openly. Was it really the Witch Cult lying in ambush?

Though Subaru had lost his voice at the too-soon turn of events, the contours of one of the vague silhouettes gradually grew more distinct, finally becoming a clear figure. This figure stood right in the middle of the road, waving both arms and loudly calling for the dragon carriage to halt.

"Heyyyyyyyy! Can you stop your land dragon so we can trade information?!"

The man, with a delicate face and gray hair, was Otto Suwen, traveling merchant.

2

"Ahh, I'm so glad. These days, most people are heading to the royal capital, and there's precious few coming out of it. So I thought I'd ask you a couple of things if possible."

With the dragon carriage stopped, Otto came to greet Rem and Subaru with a handshake and a smile as he spoke. He seemed neither drunk with wine nor in sorrows about the world. He didn't strike Subaru as a wounded man. Rather, Otto the peddler felt alive and well.

The memory he'd expunged of Otto desperately trying to stop him the first time around returned. Subaru tried to wash away the bitter taste of it while surveying the people behind Otto.

"Is everyone in this whole group a traveling merchant?"

"Indeed they are, every last one. We're headed to the capital with a yearning for profits in our hearts."

Otto replied to Subaru's question with an amiable smile.

There were various dragon carriages stopped on the side of the highway, and the men, presumably the dragon carriage owners, were gathered together. There were more than ten of them, ranging from the young to men in their forties.

Judging that Otto, Subaru, and Rem had concluded their pleasantries, they congregated around the latter two, introducing themselves by name as they began establishing the topic of conversation. The contents mostly concerned the current situation in the royal capital and changes thereof. Furthermore, the merchants spoke mainly of things like trends in coinage prices and the atmosphere in the marketplace.

Put bluntly, every minute wasted there was precious. Now that he had confirmed Otto was safe, he would have been happier to pass on such mundane conversation and leave. But…

"You'd head out now…? Isn't that dangerous? It's night already. We plan to camp here tonight. You could remain with us if you like."

Just as Otto said, the sun was already sinking in the west, with night creeping over the highway. The Liphas Highway would soon be subsumed by night. They would have only the light of a magic crystal lamp and the stars to rely upon.

The traveling merchants had already begun preparing to camp, lighting a brilliant fire in the center of the group. With this many people, even wild beasts and bandits appearing along the highway could surely do little. But even time spent in safety was time Subaru could hardly afford.

"So you say, Otto. You're just trying to pawn off some of that oil you bought at the wrong time, aren't you? Don't pull that oh-so-friendly face on me!"

The instant Subaru declined the invitation, a chorus of voices started needling Otto, and raucous laughter spread through the group. Otto, the butt of the joke, pursed his lips and made a sour face.

"That is not my motive at all. This is purely well intentioned. Well…you'll need food and lanterns. Though I grant you…if I could interest you in even a small bit of oil, I would like that very much."

As Otto lowered his shoulders and voiced his obvious dismay, Rem inquired, "What is this about oil?"

"Oh, I simply wound up getting something of a short straw. At present, the merchandise I am carrying is a somewhat large quantity of oil. I'd really meant to trade it in Gusteko for a large sum, but now, my very life hangs in the balance, and I must mitigate the loss as much as possible…"

It was plain as day that he was seeking sympathy for his plight… and a buyer for his oil. No doubt Rem understood this full well. Sympathetic as she might be, she would offer him nothing beyond perfunctory condolences.

"I do not know if I will be able to sell all this oil even if I go to the royal capital. If I sell it for the price of dirt, I will be bankrupt—bankrupt!"

Repeating himself for emphasis, he opened the door wide for a highly generous person to take all the oil off his hands. Though the man had helped him during the first time around, it was precisely why Subaru sought to avoid getting deeply entangled now. He could pray for Otto's prospects, but at that moment, Subaru and Rem's futures came first.

To get to the Mathers domain as soon as humanly possible, they could not avoid rushing along the highway at night. But just as Subaru was about to say his good-byes, he suddenly realized something.

If trust wasn't enough to put things into motion, maybe he should move them with money…

"Otto, there's something I… No, I have a business proposal."

Otto's eyes opened at how the expression on Subaru's face vanished, and the air around him changed. But perhaps sensing from Subaru's voice that he wasn't joking, he immediately adopted the posture of a salesman.

"If it is business, I will listen to anything you have to say. Dear customer—how may I be of service?"

"I'll buy every drop of oil in your dragon carriage. In return, give me a hand."

Subaru pointed to Otto's land dragon, which he remembered, and then opened his arms wide, shouting in a voice loud enough for all the merchants setting up camp to hear.

"Every merchant with a land dragon here… If your services are for sale, let me buy everything you have!"

3

At first, the merchants looked at one another and laughed at Subaru's "business proposal." But when Rem, sensing what Subaru had in mind, lifted up her sack and showed everyone the coinage within, the expressions of all the men who'd dismissed it as a joke changed in an instant. After that, Otto acted as the ringleader and recruited those willing to participate.

As a result, of the fourteen traveling merchants in that place, ten decided to go along. The conversation had a rocky start, but Otto's proposed split of the profits neatly resolved the issue.

"Everyone will entrust their cargo to the four with the largest dragon carriages. The net proceeds from joint sales in the royal capital will be distributed at a later date. The sales will offset the freight cost of accompanying Mr. Natsuki."

Thanks to Otto's skill in bringing everyone to a consensus—no doubt an effect of his desperation when faced with the chance of a lifetime—he was unanimously voted to represent the group.

Seeing Subaru with his arms folded, concerned about their departure time as he watched fellow peddlers transferring their cargo, Otto asked him, "I'm pleased that you're buying up my oil, but what do you intend to use all these dragon carriages for?"

Subaru touched his chin as he mulled over the question.

"We're on our way to the Mathers domain. I happen to be a manservant working for Marquis Mathers, you see."

"I'm aware of him. Marquis Roswaal L. Mathers, with his 'penchant' for demi-humans. They say that he is an eccentric, even by the standards of Lugunica nobility."

Had Ram overheard that appraisal, she would have no doubt been indignant. Subaru's shoulders sank at Otto's description.

"Well, no denying that. It's true he comes off as a perv."

"But he is your employer, you say? Er, I broached the subject because I rather expected a reply of that sort. Though I must confess that you do not look like a nobleman's servant, Mr. Natsuki."

"I'm still in training. I only make the grade in sewing and making beds so far."

"Either way, I'll trust your story about serving the marquis... But why hire all these dragon carriages? A marquis can surely afford his own?"

Otto's probing questions were proof that he doubted Subaru's true intent.

"Like I said, we need a bunch of dragon carriages. We have a lot to haul, so it's best to have them as empty as possible. In your case, that means having to buy up all your oil."

"For which I am very grateful. What is the freight you intend to transport, then?"

From Otto's repeated questions, it seemed he did not doubt Subaru's station. He appeared to be pressing out of simple concern that the freight to be transported might be dangerous.

"—"

There was no need to conceal it with a lie. He couldn't let this talk foster doubt and lead to the deal being called off.

"We're transporting...people."

"Don't tell me this is slave trading?!"

"Nothing shady like that. There's a village near the marquis's mansion. It's a small settlement, and the villagers put together don't even number a hundred. I wanna get those people aboard and move them out."

—That flash of inspiration was why Subaru had hired Otto and the others.

The large dragon carriage for commercial freight that Subaru and Rem were using could run with more than ten people aboard. With similar dragon carriages put together, he figured they could evacuate every last villager.

"You are not telling us to carry corpses, I take it. If so, I would have to decline with deep regrets..."

"...I want you to bring them out of there so it doesn't come to that."

In his haste to reunite with Emilia, Subaru had forgotten about the villagers. He was upset with his own lack of consideration, but coming across Otto and the others was a very considerable stroke of good fortune. Be it coincidence or fate, Subaru was fortunate to be on something's good side for once.

"Actually, we're planning on doing a large-scale mountain hunt in the area around the marquis's mansion in the near future."

"A mountain hunt, you say?"

"There's been a bunch of demon beasts breeding in the wilderness around there since way back. Barriers isolated the people from the demon beasts until now, but... Not long ago, those monsters injured some people in the village."

"And this 'mountain hunt' is the result of that? But..."

Otto couldn't quite let it go; he seemed to be having trouble with something in Subaru's explanation. Subaru remained silent as he rolled up the sleeve over his right arm, showing him the cruel scars the beasts had left on him.

Otto drew a small, sharp breath at seeing the deep wounds of claw and fang. Many more had been carved into Subaru's body that would never fade.

"In his goodwill, the marquis sent me off to the royal capital to be healed. Now that I'm partly recovered and no longer at death's door, I'm on my way back."

"I—I see... Er, but why, then, are you procuring dragon carriages along the highway without the marquis being directly involved...?"

"The marquis decided to start the hunt right away before moving the residents. That's why I want to make sure it's covered. It's not that I don't trust my master; I just have prior experience with this."

As Subaru offered that humble statement, lowering his eyes, Otto made a small sound and sank into thought.

"Understood. Sorry for prying into things you didn't want to speak about. I shall explain this to the others without mentioning the scars."

A pained expression came over Otto's good-natured face as he made a show of consideration for Subaru. No doubt he regretted unintentionally dredging up Subaru's past trauma.

Subaru thought that his sudden change in demeanor, shifting from thoughts about commerce to simply worrying about his business partner, showed that Otto was a real softie at heart.

"Don't sweat it. Please just explain it to everyone straight so that no one gets any weird doubts."

"Well, if you insist, though I'm not really cut out for that."

Making light of Subaru's decision, Otto smiled apologetically.

Subaru thought himself a far greater villain for internally making excuses.

—Namely, that he wasn't really lying; he just wasn't telling the whole truth.

4

It was another two hours until all preparations to pull out of the campsite had been completed.

After the freight was transferred to the four large dragon carriages, Subaru and the others departed along the highway by night.

There were eleven dragon carriages heading toward the Mathers domain. They might prove somewhat cramped, but they should be more than enough to get all the villagers out.

Otto called to him as his dragon carriage ran parallel to Subaru's.

"By running through half the night, we'll probably arrive in the Mathers domain near morning…"

It was the land dragons' wind repel blessings that enabled them to have a normal conversation while two dragon carriages ran side by side. They did more than nullify the effects of wind and vibrations on them, apparently.

"Sorry to make you keep running without a break."

"Not at all! I have no complaints. Now that I can dispose of my stock and defray the freight costs, I am invincible. I could keep this up for three days and nights!"

"And then you can fall asleep right after the deal is done?"

"Huh?! Did you read my mind?!"

The punch line to a classic joke was stolen right out of Otto's mouth. From there, Subaru shifted his gaze toward Rem, holding the reins beside him. He could not read any emotion from the side of her face as she stared straight ahead. To Subaru, it wasn't a very pleasant situation.

"—Subaru."

"...Y-yeah. What is it, Rem? Something's up?"

"No. It is quiet, so I wondered if you might be tired. The dust makes for poor visibility, but with other land dragons about, the path is not uncertain. If you are sleepy, it is all right for you to rest."

"I'm happy to hear you say that, but it's not cool to make you do all the work."

"But Subaru, you are still convalescing, so..."

Rem's considerate stance toward Subaru made him shut his mouth. Her manner of speaking was gentle, but there was a stubborn, steely will behind it. He keenly understood that she wished to reduce the burden on him as much as possible. But her tenacious efforts made him fearful that he didn't know her true intentions. The thorns he could not dislodge from his chest were the product of both wanting to know and not wanting to know.

"Rem, do...?"

"Yes?"

Subaru's breath caught as Rem's pale-blue eyes stared at him, as if seeing right through him. He wanted some way to redirect her attention from his doubting, hesitant silence, but Subaru shook his head, brushing aside such thoughts.

If he doubted Rem's intentions enough that it hurt, it was far better to get them out in the open.

"Rem, do you have any doubts about what I'm doing? I didn't explain anything to you. Not about the Witch Cult, not about the traveling merchants..."

He was painfully aware of how Rem had kindly indulged him in spite of his duty to explain himself. That was precisely why he was worried about how Rem felt about following him without question or debate.

Rem closed her eyes but once at Subaru's question.

"Master Roswaal told me to respect your actions in the royal capital."

"—"

Subaru's expression stiffened, the reply leaving him lost for words.

"Roswaal…told you to…?"

"Yes. He did not command me to do any specific thing, but rather, to go along with your plans in the royal capital, whatever they might be. I also planned do so as much as I could."

"Roswaal's orders…"

Rem's words somehow weren't sinking into his skull. Instead, the fact that Roswaal had ordered Rem repeated itself in his head, over and over.

Rem's lack of dissent toward Subaru's actions was because her master had directed her to shut up and obey. Did that mean, in other words, that Rem's actions to that point had not been of her own will? Hell, even her staying by his side at that very moment might not have been…

"Subaru?"

As Subaru fell silent, Rem peered at him, her shapely eyebrows drawing together. Yet in that moment, Subaru was unable to take even that expression of concern at face value.

"I-I'm all right. It's nothing."

Shaking his head to flee from Rem's gaze, Subaru gave a perfunctory reply to keep the peace.

Her caring concert, her support when he was on the brink of collapse, her being by the isolated Subaru's side, were all of these because of Roswaal's orders…? Beyond that, deep down, did Rem approve of what Subaru was doing…?

"—!"

As paranoia brought bile up from his stomach, Subaru swallowed down the acidic liquid filling his mouth. With his nausea having nowhere else to go, fright and despondency raged inside his body.

His limbs felt numb, his vision narrowed, and there was an unbearable, physical itch in his brain. His breath was ragged as he fought the urgent desire to crack his skull open and jab his fingers in to scratch at it.

He didn't want to think. About anything.

The more he thought about things, the more he mulled them over, the more he sought answers—the more distant his desires would become, the more his ideals would turn to fantasies and his dreams to hopelessness and despair.

"Subaru, did you fall asleep?"

He hated it. He wanted no more of it.

He didn't want to think. He didn't want to doubt. He didn't want to trust. He didn't want to be betrayed.

He clutched his head, shutting himself in and cutting off all responses to the outside world.

Rem called his name several times. Seeing that there was no response, she gave up after a while and shifted her gaze back to the highway.

By then, Subaru had finally, and by his own hand, become truly alone in that world.

5

"—ru. I'm sorry, Subaru. Please wake up."

Subaru sensed someone calling him and shaking him awake.

The touch on his shoulder roused him from the abyss of unconsciousness. When he absentmindedly rubbed his eyelids with his hand and opened his eyes, he found the face of a familiar girl right in front of him.

"...Rem, huh. What's wrong?"

The instant he was sure it was Rem, Subaru remembered their exchange before he slept. He felt a dull ache in his chest.

Rem, not noticing how hard Subaru was working to endure that pain, lowered her head apologetically. After another brief apology for waking him, she said, "We are about to reach a fork in the road. As it is a landmark that cannot be mistaken even in the dead of night, it should be all right...but I want to be certain before we reach it."

The area around them was filled with deep darkness. Even with Rem sitting right beside him, her face seemed indistinct. The crystal lamp hanging from the land dragon's neck and a simple light attached to the dragon carriage itself provided the only illumination. It was very little to go on—if not for land dragons with good night vision, then certainly for the humans.

"I see your point. What do you want me to do, though?"

"I want to check the map, but I cannot take my hands off the reins... I put the map in the sack at your feet. Could you get it out for me?"

"At my feet. This, huh?"

In the dark, he pulled over a fairly heavy sack. He set it on his lap and thrust in his hand to fish around, but finding what he was after proved rather difficult.

"I can't even tell what's a map and what's not. Isn't it too dark to even read it?"

"That is... Mm, that could be a problem. What shall we do...?"

"Yeah, what can we...? No, wait a sec."

Rem's expression was clouded when a light suddenly turned on in Subaru's head. Once again, he searched at his feet, picking something out of a different sack—the one with Subaru's personal belongings.

"Oh, I found it!"

He took out the object, cool and hard to the touch, and thrust it in Rem's face. Right in front of her wide eyes, Subaru pressed the power button of something he hadn't held in ages.

"It hasn't been charged in a while, so I hope the battery isn't dead... Ohh!"

After a single tense moment, the boot-up sequence appeared on the screen. A few seconds later, a dazzling light shone from Subaru's hand.

Rem looked at Subaru with surprise at the brilliant sight.

"Subaru, what is that?"

"Lost technolo… Er, future technology. A cell phone. Looks like it still has a little juice left, luckily for us."

The cell phone had been off ever since his generous use of it on the day he had been summoned to this other world. It was one of Subaru's few possessions from home. He had a few other personal belongings, but this was by far the priciest and most useful—at least, as long as its battery held out.

"I never imagined the next time I'd use it would be as a flashlight, though."

Using it in a manner inconsistent with its original purpose, Subaru shone the light of civilization upon the contents of the luggage. After he easily found the map he'd been searching for in the sack, Subaru spread it out over Rem's lap.

"I'll shine this on the map, so take a look-see."

"Yes, thank you very much."

At that moment, Otto poked his head in from the side, his interest keenly piqued.

"Mr. Natsuki, what is that? I've never seen such a thing." Leaning over from his dragon carriage, immediately to the left, he tilted his head in confusion. "A crystal lamp I have never seen bef— No, not a crystal. It seems to be made of some material unfamiliar to me."

Noticing Otto's reaction, a man in his prime with a bandanna wrapped around his head pulled his dragon carriage along the right side as well. The eyes of the driver glimmered as his gaze remained pinned to Subaru's cell phone.

Ordinarily, their reactions would have doubtlessly brightened Subaru's mood, inspiring him to casually show off and brag. However, the current Subaru was in no mood for such pleasantries.

"Sorry, it's a secret item the marquis gave to me. If I told you about it, you might vanish without a trace. Best to forget you ever saw it."

"Whew, that secretive explanation just reeks of money…"

Otto's interest seemed to have only deepened. But before a long cover-up conversation became necessary, Rem lifted her head from the map and nodded.

"I realize where we are now. A little farther and we should be able to see the Great Flugel Tree. From there, we take the road northeast and enter the Mathers domain shortly after."

"The Great Flugel Tree?"

Subaru inclined his head at the unfamiliar term. Otto raised a finger.

"The Great Flugel Tree is a huge tree found along the Liphas Highway that seems to pierce the very clouds. The tree really is huge like you wouldn't believe. According to legend, a sage named Flugel planted it."

"So that's why it's the *Great Flugel Tree*. Why'd the sage do that, anyway?"

"Er, well, this was hundreds of years ago, you see. Aside from the story of how he planted the tree, next to nothing is known about Flugel, not even why he is treated as a sage."

"The hell is that? Why treat him like a big shot if you don't even know what good he's done?"

Subaru was itching to hear the rest after Otto's incomplete account, but when he saw that Rem and the other merchants weren't adding to the story, it was apparent that his exploits really hadn't been passed down.

Subaru mulled over the thought, and around half an hour later, he saw the Great Tree for himself, to his shock.

"Whoa… Yeah, *incredible* is about the only word I can use for it."

The venerable tree, its branches rising into the night sky, towered over Subaru and the others with an overwhelming presence. Its size dwarfed the trees from his old world that were often said to be more than a thousand years old. According to Otto, this specimen was centuries old, making Subaru wonder if plants grew at a much faster pace in his current world. Before he realized it, he was seized by a considerable sense of awe.

The enormous tree had put down its roots not in a great forest, but alone in an open field. Along the Liphas Highway, there was no landmark more prominent.

Passing by the calmly towering Great Tree, the dragon carriages headed northeast in accordance with the map. As the distance to the Mathers domain lessened, Subaru finally began to feel a little regretful at leaving the Great Tree behind.

"Geez, this isn't the time to get all sentimental. Er, ah?"

If he had been less troubled, he might have taken a picture of it with his cell phone. Subaru, who was sitting on the driver's seat when he had the thought, felt uneasy as he redirected his attention from the Great Tree.

"Where'd the bandanna guy to the right of us go?"

Subaru could see no sign of the dragon-carriage owner who had shown interest in his cell phone while running on their right. Subaru checked behind him to see if it had suddenly slowed down, but he saw only the dragon carriage that had been running behind the bandanna man; he was gone from the convoy, leaving an empty space.

"Don't tell me he was so enchanted by the big tree that he wandered off?"

"What is it, Mr. Natsuki? Are you looking for something?"

"Not something—one of your guys, the one who was running on this side till just now, a manly looking guy with a bandanna. This ain't the time to go tree climbing like a little kid."

Subaru harshly answered the carefree Otto with sarcasm, inwardly scolding him for poor management. But Otto, on the receiving end of that annoyance, stared blankly and tilted his head, as if he had no idea what Subaru meant.

"What are you talking about? No one's been on the opposite side of you."

"—Huh?"

Subaru's mouth hung open, and the meaning of the reply failed to sink in.

"What are you sayin'? He was all curious and staring at my cell phone just earlier, same as you."

"Ahh, so it's called a *cell phone*? Wait, ah, can you guarantee my safety for having heard that? I don't want to disappear..."

"Don't play games with me!"

Subaru roared at Otto, who was casually ignoring Subaru's question as if he thought it was all some big joke. Subaru looked to the right again, but the gap was as wide as before, and the carriage that should have been there nowhere to be found.

"—?"

Then, as Subaru stared at the gap, his field of vision suddenly became indistinct. He sensed a blur, as if there was a haze right before his eyes. Subaru blinked several times, but that did not wipe away his unease.

The dark empty space continued to run parallel to Subaru and Rem's dragon carriage. The darkness was terribly ominous, and he couldn't help the nervousness welling up inside him.

That was why Subaru opened his folded cell phone, shining light upon the gap to drive away the darkness.

He meant to look for a trace of the person who should have been there, and to ascertain the source of the uncanny feeling that just wouldn't go away.

And within the shining light—

"...Ah?"

There, floating in space, Subaru met a truly gigantic eye.

The next moment, something roared, and mist covered the Liphas plains.

—Mist.

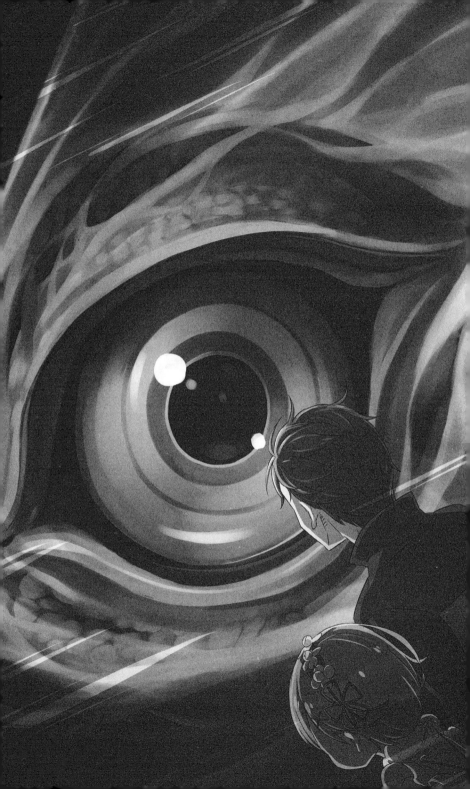

6

Bathed in a powerful gust of wind, Subaru felt like he'd been smacked in the face.

"—!"

Pounded by the gale, Subaru's body floated up, in danger of being tossed from the driver's seat altogether. He instantly reached out, but his fingers found nothing to grasp; Subaru's body flew straight forward, hurtling toward the darkness—or it would have, if she had been a moment later.

"Subaru!!"

His collar was grabbed from behind, forcefully pulling him back down. The hard impact of his butt upon the seat made him see stars; amid them, he saw Rem, holding him down while handling the reins.

Rem's mouth was open as she abandoned her usual neutral expression, howling desperately. Her shouts became a chant. Mana gathered according to Rem's will, transforming the world around them with magic to create spears of ice as long as Subaru was tall.

In the blink of an eye, three frozen missiles formed in mid-air, shooting out like arrows with incredible force. The ice spears raced through the sky, landing with a sound like steel smashing stone—and the darkness before them was shattered.

"Oh, wahhh?!"

The next moment, Subaru was grabbed by his neck once again and instantly hoisted straight up.

As he floated upward and away from the driver's seat, he saw the dragon carriage beneath him. The land dragon, not realizing its passengers had vanished, continued kicking up dust as it sprinted along the highway with all its might.

In the next instant, a hit from the side with enormous mass behind it reduced the dragon carriage to splinters, sending the land dragon hurtling along with it. The unadorned vehicle for hauling commercial freight was torn apart like paper; the huge animal, slammed into the ground, burst apart from the impact, turning into a smear of blood, innards, and fragments of flesh on the highway.

Subaru's mind went blank from the overwhelmingly unreal spectacle.

"Left—!!"

He thought he heard a shout from right beside him. A second later, his body landed on a hard floor. The dull pain coursing through his shoulder and hip dragged his mind back to reality.

However, the blows assailing him one after another gave him no opportunity to lift up his head. The dragon carriage he was now riding made a sudden turn, and the centrifugal force flung Subaru to the side. When the vehicle tilted, the rope wrapped around his fingers was the only thing keeping him from being hurled right out.

Turning his head, he came to realize that he'd leaped onto Otto's dragon carriage.

Wrapping the rope for securing freight around his wrist, Subaru tried to get up amid the shaking.

"No, Subaru, you mustn't! The dragon carriage's blessing has given out. It's dangerous for you and Rem to get up!"

When he looked, Rem had impaled the floor with her own right arm to support herself. It was difficult for her to keep steady during the rocking, even with her physical abilities.

Without the effects of the wind repel blessing enveloping the land dragon, Subaru's body was mercilessly subjected to the ferocious wind and shaking. He grew ill; he couldn't even try to stand.

Rem had clutched Subaru and leaped from their dragon carriage to Otto's. If she'd made that decision even a second later, she and Subaru would have shared the same fate as the pulverized cart.

"Wh-what happened?! What the hell's going on here?!"

The overwhelmingly destructive change had happened in mere tens of seconds. Subaru couldn't even begin to wrap his mind around the sequence of events.

"Don't you get it?!"

Otto responded to Subaru's confused question in a near scream.

When Otto looked back, his face was white as a ghost, his teeth chattering as he pointed to the sky.

"The fog appeared! That giant thing swimming in the sky can only be one thing!"

It was as if Otto was convincing himself because he refused to accept it; he grudgingly shook his head, convulsing with fear as he desperately drew air into his lungs and shouted with all his might: "—The White Whale!!"

As if responding to Otto's shout, the White Whale's roar shook the air, echoing across the plains.

—The White Whale.

Subaru knew he'd heard the name during the first time around. The name of the monster shrouded in mist that had shut off the highway.

With the highway blocked due to this creature, he'd had to take a huge detour to get back to the mansion. One might say it was the reason he didn't get back before the Witch Cult's onslaught.

But until that moment, Subaru had never laid eyes upon the monster itself. Furthermore, Subaru had forgotten its existence; he couldn't deny that he'd been too naive. Namely, that…

"How could it come out like this, right now?!"

Subaru knew that the highway was closed whenever the White Whale appeared. The first time around, the blockade had occurred on the third day of Subaru and Rem's journey back due to the appearance of the White Whale's mist along the road. And that moment was the night of the second day—no doubt the royal capital would be informed of the appearance of the mist in the morning, with the highway sealed during that day.

That night was the only one when they were unaware of the White Whale's presence, and they had blundered into the menace.

"To think…running into the Wh-White Whale… O Dragon, O Dragon, please deliver us…!"

With hollow eyes, Otto murmured a prayer to the Dragon in search of salvation. As Otto lost the will to fight and even his very spirit, Subaru saw with his own eyes how, among traveling merchants, the existence of the White Whale was synonymous with absolute terror.

The previous time around, Otto had indicated how the White Whale was an evil omen among all merchants.

Otto's lips trembled, his mind somewhere else as he managed the reins. His land dragon, sensing the presence of the White Whale, had fallen into a state of terror, exhausting its remaining strength to kick the ground and propel them forward at an unsustainable speed.

The White Whale had sunk into the night, its giant body nowhere to be seen.

"Shit... Just when it starts coming after us, the fog comes out...!"

Subaru scowled as he felt cold droplets of sweat on his brow, wiping them off with the palm of his hand. With few sources of light to begin with, the emergence of mist made maintaining visibility all but impossible.

Subaru looked behind, to the side, and above, searching for any trace of something that resembled a fish.

"Rem! Do you see the White Whale?!"

"I cannot; it is too dark! But...!"

Rem replied bitterly to Subaru's question, but for some reason, she trailed off. The catching of Rem's breath tugged at Subaru, but when he tried to look at her, all he could see in the deep mist was a silhouette; he couldn't tell what was on her face. The mist grew even thicker, to the point that he wasn't sure where his own hands were.

"___"

When Subaru had first met the White Whale's gaze, it was bigger in circumference than Subaru's arms could reach. If the giant eye was anything to go by, the White Whale had to be truly as large as the name implied.

It struck him that such a monster was hiding without any sound or sign of its presence, and it was able to swim freely through the night sky. They'd lost sight of the White Whale in the deep fog, a fact that aroused even greater terror.

"But I believe my preemptive attack struck... It is possible the creature has retreated."

That was surely too optimistic.

The might of the ice spears Rem had rammed into it with her

incantation was on par with the most powerful magic Subaru had yet seen. If he were ever the target, it'd be enough to kill him three times over.

Perhaps even a gigantic creature like that might hesitate to pursue them too far.

"What happened to the other dragon carriages?!"

"They seem to have scattered and run for it. If you split up and flee the instant the mist arrives, you might be able to escape without the White Whale pursuing—if you're lucky."

No doubt it was standard operating procedure when encountering the White Whale.

It made sense. Certainly, the dragon carriage that had been running parallel to theirs was nowhere to be found. The other vehicles that had followed behind them until that point seemed to have obeyed the unwritten rule and scattered to the winds.

—Subaru clenched his teeth at the fact that he'd lost the carriages he'd worked so hard to obtain.

The timing was a disaster. His plan to evacuate everyone in the village had fallen to pieces once more.

"No point crying over spilled milk. Anyway, right now I've gotta focus on a way to get out of this fog..."

As the rocking jostled his internal organs, Subaru pushed aside all other concerns until after they escaped. They had few cards to play to deal with the immediate crisis. Now that his own dragon carriage was unavailable, he needed at least Otto's to get back to the mansion. That was why, right then, they had to get past that dangerous fog—

"—!!"

A mouth cavity lined by giant teeth resembling rows of millstones suddenly opened wide before their very eyes.

The overpowering violence of the sound and the blast winds of its thunderous roar sent the land dragon reeling. The ground split, tripping up its feet, and the dragon carriage's wheels lifted as the wagon tilted far to the side. The canopy holding down jugs of oil broke, and the cargo went flying outside; Subaru, holding his cord, was in danger of being thrown out himself.

Subaru desperately clung to the wagon as he saw the enormous mouth lined with filthy teeth in front of them bearing down, seeking to swallow them whole.

It was in that moment that Subaru truly grasped just how little he'd understood.

And now, in that instant, plunged into that encounter with the White Whale within that deep nighttime mist, was the gambling table upon which they would wager their survival.

"—Roaaaaa!"

The instant the maw came to swallow the dragon carriage, there was a great shout as something shot into the air from the wagon's floor. Rem had leaped, shooting in front like a bullet, shattering the floor in the process. From the hair under her hairpiece, buffeted by the blast winds, a sharp horn protruded as she entered her Oni state. She swung her personal weapon, a spiked ball on a chain.

"—Slip past it on the left!"

"Left, left, left, left, left!"

The iron ball smashed straight down into the White Whale's upper jaw, sending a pitch-black cloud of blood spurting forth as the enormous, yawning mouth snapped shut. The lower jaw gouged out the earth, but even so, momentum continued to propel the giant head forward. Otto poured his entire being into controlling the land dragon, slipping right past the side of the head. However, the wagon behind the sprinting animal could not completely evade the gargantuan body to its right; the two met, kicking up a sound like that of rubbing against solid rock.

With a heavy *creak*, the wagon lost a wheel; without that balance, it flipped right over. Naturally, Subaru, who was atop it, was powerless to avoid being tossed toward the ground in the process.

—*Am I gonna die?*

Just before his inability to respond led to his death, a silver snake wound around Subaru's chest with a loud roar. Subaru was forcefully dragged up from his steep descent and plopped headfirst onto the driver's seat.

"Take thiiiis—!"

After dragging Subaru up with the iron ball in her right hand,

Rem smashed the joint connecting the luggage compartment to the driver's seat with her empty left hand, grasping the edge of the separated section. Instantly, the land dragon pulling the dragon carriage let out a painful neigh from the strain as the parts of the large commercial freight vehicle were torn apart.

Even if half of it was gone, it was a supersize bullet made of almost as much wood as a log cabin. It squarely struck the White Whale's straying belly. The White Whale thrashed, its tail blasting apart the earth and the trees, kicking up clouds of dust.

"D-d-did you get it?!"

Even if Otto didn't know what had just happened, he'd surely noticed the fact that most of his dragon carriage was missing. His voice was tinged with bitterness as he sought hope that would warrant the sacrifice.

A roar made the air tremble as an even worse mist blotted out the light. From the pressure bearing down on them from behind, one known as absolute despair, he knew that hope had been shattered.

"Wh-why is it only after us...? Aren't there other carriages?!"

Otto let out a lament as he cursed the misfortune that had befallen him. He blamed the sheer irrationality of the other eight carriages being ignored while his was attacked. Subaru felt the same way, but he swallowed his complaints when Otto launched a string of curses. He felt like he was getting a good, hard look at an ugly truth—against the Witch Cult, he and the others Subaru brought along would have served only as sacrificial pawns, or perhaps meat shields.

"Besides, cursing my fate won't change a thing..."

The menace of the White Whale continued to press upon them from behind, swimming through the sky faster than the land dragon. Even though the land dragon was running with a lightened load now that they had abandoned the freight, it was only a matter of time before the whale caught up.

"Think, think, think. There has to be a way, something, something...!"

Subaru desperately put his head to work, but no plan for a counterattack came to mind. With a sense of urgency weighing on him and the night mist so thick that he couldn't see his own feet, Subaru couldn't find even a single hint.

And as time idly wasted away, fate forced yet another difficult choice upon Subaru.

The carriage was heavily rocked. As Subaru clung to the floor, Rem approached. She should have been shaken, too, but she didn't seem bothered by it as she nestled close.

"Subaru. Please take this."

"What?! Did you think of something?! Now we can do something ab—"

Believing that Rem might have come up with an off-the-wall plan to escape the crisis, Subaru lifted his head as she pushed a small sack onto him. From the heavy weight, he immediately realized it was the traveling money.

What use would money have at a time like this…?

Feeling a deep chill at Rem's offer, Subaru's cheeks stretched into a stiff smile.

"R-Rem…? I know there's a coin-toss skill to at least knock someone off balance, but that's just in games…"

"I will get off the dragon carriage and counterattack. During that time, please cut through the mist, Subaru."

Though Subaru tried to deny reality with a joke, the firmness of Rem's voice shattered the effort.

Rem turned, facing Otto instead of Subaru.

"Master Otto. Please take care of Subaru. He is able to pay the promised reward— Cut through the mist and report the appearance of the White Whale to the Mathers domain."

Otto, not having heard the previous exchange, replied, "R-reward…? There's no time for that! Right now, our v-very lives hang in the balance!"

Despite his protest, Rem was relieved to see that he was earnestly making his land dragon run so that he might live. Her lips softened as she looked back at Subaru.

"Subaru, please forgive me. I am not very bright, so this is the only plan I can think of…"

"W-wait, Rem! You said to report about the White Whale showing up, didn't you? Don't tell me...you don't plan on coming back alive?"

Subaru desperately tried to make Rem reconsider the tragic decision she had made.

Even though the darkness that had befallen them continued to blot out the rest of the world, for some reason, the only thing he could see clearly was Rem's face before his eyes.

"I won't let you go! I won't let you! If you... If you die, too, I'll...!"

As Rem stood before him, Subaru dropped the money sack to his feet, putting his hands on Rem's hips and pulling her to him. He wrapped his arms around her petite figure so that she could not withdraw. If he loosened his arms, he would be releasing Rem's life to fly away, too.

He had to at least stop that. At least that—

"Ahh..."

With emotions raging within her, nearly enough to bring her to tears, Rem let out a heated breath as she accepted his embrace. As she looked up at Subaru, holding her in his arms, she lowered her gaze with a charming smile on her lips, seemingly enthralled by the sound of his voice.

"I was surely born for this very moment..."

"What are you sa...?"

Saying, but his mouth wouldn't form the word.

Something hit the back of Subaru's neck, and it seemed like the whole world had turned upside down. Rem had stretched out an arm, as if to hug him back, and delivered a chop to the back of his head. Strength drained from Subaru's body, and he crumpled against Rem.

"Re...m... What did you...?"

Not only was the swaying of the dragon carriage affecting his vision, but it was swallowing his fading consciousness as well. Subaru desperately clung to Rem as it became difficult to even hold his head aloft.

Rem gazed affectionately at Subaru as he struggled. Then, she

gently brought her lips to Subaru's ear, whispering as if to reach the last remaining shred of his consciousness.

"It's all right, Subaru. I will always be watching you from behind."

You don't need to do anything. Just always be right there behind me.

Those had been Subaru's words to Rem on the morning of their departure.

Hence, just as he had said, she now stood behind him—as his rear guard.

"No…I never intended…"

"Subaru. I—"

His mind fell away.

It grew distant and went white.

For a moment, he felt like someone was embracing him strongly.

He felt something soft touch his forehead and then immediately depart.

And that was the last thing he knew.

7

—.

——.

———Ah.

He could feel the repeated rocking and jolting of the carriage, as well as something bumping into his head over and over. Gradually, it called to Subaru's blanked-out mind, bringing him back to reality.

He tried to lift his head and sit up, but the rocking was fighting him. His hand was slippery, and he was about to fall onto the floor headfirst once more, but this was averted because something heavy was pressing down on his belly.

The pressure on his gut came from something hard. When his hand touched it, he knew from the texture that it was money of some sort, and the memories from just before his consciousness faded rushed from back of his mind.

"—Rem?!"

"Mr. Natsuki?! You're awake?!"

Subaru cast aside the bag of traveling money on his stomach, remaining seated and leaning back on his hands as he looked around. The world was still mired in darkness, but the sound of violent shaking told him that he was still on the dragon carriage.

And noticing that Subaru was up, Otto turned his head to check on him. Subaru was trying to get up when Otto raised his voice, still looking back from the driver's seat.

"Please do not move! You hit your head and the carriage's blessing has been gone for some time. Even now, the land dragon is running with all its strength; I have no time to be concerned about you, Mr. Natsuki!"

"Never mind any of that! Rem, what happened to Rem?!"

Shouting back, Subaru searched every corner of the driver's seat for the girl. Without the wagon, the dragon carriage was very cramped. Anyone would understand in an instant that there was no need to search.

Yet even so, until he checked for himself, he just couldn't accept that she wasn't there.

"Answer me, Otto. What happened to Rem...?!"

"That young lady..."

Realizing that Subaru's voice was rough, agitated enough that he might pounce at any moment, Otto no doubt hesitated to reply because he knew how dangerous things were.

"...disembarked from our dragon carriage to engage the White Whale...so that we could have a chance to escape."

This told Subaru that the exchange just before he'd lost consciousness was no dream or illusion but fact.

"—"

Having dragged the answer out of the man, Subaru sucked in his breath but once. Then, he said, "Turn back."

"...Huh?"

"I said, turn back. Rem—we have to save her! Turn back right now!"

Subaru leaped into the narrow driver's seat and grabbed Otto by his collar. Confused and still occupied with controlling the land dragon, Otto was unable to respond to Subaru's act of violence. His face went pale as his collar was grabbed.

"A-are you serious?! Turn back... Turn back and do what?! Did you not see how terrifying that monster is?! It's suicide!"

"I'm telling you to go back to where we saw the monster so we can save Rem, damn it!!"

When Otto refused his command, a vein bulged on Subaru's forehead as he shouted in anger.

The menace of the White Whale had been burned into Subaru's very eyes. The giant creature swam through the air faster than a land dragon could run; a single, casual slap of its tail could rend a carriage asunder. Even within the blinding mist, it unerringly located its prey; even Rem's magic hadn't inflicted any damage.

Without doubt, it was the largest and mightiest of all the foes he had seen since arriving in this other world. Compared to the menace it posed, dealing with Elsa, classified as a human being, and the pack of countless Urugarum was far easier to plan for.

But he couldn't even dream of a way to defeat a monster on that scale.

"And Rem couldn't, either... We can't just leave her. If we do that...!"

Subaru was well aware of how strong Rem was in her Oni state. But his familiarity with her abilities meant he could plainly state that it meant nothing before the might of the White Whale.

If he left Rem behind, he would lose her for certain. Then everything would be pointless. Then there would be no meaning in Subaru surviving. Rem was an irreplaceable part of the future Subaru desired.

If she wasn't there, Subaru would lose sight of even his own self. He would have no one to accept him. Subaru needed her to give him affirmation.

"I won't let her sacrifice herself to buy time! Turn back right now, Otto! If you don't..."

"Have you lost your mind?!"

However, Otto's angry shout interrupted Subaru's plea. Still grasping Otto's collar, he felt a squeeze on the back of his wrist; in the next moment, he was slammed against the driver's seat back first.

"Agah!"

"You think you can force a traveling merchant tearing down a highway without a blessing? You underestimate me!"

With Subaru facedown, Otto twisted the wrist in his hand, straining Subaru's shoulder to its limit—still grasping the reins with his other hand all the while.

"At any rate, calm down! Look at yourself. What can you do in a state like this? Do you plan to put to waste the feelings that girl left behind?"

"Don't you talk about Rem! You left her… You left Rem to die! You have no right to talk about her! Turn back! Save Rem right now…!"

"Ahh, goodness! You're not listening! Please regain your composure!"

Subaru chewed Otto out as he writhed, struggling to get his pinned arm loose. Meanwhile, Otto gazed at the road ahead as the land dragon ran down the center.

"You still don't understand how terrifying the White Whale is?! There are many tales of those who tried to kill it, ever since it descended upon the world centuries ago! Don't you get it?!"

Misery clouded Otto's face as he ranted at the obstinate Subaru.

"They couldn't kill it, even with hundreds challenging it all at once! We don't even have weapons or power to fight with, so what can we do?! Stand before it and rescue the girl?! We can't do that! There's no way!"

"Shut up already! I've heard all that bef—"

"Then it should be obvious! Even when the Kingdom of Lugunica assembled a great expeditionary force to quell it, the monster killed the last Sword Saint! We can't beat it!"

Otto's face trembled with bitter regret as he unwillingly confessed the truth. Otto, too, held great rage toward the White Whale that would never fade. But even so, the menace of the White Whale that stirred his anger was untouchable for man.

To teach the ignorant Subaru the error of his ways, Otto had to force himself to acknowledge the enormity of the White Whale, experiencing heartbreaking pain in the process.

"It killed…a Sword Saint…?"

As Otto bared his soul, a part of the story Subaru had never heard before took the wind from his sails. *Sword Saint*—that was the title granted to the most powerful human being Subaru had laid eyes upon since being summoned to that world. To Subaru, it was the very symbol of strength without equal.

It was not for certain that the previous Sword Saint could not boast the same strength as Reinhard, the epitome of "The Mightiest of All." But if the person bearing a title equal to Reinhard was someone with comparable power, and the White Whale killed that person…

"It's stronger than Reinhard…?"

A monster surpassing the mightiest of all beings could only be called the worst of all calamities.

In short order, Subaru lost the baseless feeling of urgency pressing against his spine. Without the thing pushing him forward, Subaru realized that he lacked the strength to even sit up.

"What am I doing…? This ain't the time to be lying down on the j…"

He wanted to save Rem. He wanted to rescue her. If he didn't turn back now, that wish could not be granted. Yet, even though his heart understood, none of the will to fight reached to his limbs. His soul was too weak.

Otto released Subaru from the hold, and with pity in his voice, he said, "I am weak, and so are you. That is why we cannot save her—we cannot hold a candle to her strength."

—But deep down, Rem wasn't strong, either.

Even though Subaru knew that, surely had always known that, he could say nothing.

He hung his head as the shaking dragon carriage jostled his body. The land dragon continued forging ahead straight through the night mist.

Rem remained behind them, abandoned as the dragon carriage grew distant, pulling Subaru farther and farther from her.

"—"

He stayed bent over like that as time passed—maybe five minutes, maybe ten.

"Mr. Natsuki, that's…"

Otto, having made the land dragon run in silence until then, seemed to doubt his own eyes as he called out to Subaru. Subaru lifted his head and clawed his way to sit beside Otto on the driver's seat, looking in the same direction—and found a light flickering amid the darkness.

"There is mist in the way, but…that is the light of a crystal lamp!"

"We made it…out of the mist…?"

"Even if we have, we are still on the highway at night, so any light is unnatural. It's probably someone who was caught in the mist, just like we were…!"

As if to support Otto's deduction, the other party seemed to have noticed them, too. About half a minute later, a dragon carriage, and the man driving it, emerged from the mist.

"F-finally someone…! Hey, this is just mist, right?! Don't tell me this is the White Whale?!"

The man in his prime was frothing at the corners of his lips as he desperately shouted, falling into a state of terror. When he saw Subaru and Otto in the night mist, he must have clung to the hope that they were saviors of some sort. Tensely, he tried to deny the obvious, but Otto shook his head.

"I'm afraid that it is. We have already encountered the whale ourselves. Fortunately, we should have shaken it off by now, but until one leaves the mist, you never know where it will appear."

"F-for real…?! Ahh, this is terrible. Why, why did this happen to me…?"

After a sidelong glance at the man clutching his head, lost in his personal lament, Subaru glared at Otto, seated beside him—his use of the word *fortunately* sounded like Otto had already shed his guilt at leaving Rem behind.

"Otto, watch what you say."

"What is it, Mr. Natsuki?"

"I'm telling you not to make light of things. 'Fortunately'…? That ain't funny. What do you think Rem went through when she…?"

As far as leaving Rem was concerned, Subaru and Otto stood in the exact same place. Despite that, Subaru was angry when he thought about Rem—an effort to assuage his own feelings of guilt.

Subaru understood. He'd understood all along. The idea that Rem, left behind, would stand before the White Whale, exercising her wits, and survive—it was nothing but a fantasy, not even wishful thinking.

There, inside that mist on the third time around, Rem had died— again—to save him…

"Rem? Who is that?"

His thoughts of Rem's tragic resolve were undermined with shocking ease.

"—Huh?"

"Er, I mean, who is this Rem? There was no one by that name among the traveling merchants who scattered… Of whom are you speaking?"

Otto tilted his head, not understanding what Subaru had meant.

To Subaru, that casual treatment toward her existence was like trampling mud all over her noble spirit.

—He swung his fist into the side of Otto's face at full force.

Instantly, the reins communicated the chaos atop the vehicle to the land dragon, resulting in the dragon carriage swerving violently to the right. Having lost his footing, Subaru crashed backward onto the driver's seat as the man he'd just struck hit the seat on his side.

"Wh-what was that for?!"

"Don't mess with me!"

Unbelievable, said Otto's wide-open eyes in response to Subaru's act of violence, but Otto's words and actions were just as unbelievable to Subaru.

"What the hell are you saying…?! Asking who Rem is? She's the girl who stayed behind so we could get away! Don't mess with me! Do you have a death wish…?!"

"I'm telling you, I don't understand what you're saying!! You're just spouting strange things all of a sudden... Did seeing the White Whale drive you mad?!"

Even in the face of Subaru's accusation, Otto proclaimed his own innocence.

Subaru's field of vision was dyed crimson by fierce, irrepressible emotions. The passage of every second felt agonizingly slow as the bloodlust seething through him commanded him to snap the slender neck of the man before him. And just as his hands stretched out to wring the life out of the ingrate—

The man in the dragon carriage alongside them, in shock as he saw the angry quarrel on the verge of escalating to murder, shouted to try and stop them.

"What are you two doing?! This isn't the time to argue! We have to get out of the m—"

But his voice did not reach the two and was lost in the heat of the moment.

It was man's next action after he spoke that broke up the ugly dispute.

"Getting out of the mist and running from the White Whale comes first, doesn't—?"

The man was continuing his realistic, heartfelt logic. Behind him, the dragon carriage was sucked into the giant mouth of the White Whale, vanishing from Subaru's and Otto's field of vision in the span of a single second.

The head of the White Whale turned upward, swallowing the dragon carriage and land dragon whole in a single, enormously weighty bite.

As wood and steel were crunched together, the land dragon let out a death cry as its flesh was ground between the millstone-like teeth. The great scream and the sound of its annihilation drowned out the voice of the man, no doubt similarly turned to mincemeat.

"Wh...y—?"

The silent approach of the enormous creature shocked both

Subaru and Otto beyond words. Otto's knees trembled as he beheld the awesome spectacle of the White Whale once more; Subaru's eyes were wide, unblinking.

"Why are…you here…?"

The White Whale, still alive and well, did not pay the slightest attention to the two little people right beside it as it licked its lips, savoring the dinner spreading through its mouth.

"Your being here…means…"

What happened to the girl who had stayed behind to draw away the monster? With the overwhelming creature before him, he couldn't help but demand an answer.

Naturally, the White Whale offered none. Having finished its chewing, it moved its giant eye down to look at the dragon carriage beside it—and Subaru—as it assessed its next prey.

"Uaaaaaahhhhh—!!"

Otto shouted, cracking under the pressure before the creature even moved.

The land dragon, also panicking due to the White Whale's presence, increased its pace to a gallop without a command from its master. The distance between them and the monster widened in the span of an instant, but then the White Whale swam faster.

"Why, why, why, why…? We should have shaken it off; why is it…?!"

On the driver's seat of the accelerating dragon carriage, Subaru remained sunk in despondency. Otto, driven to the edge of his wits, wailed as they cut from the right of the head to the left.

"Why is it after only us this stubbornly…?! In all this darkness… Why…?! Do I have s-some sort of target painted on my back…?!"

Otto wailed as he took the crystal lamp attached to the dragon carriage and threw it away. Even if it was futile, he wanted to hide from the White Whale's eye even if only for a tiny moment longer. But Otto's shout suddenly called an image to the back of Subaru's mind.

During his lament, Otto had wondered aloud if there was a bull's-eye on the two of them that the White Whale was doggedly following. If there was any reason why it was so focused on them, then—

"It couldn't be…"

Subaru pulled himself up to the driver's seat, doubting his own eyes as he stared toward the White Whale swimming behind them. Within the night mists, the darkness all around obscured the creature's giant frame. However, when Subaru strained his eyes, he could just make out something on the head of the White Whale facing them.

He saw a twisted, spiraling horn protruding from its head.

—With his own eyes, he'd also seen horns on the Urugarum, the wild demon beasts living in the forest around the mansion that resembled oversize dogs. And he'd learned from experience that those demon beasts, said to be born from the power of the Witch, were attracted to her scent, given off by Subaru. In other words…

"…That monster…the White Whale is a demon beast, too…?"

When he voiced the hard-to-believe possibility, he shook his head at the unpalatable reality. But when he thought about it, everything fit.

It explained why the White Whale had found their dragon carriage first out of all the ones that had scattered. It explained why it had obstinately pursued Otto from the moment Subaru had come aboard.

It explained why the creature had pursued that dragon carriage after Rem had resigned herself to death to buy them time.

He recalled how Rem had hesitated to tell him something about the White Whale as it pursued them through the darkness. That was when Rem had realized it.

"The White Whale…is drawn to my body…?"

The White Whale had assaulted them in pursuit of Subaru—in pursuit of the scent of the Witch. Rem had realized that fact before anyone else; to protect Subaru, she'd disembarked from the dragon carriage in a bid for more time.

To protect Subaru. For Subaru's sake alone.

"No, Rem… Because of me… Because of me…!"

Subaru lowered his head and sank down, fighting back the overflowing sorrow within him. The knowledge that Rem was gone, and that he bore all the responsibility for losing her, weighed heavily on both Subaru's mind and body.

"Mr. Natsuki…"

Stricken by despair, Subaru felt Otto pat his shoulder from behind. His fingers were shaking, his voice dry. He trembled as he looked in Otto's direction.

"Otto, I…"

"Please die."

The next moment, the shove to Subaru's shoulder easily sent him tumbling from the dragon carriage.

"—Huh?"

His field of vision inverted as he violently tumbled down, losing track of which way was up. Amid the chaos of his vision, he saw Otto loudly laughing. His mouth was open so wide that Subaru could see his white molars, spit dribbling from the corners of his mouth as he spoke.

"I-it's your fault! I-if you're why it's after us, then take responsibility! Ah-ha-ha! Die! Die and save meee!"

Hearing Otto's maniacal laughter, Subaru realized that his mind had completely snapped. Otto had been driven to the edge. Overhearing Subaru's frail murmur, he clung to the tiniest of hopes, not bothering to ask for confirmation before shoving him to his doom.

Right around the time Subaru realized this, his body reached the ground.

His back slammed mercilessly against the earth. Without hyperbole, the pain was like he had broken every bone in his body. Crying painfully as his internal organs were crushed, he spat out blood and kept rolling.

The impact was hard enough to dull even his ability to register pain.

Subaru vomited bile and blood over and over, raising his wobbly head. He could hear the far-off, fleeing dragon carriage from which he had been shoved.

Oddly, no words of reproach came to mind.

Granted, he was in far too much pain and suffering to voice any complaint, but even ignoring that, he just didn't have the heart to fault Otto. The merchant had merely been in the wrong place at the wrong time and shoved off Subaru in a desperate struggle to survive. Maybe Subaru forgave him because he could hardly have been expected to do otherwise.

"Ehuh! Guheh!"

Such sentiments, the taste of blood filling the inside of his mouth, the ferocious pain his body was trying to remember...

"—"

...all these things were forgotten when the overwhelmingly huge creature showed itself before him.

—With a single glance, Subaru came to understand just how foolish it was to defy this awesome and terrible menace.

As Subaru lay prone, the White Whale was close enough to touch, expelling putrid breath out of its incomprehensibly huge mouth as it examined the tiny being before it. To the body of a diminutive man, a mere exhalation from the White Whale was a ferocious gale. Subaru, unable to support his own body, was sent rolling across the ground with that single burst of air.

"—"

Then, while Subaru writhed with agony, the White Whale remained silent as it looked down at him, almost as if toying with him.

A word like *careless* did not apply to the creature as it casually loitered in place. The difference between them was simply that great. It would have been like an ant challenging an elephant or a man challenging a whale under the ocean's waves.

Inside Subaru's head, overwhelmed by pain and nausea, he knew he was feeling death drawing near. It was a feeling of despair that he had felt several times over.

Slowly but surely, he was keenly aware of the despondency from what he had lost and his helplessness, that once more he had left the things he had to do unfinished. The emotions came to him like old friends, wrapping their arms around his shoulders like best buds as they laughed at his embarrassing troubles and his laughable struggles.

He no longer had any idea what had gone wrong. But now that Rem was lost to him, Subaru had nothing left.

He chuckled at himself for his ridiculous attempts at resistance and survival, even in his pathetic state.

Stupid. Worthless. The lowliest of all lives, with nothing left to do whatsoever.

He felt the White Whale, right before him, drawing its nose close.

Its open mouth was lined with the unyielding teeth that had chewed up even hard-scaled land dragons with ease.

These teeth would bite down on him, chewing and grinding his flesh, bones, and very soul.

His lips quivered, trying to say something defiant, like, "Kill me already," or, "Hurry up and do it."

"I don't…wanna die…"

This time, Subaru truly despaired at how he was too weak to manage even that.

Inside his chest, a sense of powerlessness like none he'd ever had before impaled him like a cold blade. His blood froze throughout his body. He despaired as everything in front of him turned black.

"N-no…I don't wanna die! Save— I don't wanna die… I don't wanna die, I don't wanna die… No, no, no… Save me, Rem, save me…!"

Tearful words and whimpers poured out of his mouth as the inevitable end to his miserable life drew near.

It was pathetic. Repulsive. It could be called only a truly shameful sight. Anyone would avert their eyes at the spectacle and scoff at him. No doubt it would have hurt to even watch. He could not cling to life like this and hold on to his dignity as a human, too.

It was wretched. Even bugs were more adorable and lived with more pride. This self-pitying boy, too filthy to count as a higher life-form worthy of respect, was truly "the greed of a pig."

"N-no…I don't wanna die… Save me…"

Even so, he crawled in an effort to escape, grasping for whatever possibility might let him keep his life.

His body, its strength exhausted, would go no farther. His fingertips merely pawed at the grass, lacking the power to claw the soil. Even the will to cry was now lost to him. Rolling onto his side was his final act of physical resistance.

"I don't wanna die...!"

Then he rolled onto his back, a plea for his life trickling out of his mouth.

That was his final struggle to live.

He could do nothing more. He could think no more. He could only await the inevitable.

Yet even so, no matter how long Subaru waited, the blow that would end him never arrived.

Though his old friend, the aura of death, preceded the bite that would be his violent end...it never came.

The terror of knowing the end was near, but not when, was something that easily wrecked the human heart. As unendurable terror gripped him, Subaru forced his trembling body to comply. His gaze shifted around, and he sought an end to his despair, when...

"...Eh?"

...he realized that the White Whale, supposedly drawing nearer with every moment, was nowhere to be found.

8

From there on, desperately clinging to life was the only thing that kept Subaru going.

"I don't wanna die... I don't wanna die, I don't wanna die..."

He was out of breath, tottering on his feet, with droplets of blood in his eyes clouding his vision. But Subaru took no heed as he ran. It changed nothing; he'd been lost in darkness and mist to start with.

Within the embrace of the moonless, starless night, Subaru couldn't even see his own feet. Or perhaps the White Whale had swallowed him long ago and he simply hadn't realized it. Perhaps, even in that very moment, he was in the belly of the demon beast, running only toward his own doom…

"*Hic.*"

Amid the darkness, Subaru kept running and running, all alone.

He had lost Rem, Otto had abandoned him, even the White Whale had left him behind.

He didn't know why *I don't wanna die* was the only thought he had.

What meaning was there in living? What meaning was there in not dying?

Perhaps the incoherent thought rose to the fore as a simple, instinctive means of protecting himself from fear and pain. It was disgusting how, even at that juncture, his self-pity was at work.

"—Ah?"

As he berated himself to no end, the mist suddenly, and without the slightest fanfare, fell away.

Subaru crumpled to the ground with an expression of disbelief at the abrupt end to the darkness that he thought would continue forever. Soft moonlight poured down on him as it sunk in that he had survived.

Subaru, feeling blood flowing through his limbs once more, stretched both hands toward the night sky. What made him do so was not unbridled joy at grabbing hold of life.

"I did it again…"

He despaired at himself, having once more cheated death after another wretched struggle.

Having obtained the life he had so craved, Subaru could take little joy in it. An unquenchable sense of guilt burned in his chest, and his shame at forgetting about her almost made him crave death again.

"Rem… Rem…!"

Covering his face, he called her name as irrepressible hot tears continued pouring out from him. In so doing, Subaru sought her forgiveness so that his own soul might find comfort.

He rubbed his head against the soil as he wept. He didn't know how much time passed like that until he heard a slow creaking sound drawing closer to the hunched-over boy.

"Y-you're…"

It was a land dragon, pulling the bloodstained remnants of what had once been its carriage.

He remembered it. There was no mistake—it was Otto's land dragon. But there was no sign of the young man who had shoved Subaru off.

"Why are you…? Where is he? Where's Otto?"

Though he voiced the question, he of course received no reply. The land dragon tottered closer; Subaru, in turn, rose and walked toward it. As Subaru looked up at the cruelly damaged animal, he realized it.

—The driver's seat was stained with blood, impaled with crucifix-like daggers.

Someone had attacked when they'd left the mist.

Subaru couldn't even imagine what despair Otto must have felt, having gone mad and even leaving Subaru to die in his efforts to escape with his life, only to be ambushed afterward. But the fact that his land dragon was alone made it all too clear what had resulted.

"…Let's go."

With a muted murmur, Subaru dragged his pain-racked body up onto the driver's seat. Grasping the reins with his right hand, which was somehow still functional, he did as he'd seen others do and ordered the land dragon to move out with a flick.

Sensing someone not his master through the reins, the beast looked up at Subaru with its round eyes, seemingly at a loss. But when Subaru flicked the reins once more, it gently began moving down the highway.

—Under the gleam of the silvery moon, the land dragon smoothly ran along.

The man and land dragon, having both lost someone precious, were licking each other's wounds in a sense as they bathed in the soft, soft laughter of the moon and the stars.

Gently, gently, the land dragon continued to run.

And kept running.

CHAPTER 4
WON'T LET ME SAY THE WORDS

1

Making creaking sounds, the land dragon continued moving forward.

Subaru's mind was hazy; leaning deep into the driver's seat, he was the driver in name only. It was partly fatigue, partly the effects of his wounds, but it was chiefly the wearing down of his spirit.

His broken bones and cut forehead had not healed; his dislocated left shoulder was crying out painfully. His broken teeth felt extremely unpleasant; his clothes, filthy from blood, mud, and urine, transferred the chill directly to his skin.

—Why had he survived?

Protected by Rem only to lose her, abandoned by Otto, spurned even by the White Whale that had spared his pathetic life. He'd blundered his way along the highway through the night mist, breaking free of it and thus prolonging his life.

Just where would this path lead him and the surviving land dragon? And once he arrived, would there be anything he could do?

The desire to protect someone, to save someone—he'd trusted it was that feeling that had spurred him forward. Yet, having seen things he wished he hadn't, he knew he had simply been consoling himself with pretty words.

He'd come to realize that he needed his own life above all else; he was a lump of flesh wrapped up in self-pity.

When they'd left Rem to face the White Whale, and Subaru had ordered Otto to turn around, maybe he'd only pretended his heart was broken by Otto's rebuttal but was actually relieved deep down? If it was an opponent even someone like a Sword Saint could not defeat, going back meant only a dog's death. Rem wouldn't want that.

—So he'd told himself he didn't need to go back. He didn't need to die.

As a matter of fact, Subaru hadn't gone back to save Rem; he'd even begged the White Whale, the purported target of his hatred, for his own life. He'd shouted, *I don't wanna die*, as he fled in a daze, peeing on himself all the while.

At the time, Rem's safety or lack thereof never entered the back of his mind even once. Rem had done a pretty stupid thing, throwing her life away for a man like him.

"But…the stupidest thing is…"

There was no Rem anymore. Otto was gone, as were all the other traveling merchants. Subaru was alone, save for the land dragon silently continuing to advance along the well-maintained highway in search of human civilization.

It didn't matter where. Subaru just wanted it to bring him somewhere.

Subaru grew apathetic, releasing his hand from the reins as he collapsed onto the driver's seat. As he rolled onto his side, he could see the crucifixes still jabbed into a hard-to-see nook. It was evidence that Otto had been attacked by Witch Cult adherents he'd apparently encountered after slipping past the mist.

All that time, Subaru had been wondering if the Witch Cult would appear before him as well; would he meet the same fate as Otto? Would his meaningless life be cut down as well? Or if it came to that, would he be spared once more, even if he was face-to-face with Petelgeuse?

"Petel…geuse…"

Haltingly naming the object of his hatred, Subaru knew just how hollow his own heart was. Even when voicing the name of the mad-man who'd brutally murdered Rem, mocked Subaru, and was the root of all evils, Subaru's heart didn't feel a twinge, even though only a few hours prior, Subaru's anger toward him was the only thing keeping him going.

"What the hell's wrong with me...?"

The dragon carriage's wheels creaked; an extremely high-pitched sound clawed at his eardrums. Almost in pain from the discordant sound, Subaru grimaced and sat up.

"A forest...?"

The land dragon had stopped its walking some time before. When he observed his surroundings, the land dragon was clawing at the ground of a woodland road surrounded by trees. Apparently the sun had risen some time ago, because white sun rays from above were baking Subaru's body.

Now that he'd noticed it, Subaru savored the heat on his skin, soaking it up like a wick, when...

"—Ah, Subaru?"

...he was surprised to hear an innocent, high-pitched voice call him by name.

A number of diminutive figures had climbed onto the stopped dragon carriage, peering down at Subaru as he sat on the driver's seat. They pointed at Subaru and began to laugh at the sorry state they'd found him in.

"It really is Subaru." "What's wrong, Subaru?" "Subaru, you're filthy." "You stink, Subaru."

But these were not laughs of ill-willed mockery but rather, warm chuckles reserved for those whom they bore deep affection.

"Y-you're..."

He knew their faces. He'd seen them several times in the last few days. He'd seen them contorted in pain and agony, never to smile again.

These were the grinning faces of the children living in Earlham Village, on the outskirts of Roswaal Manor.

In a daze, Subaru lifted his head and saw that there, ahead on the woodland path, was the human civilization he'd sought.

He had finally arrived at the place he'd longed for, that he'd craved so much.

Subaru had made it back before he'd surrendered completely to despair and lost everything.

"Subaru?" "Er, what's wrong?" "Ahh, look out!"

The children's voices rose. Subaru knew what they were trying to tell him. Regardless, his head had already grown heavy, and he could no longer support his body.

Something stretched taut made a sound as it snapped, and once again, Subaru's mind fell toward a dark, quiet place, as if he were trying to shove all his troubles away.

"Wait a— Don't fall—"

—He fell.

2

When Subaru opened his eyes, the first thing he saw was a familiar white ceiling.

The plain room, adorned with only a crystal lamp, was something of a rarity among the dazzlingly ornamented rooms of the mansion. When he was here, he could feel at ease as the rank commoner he was. And so he had taken a liking to it, selecting it as his own room.

Under his head was one of the pillows so eternally soft that he could never get used to them. The fact that sheets had been meticulously pulled up to his shoulders made it clear that someone had tucked him in as he slept on the bed.

It was Subaru's nature to become alert as soon as he opened his eyes, no matter what the situation. He looked around the room, seeing for himself that it was indeed where he always woke up.

"—Ah."

There was a girl sitting near the side of the bed, her eyes quietly lowered upon a book.

She wore a customized, very exposing maid outfit, with black as its chief color. She had a white flower hair ornament and a lovely face; the sharpness of her stiff, beautiful features displayed her inner refinement.

The instant Subaru realized she was there, he practically leaped up into a sitting position, taking her hand into his before she even realized he was awake. Her face registered surprise…

"—Do not touch me so casually, Barusu."

…as her cold, blunt words; the tone of her voice; and the feeling of his hand being shaken off shattered his illusion.

In that instant, he realized that the girl before his eyes had pink hair. His reunion with someone precious whom he had lost was nothing but an illusion. This was the older twin sister of the girl he longed for, two peas in a pod, differing only in hair color.

"I can understand you are happy at seeing me after several days, but to leap at me by instinct is less like a man and more like a male. It is indecent."

Ram glared reproachfully at Subaru, shifting her chair away as if to distance herself from the bed. The frigidity of her gaze and voice drilled into him that this was not her look-alike younger sister.

"Yeah……that's right, I don't have any right to that anymore…"

Ram suspiciously lifted an eyebrow as Subaru clawed at his head, bit his lip, and hunched forward.

From Ram's point of view, she'd done nothing but greet his awakening with a suitably sharp tongue. The usual Subaru would make some sort of frivolous comeback, but he was falling silent with a grave expression.

"…I really would rather you did not make me do something so atypical, but…"

As Ram spoke, she drew near to Subaru and gently patted his head with her palm. The soft movement of her fingertips had a quiet, gentle rhythm that unsettled Subaru.

"Your face says you are thinking something rude, Barusu. You did not expect kindness from me?"

"No, I…didn't… I thought you were the type to kick me when I'm down."

"I imagine there are few maids who have as much generosity and

kindness as I. I'm too crafty to torment you in your current state, Barusu. I'll save the kicking for another time and place."

"Correction. You really are the woman I thought you were."

Ram declared that she'd redouble her antics next time, but Subaru did not sense any less affection from her fingertips.

Even if her speech was blunter and her personality was completely different, she really was Rem's sister. His chest grew tight with the knowledge that they really did think the same way. He bore the inescapable pain of what he had to tell her...

"Ahh..."

As he sank into thought, Subaru felt her fingers pull away, causing him to blurt out a sound in regret. He rushed a hand to his mouth, but Ram broke into a smile even faster as she shot him a teasing look.

"You wanted more?"

"I don't need it. I'm not some little kid...!"

"Bold words, when you look ready to bawl like a child. You're as stubborn as a little brat."

Ram slumped as Subaru gave her a sulking sidelong glance. Her condescension was fully intact as she said, "Now then, Barusu."

"..."

Ram returned the chair in front of Subaru, sitting directly opposite him and staring at him.

"—I must ask you what you have to say. Yes," she said, before launching into the topic at hand. "You were in an awful state, Barusu. You appeared at the village with an unfamiliar dragon carriage, filthy and half-dead. At first, when people from the village called for me to come over, I thought it must be some kind of joke."

In a businesslike tone, Ram recounted how she'd carried Subaru back to the mansion while he was unconscious.

"Dislocated shoulder, cut forehead... I connected the broken bones, but your wounds will open if you force yourself. I disposed of your filthy blood- and mud-covered clothes—I shall refrain from telling Lady Emilia that you relieved yourself in them."

"...Yeah, that's a big help."

Subaru's muted reaction made Ram lower her shoulders with

chagrin apparent on her face. To Ram, that last part was just a tiny bit of humor, but it would have been a big problem for Subaru otherwise.

"And the one who healed my wounds was…"

"Lady Emilia."

Just like that, Ram said what Subaru had feared.

When Subaru hung his head at the reply, Ram put her hands on her hips and *humph*ed through her nose.

"It could not be helped. I asked Lady Beatrice first, but she refused. Though, given how fickle she can be, I fully expected that she might decline."

"Did…Emilia say anything about me?"

"I shall tell you nothing of it. That is something you should ask her yourself."

Ram replied icily to Subaru's meek question while patting his formerly dislocated shoulder.

"I have not heard what occurred between you and Lady Emilia in the royal capital. I am not interested. From your reaction just now, it would seem that you did nothing good regardless."

"That's pretty harsh."

"I think it is a fair statement, is it not? More accurately, you are afraid that I will address the main topic of concern, and you wish to clumsily put it off as long as possible by talking about something else."

"Uhh…"

Unable to even manage a proper groan, Subaru understood what Ram really wanted to hear. After all, the individual who should have returned by Subaru's side was absent. Naturally, he needed to tell her about that first.

He wondered if it was Ram's kindness or her strictness that made her broach the conversation when Subaru had said nothing of it himself. It was probably both.

He couldn't allow her benevolence to spoil him forever.

"—Rem is dead."

The instant the words were on his lips, Subaru felt something inside him gently come loose. The instant he made the confession, the weighty mass in the innermost depths of his chest broke apart and sank into his stomach, demanding acknowledgment from him.

The hot sensation he felt through his forehead told him exactly what that mass was.

—*I've lost Rem.*

A flood of tears poured out of him.

And he realized it. Only then did he realize: Subaru had let Rem die, over and over.

Including the previous mansion loop, this made the fourth time Subaru had let her die, four times Subaru had felt her passing. Finally, it sank in that he had let Rem die four times over.

And yet, that was the first time Subaru had shed tears over her death for her sake. Not out of self-pity, not out of guilt, but purely for Rem's own sake.

"I…couldn't do anything. On the highway, the mist… The White Whale showed up. Then, so I could get away, Rem… But I was left behind in the mist…and then, finally…"

He couldn't put what he wanted to say in proper sentences. With periodic sobs, his account jumped from idea to idea, failing to arrange the topics in an orderly manner. Unable to keep his excuses at bay, Subaru grew afraid, feeling that he had somehow sullied Rem's final moments.

He acknowledged his crime. He would accept his punishment— one befitting an unsightly man such as him.

That was why he had to explain everything as clearly as possi—

"Who is Rem?"

—.

——.

———.

"Ah, er, huh…?"

He didn't…understand…what was being said to him.

Unable to grasp the meaning of Ram's question, Subaru made incoherent sounds in response.

Who is Rem? What did that even mean?

But seeing Subaru lost in doubt, Ram cocked her head and opened her mouth once more.

"Barusu. Who is this Rem?"

Her eyebrow hadn't even twitched at the mention of her twin sister's name, and now she was asking who she was.

"Wh-whaddaya mean, who…? Don't say stupid things like that! It's the name of y-your little sister, isn't it?! Rem, right? R-e-m. Rem! This isn't the time for j—"

"My little sister…?"

Ram put a finger to her lips, closing her eyes as she seemed to sink into serious thought. Subaru had seen the gesture before, but in his present state, it was extremely difficult to endure. He felt the urge to yell, *What the hell are you doing?!* and punt Ram all the way into the mist at that very moment.

"My little sister, Rem. Ahh…"

"You remember now?!"

"I cannot remember what never was. I have no little sister. I have always been an only child."

Subaru's face went very pale as Ram's plain statement defied his every expectation.

"That's crazy… What are you saying…?"

"—I do not have a little sister."

"Don't mess with me! If Rem didn't exist, what happened during that mess with the demon beasts in the forest?! You, Rem, and I went there and…"

"Truly, what is wrong with you, Barusu? I am loath to admit it, but half the credit for exterminating the Urugarum pack is yours. The remaining half goes to my own efforts and Roswaal's power… There is no place to slip in some long-lost little sister named Rem."

Even when hearing Subaru's protests, Ram obstinately refused to acknowledge her little sister's existence. Inside of Ram, things that had most certainly happened had been overwritten with false memories.

He didn't know what it meant. He didn't know why she was answering him in that manner.

"This ain't funny….Not even a nightmare…would have a script this bad…"

"As always, I am quite serious. It's you who's dreaming, Barusu."

"Dreaming… Dreaming? You're saying I'm dreaming?! Stop messing with me!"

With Ram completely at sea, Subaru pushed aside the sheets and got out of bed. His endurance hadn't returned; his lower body wobbled as he walked out, driven by his fierce emotions.

"Barusu, you should not be up y—"

"Shut up! Be quiet and…come look!"

Ram extended a hand toward his tottering body, but Subaru brushed it aside angrily.

Subaru had been sleeping in his bedroom on the second floor of the mansion's east wing. Rem's room was on the third floor, so he walked to the stairs leading up in search of some trace of her.

"Your endurance has not returned. If you continue to force yourself and collapse, it will only cause me trouble."

Ram followed behind him, speaking to him, but Subaru, his shoulders shaking in anger, had no intention of listening. Taking more time than usual to climb up the stairs, Subaru headed straight down the third floor corridor of the mansion before stopping in front of a room—Rem's room.

Once Ram saw it, surely her ridiculous notions would shatter into dust.

Subaru grasped the doorknob to the room and marched in. He didn't hesitate. If he did, Subaru's timid heart would let him make more excuses. He had no time to be worried or conflicted.

The room he stepped into was plain but decorated in a reserved, feminine fashion—

"…No…way."

There was…nothing.

The space he'd just entered had a made bed and a little table, no different than any of the other empty rooms. Rem's had been simple, but this was different, completely devoid of personality. The little feminine touches and decorations had certainly been in hers.

"This can't be rea…"

Looking around the room, Subaru couldn't believe it and rushed out into the hallway. Ignoring Ram's gaze as she stood beside the door, Subaru counted the rooms from the stairs to this one. He'd made no mistake. There was no way he could have. He could find the place with his eyes closed.

—Then why…?

"C-could it be Beatrice? Maybe she shuffled the spaces around on me like that first time…"

"Barusu."

"That's right! That has to be it! Why that little— Playing her games to make fun of me…"

"Barusu, stop it."

Seeing Subaru grow hysterically desperate, Ram quietly dropped all hint of affection. Shocked, Subaru looked at Ram. She gazed back at him, the almost unthinkable, plaintive look in her eyes expressing just how much she was concerned for his well-being.

But it was wrong. That wasn't what Subaru was looking for.

"Rem… This is her…"

"—There has never been such a person at this mansion."

Ram shook her head, her eyes clouding as she said, as if to slap him to his senses, "I do not have a little sister."

And so she finally destroyed his doubts.

3

He'd meant to own up to his responsibility, to bear his crime on his shoulders. He had meant to accept that all-too-heavy burden, the responsibility he wished to cast aside and flee from at that very moment, and face up to Rem's death.

"I—I…"

Did he not even have the right to mourn Rem's death and plead for forgiveness?

He'd done things thinking it was for Emilia's sake, but she hadn't accepted him; their feelings were at odds and still remained on different trajectories. Rem, who'd thrown everything away for Subaru's sake, had expended her life in heroic fashion as the world repeated itself. And yet, the world had robbed Subaru of the duty to shoulder the responsibility of her life.

Time, the world, the Witch Cult, the White Whale—various obstacles stood between Subaru and what he desired. Why was the world so cold to Subaru, betraying him and all his feelings?

That was, that was—

"Barusu, please return to your room."

As Subaru stood dumbfounded in the unoccupied quarters, Ram spoke thusly to him. With Subaru rooted to the floor, Ram, standing beside him, pressed a hand to his back to lead him out of the room and said, "You must be confused about many things because you are tired. Head back to your room and keep dreaming in bed. I have things to do, so I cannot stay with you like this forever."

Even though Subaru was beaten down, Ram's decision was strict toward Subaru. She meant to carry out her assigned duties without coddling him any further.

"Back to your room, and sleep."

Repeating the command one more time as she left, Ram went down the stairs and vanished from view.

Certainly, if he slept as she said, he might be able to escape that sense of alienation. It was all a bad dream, surely. He was dreaming, so he'd go back to bed to dream.

He should just run away, run away, run away. He'd fled all the way to where he stood now. If he kept trying to get away, like he always had, like he always would—if he ran and ran and ran and ran, then—

"Then...what...?"

Subaru murmured, his foot stopping just as he was about to take the stairs down.

Judging that he needed to escape into a dream, he'd dragged his feet over to the stairs. Slightly raising his jaw, Subaru looked at the steps up to the next floor.

No matter how far he fled, it'd all be the same. And Subaru would have betrayed Rem again.

Rem had protected Subaru, gambling with her own life so that he might escape from the White Whale… And for what?

So that Subaru could finish what he'd started.

For his goal of saving the people precious to him from the evil clutches of the Witch Cult.

If he abandoned that objective then and there, letting go and fleeing into his own mind…

"That's…a lot lower than begging for forgiveness…"

Subaru turned away from the stairs leading downward.

This time, there was no hesitation in his gait. Subaru put his foot on the first step and went up, not down, because that was where he would find the reason for his return.

Stepping firmly upon each step, Subaru slowly headed up. Arriving at the topmost floor, he breathed out as he found the door he had been fighting toward this whole time.

When he reached for the doorknob, Subaru realized that he was oddly calm. It seemed unreal how much his heart had quieted down after its frantic pounding when he'd burst into Rem's room. He wondered if he had actually calmed down or if he had moved beyond stress entirely and sunk so far that he could no longer hear its powerful thumping.

But: "Rem, lend me…your courage—"

When he voiced that name, Subaru felt his hand become stronger. That strength transferred to the doorknob; he gently opened the obstinate-seeming door. And on the other side of the open entryway, a girl was sitting at the desk, looking back toward him as she said, "—Subaru?"

When Subaru heard the chime-like voice calling out his name, he closed his eyes. He finally remembered the deep emotions rushing through his chest that were difficult to put into words…and that he had returned for the sake of hearing her voice.

She was a girl with fluttery silver hair, pale skin, and violet eyes.

Sadness marred her fleeting, beautiful features. The girl—Emilia—rose from her seat and said to Subaru, "...Why...did you come back?"

It was not the words themselves but the trembling tone of her voice that robbed Subaru of all thought.

Here was Emilia, lacking all strength in her eyes, her lips quivering.

It had been a little while since he had seen her. He felt like she was thinner than when they had parted. Both her voice and her eyes were clouded with fatigue, enough to suggest she hadn't been getting any sleep.

She'd probably been backed into a corner, her spirit worn down by external influences.

Thus, Subaru stepped forward, ignoring Emilia's question as he offered her his hand.

"Come on. You can't stay here."

Subaru's forceful behavior surprised Emilia; she pulled back slightly from him. When the original distance between them was restored, Emilia shook her head toward the troubled boy.

"Go where...? No, why?"

"Anywhere will work, as long as it's not here. If you're gonna ask what it's for, my answer is that it's for your sake. I came back for your—"

"This again, Subaru?"

Emilia seemed disappointed in his reply as he spoke.

Her velvet eyes watered slightly, glaring up at him through her lashes and cowing him into silence.

"Returning all of a sudden, covered in wounds and making everyone worry... Aren't you supposed to be undergoing treatment from Ferris in the royal capital? Why are you here now?"

"A lot happened! There's a mountain of things to explain, but I don't have the time to do it right now. Please listen to me. We have to get out of this mansion this—"

"I told you I can't, didn't I? I can't trust you like this, Subaru... I told you."

Grudgingly, Emilia shook her head and rejected him with a trembling voice. It was a direct continuation of their exchange back in the waiting room at the royal capital, without the slightest progress. Subaru had been unable to convey to Emilia his willingness to do anything for her sake, and he had failed to understand why Emilia refused to understand how he felt. But one thing was different from before.

"I'll drag you out of here if I have to. In a few days, you'll know I'm right whether you want to or not, so…!"

"Wait. Wait, Subaru. What's wrong? This isn't like you, Subaru. I… And yet—"

"Just shut up and listen to me!!"

The instant he shouted, Emilia's shoulders trembled. Before her unbelieving eyes, Subaru's ragged breaths came with as much force as his angry yell, and he glared intensely at her.

"You can't stay here. You'll regret it. I know you will. It won't help anyone. It won't save anyone. I don't want to suffer anymore. I don't want to cry anymore!"

"What are you talking about…? Subaru, I don't understand."

"Shut up! If everyone would just… If you do exactly what I tell you, it'll be all right! Everything will turn out okay. It's true! Why doesn't anyone understand that…?!"

Subaru clawed at his head, raising his voice—not toward Emilia but at the irrationality of the situation.

No doubt Emilia could not understand the meaning behind Subaru's angry outburst. But this was the only place where he could express these curses aloud. Only before Emilia could Subaru vent about all the senseless things he had encountered and bring out all the ugly emotions he had borne with such difficulty.

Seeing Subaru plead in a tearful voice, Emilia lowered her eyes in sadness.

"I'm sorry, Subaru. I don't get what you're saying. I really can't understand it."

Emilia's eyes remained lowered as she softened the tone of her voice in an effort to soothe Subaru's spirit.

"I want to understand. But even if I could understand with time,

I can't give you that right now… There are so many things I need to do. That's why right now, I—"

"It'll all go wrong."

Subaru interrupted her show of concern with a few short words, trampling upon Emilia's feelings.

Hearing the malice filling his voice, Emilia was in shock, blinking as he repeated the words.

"It'll all go wrong. You're no good. You'll fail. There's no way you could do it. There's no chance. You're all talk. Totally beyond saving. No one can rescue you. You'll just keep doing rash and reckless things, and the number of corpses in the pile will be the same. That…is your future."

The satisfaction filling Subaru's body was pitch-black, mean, ugly, and contemptible. As each word that fell from his mouth sounded in Emilia's ears, the pain on her face let him truly see the effects of jamming his feelings like blades into the weak points of her heart.

At that moment, Emilia was forced to pay attention to everything he said. In that instant alone, he took morbid joy in the fact that she could not ignore him.

He'd rejected her determination, laughed off her resolve, callously trampled on her actions, scoffed at her past idleness, and prophesied a completely dark future. As Subaru watched Emilia, stunned by all he'd said, his heart—

Quietly, Emilia murmured, "Why?"

Grief at Subaru's heartless words, along with pain at his description of an inescapably dark future, caused Emilia's expression to stiffen. But even then, her violet eyes remained unclouded. Captivated by the haunting, dimmed gleam of her eyes, he watched the world reflected in them—in other words, Subaru himself, as seen by her. Then, "Why do you look like you're crying from so much pain, Subaru?"

—Only then did he realize that a twisted smile had come over him while his tears poured out.

He knew that everything he'd said had been thrown back in his face.

Reflecting upon each and every word with which he'd crushed

Emilia's feelings, eyes running all the while, he realized they amounted to nothing. With everything he said, Subaru had managed only to slice himself to ribbons.

Determination, resolve, actions, past, future—Subaru's had been rejected as much as hers.

He felt like it was futile no matter how hard he tried.

He knew that he was seized by an urgent need to do something. As for what he was struggling against, he had no idea. He knew only one thing.

"She...she brought me this far... No. She stayed with me this far, and there are things I have to do for her..."

"Rem?"

Subaru anxiously searched his heart for the original feelings that had brought him to where he currently stood. Emilia, listening to his seemingly meaningless utterance, tilted her head slightly.

"—"

His breath caught.

The way Emilia had said her name.

It was clearly how people sounded when they were confused.

"—You too."

"Hmm?"

"You've...forgotten Rem, too—"

Not only had her own twin sister forgotten her existence, not only had all traces of her vanished, but the person who was the entire reason for Subaru's return didn't remember her, either, even though Rem had staked her life on making it happen.

The days she had spent, the time, the feelings, the way she'd lived, all had vanished. Her smile, her anger, her tears, the touches they'd shared—what had happened to all the things that made her who she was, that were firm proof she had lived?

"—All right. I'll tell you everything."   ·

"Eh?" Emilia responded, surprised by Subaru's words. Looking up at her beautiful, refined face, Subaru found anew the source of the emotions that had driven him to such lengths.

If the alternative was for Rem and her feelings to vanish into the ether forever...

"It's better to get everything out, even if it makes me cough up blood."

Subaru had decided.

He'd reveal it all. He'd tell her the truth about what clouded the depths of his spirit.

Emilia, seeing that the look in Subaru's eyes had changed, swallowed stiffly.

Standing before her, Subaru put a hand to his chest. His heartbeats were fast; he knew and feared exactly what was about to happen, what the result would be.

That pain. Pain enough to drive a man mad.

The suffering of those ministrations on his heart, the sensation of it being crushed, his inability to even let out a sound, continuing on and on, never knowing when it would come to an end...

But he had thought about this, too.

As if I care. I don't care. What's that pain compared to this suffering right now?

She couldn't trust him. She couldn't understand him. If he would have to endure the suffering of no one remembering Rem on top of that, mere physical pain paled in comparison.

—If you're gonna come, then come, damn it. If it's my heart you want, you can have it.

"Emilia."

"Yes?"

"I've...seen the future. I know what's gonna happen. And if you wanna know why, it's because...I can Return by Death—"

The instant he reached the verge of revealing everything, the world indeed came to a halt. As he'd expected, everything gradually slowed, finally stopping altogether. In that instant, the environment lost its color; all the sounds he had heard to that point vanished. The wind, his breath, his beating heart—all grew further and further away and did not return.

With all five senses deserting his mind, Subaru was isolated from the world.

—Then, as if unable to leave him alone in his solitude, the hands slowly appeared, bearing their unsought benevolence.

The black cloud that spawned seemed to slide through the air as it wriggled, shifting to form arms. In past times, only the right arm had the well-defined contours of a limb. But as the frequency of the evil hands' occurrence had increased, they formed a left hand as well with disturbing speed.

Both hands drew near to Subaru, with the left stroking his cheek, seemingly fond of him. The right rudely refused to be patient, plunging into Subaru's chest, slipping past his ribs, and gently enveloping his heart.

The frightening sensation of that alien limb softly, gently toying with his heart coursed through his entire body.

Unlike the unimaginable pain inflicted on him previously, the blackness that held Subaru's life in its hands seemed to be craftily manipulating his ultimate fear to break his determination and resolve.

With the impending agony failing to arrive, a new fear began to quietly take root in Subaru's mind.

He'd made his peace with the excruciating discomfort and had sworn to endure it. The evil hands seemed to be mocking Subaru's determination, delivering no more pain to his body and mind than pinpricks, and relying on his imagination to fill in the rest. It was that way of inflicting pain, so different from what he'd expected, that made the immobilized Subaru want to scream. But he clenched his unmoving teeth and rejected the urge.

He was in pain, afraid, ignorant, but Subaru did not allow that suffering to affect his spirit. If he failed, he would gain nothing. If he failed, he would never be forgiven. In a world where no one remembered that Rem had ever existed, Subaru had nowhere left to beg forgiveness for his responsibility in her death, save the confines of his own soul.

If the hand wanted to inflict suffering, he would let it carve as much into him as it pleased. But that determination was the one thing that would not shatter so easily.

Subaru glared at the evil hand toying with his own heart, holding his breath as he waited for the inevitable moment. But the hand made no move to do so. If it could do the deed anytime, it could also delay as long as it wished.

In that world of stopped time, all he could do was wage a war of attrition until his mind was worn away. Even if Subaru's determination held firm for the moment, it would eventually falter, and his spirit would be subsumed and broken.

—If that's what it thought, it had another think coming.

He'd endure the agony, no matter how many hours or days it might take. He hadn't died over and over for nothing. If it wasn't going to kill him, he'd endure anything mere pain had to offer.

Such was Subaru's resolve—

"—Ah?"

Suddenly, something began to animate that stilled world.

All traces of the looming pain, of which he'd received only a preview, vanished from his world. Subaru and his resolve were left intact as sound, color, and time returned. A flood of sounds—his breathing, his heartbeat, of moving things moving in the world—swirled around Subaru, as if that other realm had spat him out in derision.

Perhaps the evil hand had judged that it was futile in the face of Subaru's obstinate resolve?

Like hell, thought Subaru. His repeated suffering at those hands led him to scoff at the notion. Even then, he felt the black cloud's right hand softly grasping his heart. If it'd squeezed, Subaru would that very moment be—

"—"

At that point, a doubt crept into Subaru's thoughts.

Subaru had a firm memory of that abominable right hand touching his heart.

But what had the left hand been doing during that time? At first, it had touched his cheek, but after that—

"—Hu."

Before he could find an answer to his question, Emilia, standing before him, seemed to murmur something.

Her voice roused Subaru to his senses. He recalled the rest of the sentence he had started before time had stopped. Though his sudden release from the nightmare had thrown him off, if violating the taboo would bring no further price, he needed to concern himself with it no further.

He'd reveal everything, sharing with her what lay moments into the future, so that Subaru, and everyone, could get the world they hoped for. Finally, his determination to see that through would bear fruit—

"Ahh."

A moment before he could, Emilia's body abruptly leaned forward toward Subaru, who was standing just in front of her.

Subaru instinctively reached a hand out to catch her. Her breath caught a little at the soft, warm touch against his hand when…

Splat.

"—Eh?"

Splat, splat, splat.

"—Emi…lia?"

Splatsplatsplat, spurt.

Emilia made strange sounds while she embraced him as an enormous amount of blood poured from her mouth.

—Where had the left hand gone while the right was touching Subaru's heart?

Emilia rested her head on Subaru's shoulder, continuing to cough up blood. The sheer amount coming out dyed half of Subaru crimson as her body grew lighter.

"Stop i… Wha? Wai…? Huh?"

She lifted her head, seemingly trying to stop the blood she was heaving up, but in that instant, her listless head dropped. She slid down his shoulder. Her lifeless gaze told him everything he needed to know.

Right then, before Subaru's very eyes, Emilia's life—

"WaaaAAAHHHHHH—!!"

A scream rang out.

He screamed and howled enough to tear his throat apart, as if that would let him forget everything. If it were so, he wanted it to break at that very moment, to claw at it and rip it out with his own hands.

Emilia's limp body was still growing lighter within his arms.

The blood wouldn't stop flowing out of her. Subaru's body turned redder. Redder. And redder.

—While the right hand had been touching Subaru's heart, the left hand had reached for Emilia's.

His determination, his resolve, his actions, his past, and his future had all been stomped down and mocked.

His stubborn determination, the resolve that he had only just decided would never be broken, had been smashed to pieces, and Subaru Natsuki plunged into an abyss of despair.

His scream reached higher and higher, never fading.

It had finally come to this. Subaru—

—had killed Emilia.

4

This time, he surely had no more blood to cough up, no more tears to weep. He had been wrung dry.

How much did he have to cry?

How much did he have to suffer?

Had he done something so unforgivable?

His spirit had been wounded and trampled upon. He'd been robbed of someone precious. He couldn't protect the people he needed to protect. And by his hand, the most important person to him in the world had cruelly lost her life.

—Had someone levied some kind of judgment upon him?

"I—I..."

He'd been wrong. He'd misunderstood. He'd gotten cocky.

He'd become conceited after skillfully using the curse of the Witch on his soul to turn things around before. Encouraged by the thought that he'd come back even if he died, he'd dismissed the abominable being known as the Witch along with her evil hands, and this was the result.

All those things, accumulated together, had produced the tragic spectacle now before him.

Subaru fell to his knees, resting Emilia's corpse atop them, as his hollow eyes wandered aimlessly about.

How much time had passed since Emilia had lost her life?

When he touched her cheek, it had gone cold. The heat had faded from the blood that poured from her mouth. Her soft limbs had begun turning stiff, leaving him with less and less with which to deny her death.

Subaru, understanding that, remained unable to move from the spot.

He was exhausted.

He'd suffered so much. Surely it was all right for him to stop now?

Was there any human being anywhere in that world who had undergone as much as he?

He'd made efforts unthinkable for his old self, trying to manage somehow. Even so, he'd been unable to avert the worst case, the calamity had overtaken him, and he had lost everything. Then what more could—

"—Your face seems to say, 'I am the unluckiest man in the whole world.'"

No one should have been there, so Subaru doubted his own ears when he looked toward the entrance.

As he sluggishly brought his head around, he saw a single girl standing in front of the door. She gazed at Subaru with disdain. Her long cream-colored hair was split into two beautiful rolls, and she wore an ornate dress fit for a Western doll. She had an adorable face, one Subaru had not seen upon his return to the mansion the last two times through the current series of loops.

"Bea...trice..."

"In the time since I have last seen you, has your witless face grown even more foolish, I wonder?"

Making that harsh declaration, Beatrice surveyed the tragic sight in the room.

Then she said, "Well, now you've really done it..."

With a sigh, Beatrice summed up the tragic spectacle with extreme bluntness.

Seeing Emilia immobile in a pool of blood, eyes hollow in Subaru's embrace, was Beatrice truly moved so little?

But even if animosity was the obvious reaction, Subaru could no longer manage it. Indeed, in that moment, Subaru was grateful for Beatrice's reaction, not asking him a single thing. He would have been more grateful still if she simply turned around and left Subaru there.

"Will Puckie not come out, I wonder?"

As Beatrice spoke, she walked closer and kneeled right beside Subaru.

"Even if I tell you to look, I doubt you would listen... I do so hate to get my hands dirty."

Speaking indifferently, Beatrice reached out toward Emilia. Subaru did not know what she meant to do with the deceased girl, but he made no reaction as her fingers touched Emilia's neck. Subaru, feeling uncomfortable with the action in a way he couldn't put into words, began rebuking her.

"It's disconnected, I suppose?"

But Beatrice accomplished her objective before he'd even gotten a word in. As Beatrice's hand moved away from Emilia, it held a beautiful, glimmering green crystal. This was the pendant that Emilia never took off—Puck's abode, and the physical representation of the pact formed between Emilia and the spirit. But now, it was...

"Bro...ken...?"

"A bold thing to say for the one who broke it... Though you seem to be unaware of the fact."

Gazing desolately as the two pieces of the crystal rested on her palm, Beatrice tucked the ruined thing away.

What had happened to Puck, the spirit who should have been inside the broken pendant? What had happened to the spirit who had loved Emilia, now resting in Subaru's arms, so much that he had called her his daughter? Where had he gone?

"Are you concerned, I wonder? Puckie is not dead. He has simply been returned to his true body for the moment. It is only a matter of time until he comes… But it shall not be too long, I think."

Responding matter-of-factly to Subaru's unstated question, Beatrice stood up with a slight flutter of her skirt. Subaru watched the girl's bouncing hair rolls as he took solace in her answer.

If that spirit was alive, if he would be returning here, then he'd probably…

"—Do you have something you wish to say, I wonder?"

Seeing Subaru's extremely inappropriate relief, Beatrice gazed at him evenly as she posed the question.

Subaru did not notice the feelings in Beatrice's voice. But if she was asking if he had anything to say, then—

"Kill me."

—he wanted someone to end his life, then and there.

He was sick of everything. It had been one thing after another, and he was worn out.

So he wanted to die. He wanted to die and end everything. Even if he died and did it over, he'd probably lose it all again. If things started over when he died, or even if they didn't, he no longer wanted to be in that world. In a world where Emilia had died and Rem's existence had been erased, there was nothing left for him. That was why…

"Kill…me…"

…putting an end to it all was Subaru's only hope for salvation.

If there was someone out there who would hear his plea, he wanted his good-for-nothing life plucked away. He had trod the dignity of his life underfoot, rendered everyone's feelings meaningless, and abandoned everything in a pathetic effort to save his own life, and he wanted to be burned away and utterly destroyed.

Surely the girl with supernatural powers standing before him could grant that much.

Beatrice surely hated Subaru. If she listened to Subaru's request, there was no doubt he could expect a cruel punishment that matched the gravity of his crime.

He was a foolish human being. Dying nine times over had done nothing to change that. Why not cut him down for the tenth time, then? Now that the benevolence of God, Goddess, Buddha, and Witch were exhausted, there was no better time.

Hence, "Kill me here, please."

Subaru earnestly pleaded to Beatrice as he embraced Emilia's remains.

If this was going to be the end, he wanted it to be with Emilia in his arms.

Having achieved the worst of all worlds through his self-interested efforts, Subaru would indulge himself to the bitter end.

Subaru squeezed Emilia harder, closing his eyes as he waited for the end.

He imagined he would soon fall into that silent time.

"...t to."

Subaru, having selfishly decided to end it all, abruptly heard something.

"—Eh?"

It was a small, frail, halting voice.

Without thinking, Subaru let out the breath he had been holding and opened his eyelids to look up at her. As before, Beatrice was standing in front of him, gazing down at him all the while.

She embraced her tiny body with both arms, biting her trembling lips as if she were freezing.

"To ask Betty to kill you... Is that not too cruel, I wonder...?"

She said it with a tearful look and a choked voice, leaving Subaru completely at a loss. No matter how many times he blinked, Beatrice's thick sorrow would not vanish.

The girl Subaru knew would never wear that expression. After all, she was supposed to hate him. Even though she was always blunt, she'd put up with Subaru because she had some goodness in her, but he thought she was someone who could heartlessly lay into you by nature.

Even though he thought she might not readily accept, or might even turn him down, he expected it to be accompanied by disdain and mockery.

"You don't understand… You don't understand anything…!"

Subaru had never dreamed she would refuse to kill him with such a sad expression.

"B-Beatrice…?"

"Shall I refuse every single thing you ask, I wonder? If you want to die so much, go die by yourself… I refuse to do it."

Beatrice shook her head and covered her eyes with a hand, suppressing the emotion on her face. Hiding her welling tears rather than letting them fall, she turned that hand toward Subaru.

"What are you…? Everything is—?!"

In that instant, the world began to distort. Everything around Subaru warped, and a crack appeared.

These were preludes to the destruction of the world, or so he thought, instantly clutching the body in his arms close to him. Looking down at him, Beatrice spoke again with cold eyes.

"If you're going to be this useless, having you here is a bother— At the very least, perhaps I can protect this mansion, I suppose?"

"What are you say—? No, Beatrice, you're…!"

"—Do not think Betty is like Roswaal. Pain, anguish, suffering, sadness, fear… Perhaps Betty hates all these things?"

She replied to the question that was not a question with an answer that was not an answer.

Space distorted, and the resulting fissure enveloping Subaru brought him beyond the reach of all known physical laws.

It didn't hurt.

"If you are going to die, can you do it in a place where Betty will not see, I wonder?"

Though her final murmur was cruel, she could not conceal even a tiny fragment of her desolation.

He could say nothing. He understood nothing. But her emotions did tell him one thing.

—Subaru's decision and behavior had made Beatrice sad.

The distortion reached its zenith, and then it snapped back to normal. Something like static ran across his field of vision as the world was instantly swept away; in the next moment, the distorted air succumbed without a trace and vanished.

The gouge in the bloodstained floor was the only sign that Subaru and Emilia had ever been there.

Beatrice watched the two vanish before leaning back against a wall with a tired look. She sluggishly raised her palms, lifting them over her eyes as if that would hide the world from her.

"—Mother. How much longer must Betty…?"

The murmur of the girl left alone in the world petered out, reaching no one.

5

—Without warning, Subaru was cast out of a rip in space, plunging headfirst onto mossy plants.

"Bwah!"

Subaru spat out saliva that tasted like dirt, then lifted his head and looked around. Bunches of trees appeared in his dim field of vision. Surrounded by nature in all directions, Subaru realized that he had been cast into the middle of a forest.

"A forest at night…? Somewhere in the mountains…?"

He was only able to see at all because the moonlight was unhindered.

A cold breeze rustled the leaves of the many trees, with the sounds of insects dominating the gloomy forest under the twilight sky. The fact that it was night outside the mansion made Subaru aware that he'd slept for more than half a day.

"Teleportation…or something like it, I guess?"

The air had bent, and right after the resulting fissure had swallowed him up, he'd been dumped out into the forest. Using the Passage magic spell, Beatrice was able to freely rearrange where each door in the mansion connected. Maybe there was no reason to expect she couldn't relocate people one by one if she had a mind to.

But even if he could understand that much, he still had no idea what Beatrice had really been thinking.

Even then, the final image of her crying refused to fade from his mind.

Though she had turned him down, he had been sure she'd disdainfully leave him there. And yet, Beatrice had looked at Subaru with dejection and despair in her eyes—

"It's as if…she…"

—as if she'd expected more of him.

Subaru himself had rejected such notions, thinking them exceedingly self-serving. He'd acknowledged he was a spirit of pestilence, unable to do anything, hadn't he? He'd accepted it, hadn't he? If he couldn't expect anything from himself, no one else could, either.

Having even someone who hated him expect something of him was nothing but the height of "Pride."

—Even though he had kept running and running from other people's expectations long before he'd reached that world.

"Man, I'm hopeless, aren't I…?"

A crooked smile came over Subaru as he slowly knelt up on the grass. His legs seemed less mobile than expected. When Subaru looked down, he realized that there was something other than him weighing on his knees.

Even then, after tumbling through space, Emilia's remains continued to rest atop his lap.

"Emi…lia…"

In that world of gloom, a trickle of moonlight shone upon her pale face.

She seemed neither in pain nor at peace in death. Instead, she seemed full of conflict, unable to understand the cause of the misfortune afflicting her body. Namely, how her heart had been crushed while she was still alive, in a world of frozen time.

But even if she hadn't felt any pain, that was no saving grace. There was no such thing as a peaceful death, nor was death a saving grace for anyone.

—Except for Subaru himself, in that moment.

"I'm sorry. I'm so, so, so sorry…"

As he looked down at Emilia's face, droplets fell upon her pale cheek.

He had thought his tears had run dry, but they flowed from a bottomless well as Subaru was racked with ceaseless torture.

He heard voices—voices blaming him.

The people Subaru had met were shouting down at him in frigid anger.

There was a girl with silver hair and a girl with blue hair among them—

"Someone…someone, anyone…"

—*Please kill me.*

Under a hail of shouts that would not vanish, Subaru picked up

Emilia and rose to his feet. From there, he stepped on the grass and broke branches as he began slowly walking into the forest.

He could hear beasts howling in the distance. If he met those black demon beasts now, he felt like he'd greet them with a smile on his face. He wanted them to consume his flesh, his mana, his life—anything they pleased.

For if they did not, if that did not happen, there would be no salvation for Subaru Natsuki.

"—"

Heading toward the howls, Subaru advanced into the dark depths of the forest.

He no longer felt the weight of carrying Emilia, nor fatigue from walking along the cold mountain road with poor visibility. He wondered if it was because he had a clear goal and was earnestly working toward it. That would be pretty pathetic. Nor did the word *pathetic* begin to describe his fate.

"Here... Past this ravine...and then..."

Carefully heading downhill, he climbed up the twisting tree roots as if they were stairs.

Like a candle on the verge of burning out, he was exhausting the last strength his life had to offer. But that was not the only cause of the lack of hesitation in his steps. Put simply, he remembered the path.

After all, this place was—

"Yeah, there you are."

A thin, heartfelt smile came over his lips as if he was relieved not to have missed his mark. Mad laughter came over him—the sort only a man smeared with blood and free of his sanity was capable of. Subaru knew a man who laughed like that. If he looked in the mirror at that moment, he'd probably see the same smile on his own face. Seeing such an expression ate away at your mind, its sheer malevolence giving rise to a physiological sense of revulsion.

But those to whom he turned that crazed smile were accustomed to the sight.

"—"

Inside the nighttime forest, a group in black outfits that blended in with the darkness surrounded Subaru.

As if rising from the shadows themselves, they had silently encircled Subaru, not even allowing him to sense their auras as they continued to stare right at him. Their gazes held no hostility, nor amiability, nor malice, nor benevolence. He couldn't sense anything resembling "will" at all. Subaru, under their scrutiny, recalled his encounter with them from the first time around.

"Same thing, huh…?"

Just as in Subaru's memories, the black-robed figures all lowered their heads then and there. Like marionettes lacking wills of their own, they showed Subaru "respect" for the first time.

Subaru had no idea why they demonstrated admiration for him. All he knew for sure was that they were all devotees of the Witch Cult, and that the darkness enveloping Subaru had some relationship to the Witch they worshipped.

"—Outta my way."

Really, there were many things that he wanted to ask them. If this had happened before he'd resigned himself to death, he'd have had a mountain of inquiries. But by then, even that sentiment was a mere worthless relic.

At Subaru's brief command, the black-robed figures did not voice a single sound of dissent as they melted into the darkness and vanished. As they disappeared from his sight, Subaru noticed that the world was filled with silence. He no longer heard the howls of the beasts he wanted to come after him, nor the ceaseless cries of insects—not even the wind. It was as if all living creatures scorned the Witch Cult.

Perhaps the reason wasn't just the Witch Cult but Subaru's presence, too. Perhaps the Cult and Subaru being together in one place painted so repulsive a picture that the world itself recoiled.

—He thought that this latter assessment suited the current him far better.

A faint laugh came over Subaru as he advanced past where the Witch Cultists had surrounded him. He passed beyond the roots, stepped across the soil, crushed the tree leaves with the bottoms of his shoes, and finally, the forest opened. A rocky, sheer precipice spread out before his eyes.

"Beloved acolyte, I have been waiting for you."

Standing before the rock wall was a gaunt man bearing the same mad smile that Subaru did.

6

"My, my, my? And furthermore, furthermore, furthermore, you carry in your arms... Could that be the half-demon girl?"

When Subaru approached the rocky area, Petelgeuse cocked his head and looked at Emilia, whom Subaru held in his arms. The madman's head remained parallel to the ground as his tongue slid out in amusement, dribbling spittle.

"Heavens, for her to lose her life before even undertaking our trial... What a tragic fate! What an untimely demise! Ahh! And, and, and...what diligence upon your part! On the verge of the trial, before I even act, you have stolen the half-demon's body and life...!"

Petelgeuse shouted, hailing Emilia's death with exaggerated gestures, waving his arms around. Subaru then noticed that the Witch Cult adherents had gathered around Petelgeuse at some point, all of them on their knees as they devotedly listened to the madman's ravings.

"Me, diligence...?"

Hearing Subaru's halting murmur, Petelgeuse rushed over with jubilant laughter.

"Yes, that is right! Diligence! It is splendid! Unlike us, slow to decide, meager of wit, and lacking decisiveness, you made the Witch's will manifest before any other!"

Then he slid onto his knees and fell prostrate, virtually slamming his forehead against the rocky ground.

"Compared to you! My fingers and I were so slow, so foolish, so lacking! Ahh, forgive me! For being unable to requite your love!

Forgive this slothful, unfaithful flesh! Forgive this stupid man unable to respond to the love you bestow upon me!"

A flood of tears poured from Petelgeuse as he pounded the rock with an arm, nearly splitting his forehead with the intensity of his apology. The fervent act of self harm was accompanied by a spray of blood. Subaru could see bone from where his wrist was cut. Despite that, Petelgeuse did not cease his violent action; indeed, each of the faithful kneeling all around rushed to emulate the madman's self-destructive actions.

It was a cacophony of blood and agony—and as he watched it all, Subaru felt nothing. Even with the man he had so hated right before him, his heart was unmoved whatsoever.

"Ahh, what can I do for you, who fulfilled the trial in my place while I failed to respond to Her feelings? Tell me, please. What may I do for you, so that I may prove that my love is not slothful?"

Petelgeuse came close, the blood trickling from his head causing tears of blood to flow as he made his earnest plea.

Subaru replied, "Kill me."

Surely even the expression on that madman's face would register shock from the sudden request—

"Are you sure about that?"

—but it did not. Without a moment's hesitation, he kicked Subaru away.

The wind kicked out of him, Subaru sailed back as Petelgeuse watched him with an expression of ecstasy.

"Ahh, splendid, splendid indeed...! With the trial fulfilled in search of salvation, my actions, and those of my believers seeking salvation, may have thus become diligent...! Ahh, we are spared from being slothful! Both you and I! You have my thanks! And my diligence has earned Her love!"

Petelgeuse harbored no misgivings about the brooding Subaru's reply, nor felt a single pang of conscience over his own actions, seeing neither as contrary to the laws of the world in any way. Under the guise of diligence, his bloodlust had been unleashed.

Subaru, seeing this in the madman, closed his eyes, his heart hardly stirred.

At the very least, it was what Subaru wanted to see just then.

"Though I must say..."

When he heard Petelgeuse mutter something, Subaru felt hostility press upon his skin.

"Unable to even pass a single trial, not even facing a single Deadly Sin, bearing great expectations only to stumble over the first stone in her path..."

The madman looked down at the sleeping Emilia, sighing.

"—Ahh, you were lazy!"

He had no greater words to demean Emilia's death.

Subaru knew this, because he recalled how the madman had disgraced the life of a girl precious to him in a world long past.

"—"

Subaru opened his eyes. That instant, he saw a dark cloud approaching, taking the form of a hand. For a single moment, he recoiled from the painful memories rushing into the back of his mind.

But this evil hand was different. His body could move. His feet could move. His arms could move. Hence, his body evaded it.

As the black hand gently slid toward him, Subaru leaped to the side, holding Emilia in his arms. The hand slipped past, seeming perplexed as it vanished. Subaru's breath was ragged as he watched it disappear.

Petelgeuse stared at him, eyes wide with a fire raging in them, asking in a shaking voice, "...You. Just now, you saw my Unseen Hands, did you not?"

The madman inserted his twig-like fingers into his mouth, crushing his fingertips with his teeth one by one. As each part of his flesh burst with the horrible sound of bones snapping and fresh blood seeping out, he continued, "That will not do, that will not do at all. It is strange, it is wrong. There is some error, some mistake. My power, the power of Sloth, the Unseen Hands, Her favor bestowed unto me...! That another has set eyes upon them is unforgivable!!"

Spitting blood, Petelgeuse chewed on fragments of bone and nail as he glared at Subaru with bloodshot eyes.

In the next instant, black arms rose out from Petelgeuse's back.

Petelgeuse's shadow exploded into seven black limbs that madly danced about. A chill ran up Subaru's spine at the resemblance to the two evil hands that punished Subaru when he touched upon the taboo.

"But if I can see them, and my body can move…"

He could dodge them.

The speed of the black hands was not all that fast. Though they boasted the power to rip a human limb from limb at a distance, their greatest menace was their power of Invisibility. Their greatest advantage no longer worked on Subaru. And with the last wisps of his life burning down, Subaru exhibited physical abilities beyond his limitations.

"Whywhywhywhywhywhywhywhyyyyyyyyyy…? Why can you avoid them?! Do you see them?! This love belongs to me! To me alone!!"

"Deep down, there's only one guy I don't wanna be killed by, and that's you."

Subaru twisted to evade one hand and leaped forward to dodge a different set of fingertips stretching up toward him. He crouched instantly to avoid the two coming at him from the left and right, practically falling forward and closing the distance with Petelgeuse.

Seeing the insanity on Petelgeuse's face twist into shock, a dark pleasure filled Subaru's belly.

He'd just remembered the fact that he had wanted to kill that madman.

"—Bgah!"

Taking the shortest possible route, Subaru slammed his head into the bridge of the madman's nose, violently kicking his body as he rocked backward. The black hands flailed about, unable to strike precisely. Now blood was pouring from Subaru's forehead, too, cut by Petelgeuse's front teeth. The heavy bleeding got into his eyes, blotting out his vision on the right side.

—A moment after he noticed something sliding under his feet, it grabbed Subaru's legs and sent him flying.

The instant before he slammed against a large tree, Subaru abandoned all thoughts of cushioning the blow, clutching Emilia's remains even more strongly. Not to cling to her but to protect her.

"—Gweh!"

And so his back collided against the tree, making him feel a seemingly lethal crack in his spine. Several vertebrae broke, and his recently closed wounds opened all at once. Each one cried out in a chorus of ferocious pain as Subaru fell onto the ground, writhing, and bubbles appeared around his mouth.

"Disgraceful! Disgraceful, is it not?! Ahh, I am so relieved. Truly relieved! At that rate, I would have wallowed in idleness, all my actions rendered meaningless! But I am indeed diligent, exhausting my efforts for love..."

"Shut up, dim...wit...!"

His breathing sounded strange. He felt like he'd taken heavy damage to his lungs. Even so, he laughed and mocked Petelgeuse, bubbles of blood dripping from his lips all the while.

"What love, you moron? That so-called love you say you got... I can see it, too, can't I...? She's been cheatin' on you, sucker."

"What...are you saying...?! Saying, saying, sa-sa-sa-sa-sayiiiing... My brain, my brain treeeeeembles!"

Petelgeuse tore hair from his head as he raged, eyes wide open. He walked toward the fallen Subaru, violently kicking Emilia from his arms as if to deliberately distance her from Subaru.

Emilia's body rolled, slamming into the roots of various trees. Petelgeuse glanced sideways at it and laughed.

"Denigrating my love is impermissible! Ahh, I have decided. It is decided! Though the half-demon who should have undergone the trial perished beforehand, those sheltering her yet remain!"

Petelgeuse ranted and raved as one of his black hands lifted Subaru by his neck. Subaru's eyes snapped wide as the force threatened to rip his head off his shoulders; the brutal pain left him unable to speak.

"First, I shall eradicate those associated with the mansion; next, I shall sacrifice the residents of the village nearby for Her affection. Nothing shall remain, for any survivors would be proof of Sloth. I, the pinnacle of diligence, and my fingers shall render judgment upon all—the highway is sealed by the mist, so there is no one to interfere with my love!"

Shouting and spitting in his agitated state, Petelgeuse laid out his diabolical scheme.

"Before that, you seemed to clutch that half-demon's flesh as if it was quite precious to you... If I destroy it, I wonder what wonderful sounds I will hear you make?"

Petelgeuse's head tilted, his lips twisted, and his eyes filled with inhuman curiosity.

Five arms other than the one holding Subaru up crawled out from the madman's back, each moving independently as they wriggled their way toward Emilia's remains. One grasped each of her limbs, with the last hand wrapping around her slender neck.

"Do you see them? Do you understand what is about to happen?"

"...S...top!"

At that moment, Subaru was racked with fear precisely because he could see it. It made him remember every detail of what this man's black hands did to Rem's body when he couldn't see them. And now, those same destructive impulses were directed toward Emilia's flesh.

He had no power to prevent the vile act. Subaru's grief only deepened Petelgeuse's crazed, amused smile. All that remained was for him to cruelly rip Emilia's flesh asunder—

"—What are you doing?"

Without warning, the voice poured down from the heavens, coldly thrumming in the ears of all present.

"—!"

Petelgeuse's expression shifted, his gaze drifting around in search of the speaker. The voice had enough power in it—and well-honed anger—to make even his expression change.

Finally, Petelgeuse's gaze turned toward a single point in the sky and stopped. A second after, Subaru, still held aloft by his neck, looked at the same point in the sky, too.

"I repeat…"

An incredible number of icicles poured down, filling their vision, seemingly blotting out the nighttime sky. A breath surged, dyed white; in the blink of an eye, a cold that threatened to chill the whole world spread throughout the forest.

The black-robed figures still on their knees and Petelgeuse, with a crazed smile, over him, were at a loss for words.

"What are you lowlifes doing to my daughter…?"

—The Apocalypse Beast of Eternal Frost dyed the world white.

To Subaru, it was the being who would bring him death at the end of his tenth time—the tenth world.

7

Since being invited to this world, Subaru had experienced death time and again.

Under normal circumstances, it was an ordeal no one faced more than once a lifetime. That common-sense rule had been violated, and Subaru, who had already been granted ten opportunities to grapple with death, knew as much about it as anyone. And having come to know it so well, Subaru had become able to sense its approach.

His refined senses told him loud and clear that death was on its way.

"You lot sure like to do whatever you please."

The voice, bearing penetrating cold and oppressive might, had come from the icy veil in the sky above. The voice hailed from a small, mouse-colored cat, its emotions as frigid as the horde of sharp-tipped icicles accompanying it on its way to the ground. It was small enough to fit in the palm of your hand, with a tail about as long as it was tall. It had a pink nose and round eyes. Its short arms were folded, almost humanlike, as its expression was fraught with deep hatred.

Petelgeuse and the other members of the Witch Cult were silent before the supernatural being that spoke the language of men. And Subaru, who was with them, felt his throat closing up in shock for a different reason. He had never before seen that being, that spirit, shaking in anger like that.

As one present in that place, feeling the overflow of his anger, he knew that death had come to the world.

"...Puck."

Under the white mist surrounding the floating spirit—Puck—the forest in their vicinity let out a crack-like sound as it was transformed. The trees turned white, as if the green had been sucked out of them; their mana absorbed, leaves, branches, and trunks froze over, dead as they fell.

The ground itself displayed identical effects. First, the flowers died, then the cold crept over the soil, and finally, it reached Subaru, also on the earth, stabbing him all over with burning pain. He felt lethargy gradually rising from the depths of his body, causing his breathing to falter as his mind began to fade.

Long before, Subaru had experienced being forcibly robbed of his mana at Beatrice's hands. The angered Puck was employing that power on a global scale, turning the world's power into his own.

Beside Subaru, holding back a whimper, Petelgeuse backed up a step with heavy sweat on his brow, and the kneeling Witch Cult was gasping for oxygen through their open mouths, almost like fish.

"The Witch Cult—no matter how much time passes, you never change, do you? In every age, it is you who bring me the saddest things of all."

Puck spoke as if dealing with noxious insects as he trained his eyes on a single point in the forest. Subaru, following his gaze, saw that there was a single space left that Puck's power was not affecting. Only the prone girl's corpse was protected from the end of the world.

"Ahh, my poor Lia... You died without understanding anything."

After gazing longingly at Emilia, Puck turned his eyes toward those who still lived.

"Depriving my daughter of her life is a grave crime. Do not think any of you will escape alive."

"How dare a mere spirit...! How, how, how, how, howww dare you speak?! A half-demon failing an ordeal is nothing but a filthy pretender! The blame is yours for your Sloth and inability to protect this fool! Ahh! Ahh! Ahhhhh! My brain is trembling!!"

Petelgeuse responded to Puck's threats by raising both hands to the sky, flying into a rage. The madman's bloodshot eyeballs were unfocused as Petelgeuse's welling bloodlust erupted in a geyser of froth.

"All that shall transpire, all that must transpire, the proper course of history is recorded in my Gospel! The Witch loves me, and I must repay Her with diligence! Whereas you, lowly spirit, wallow in idleness!"

Love, was it? To Petelgeuse, acts of worship toward the Witch were nothing but repaying her for her love. For the madman, actions that displayed his adoration for the Witch had absolute priority over everything else. The Witch was supreme and the Witch was the greatest. Furthermore, nothing and no one was permitted to defy his love for the Witch.

"Death to half-demons! And you, too, must pay for your idleness! The Witch's favor is the truth that lets my heart beat! All must be sacrificed for it!"

Petelgeuse waved his arms, ranting, raving, and loudly stamping his foot.

Puck looked down upon Petelgeuse's madness with eyes that were cold to their very core. They contained neither pity nor anger, only a lucid view of the low worth of the object before them.

Puck's and Petelgeuse's absolutely incompatible wills clashed, fueling each other's bloodlust.

"My fingers! This fool must pay for his—"

"Die."

The descending icicles poured down on the Witch Cult adherents, skewering them and pinning them in place. The cultists' bodies and limbs were impaled against the ground, pierced like bugs for study.

The air creaked, and the flesh of the dead Witch Cult worshippers froze over, turning the rocky area into an ice sculpture exhibit.

"—"

Instantly, without warning, Puck had taken nearly twenty lives. During that time, his gaze did not waver in any way; neither did Petelgeuse's. Unmoved by the loss of the followers who obeyed his commands, who were now literal sacrificial pawns, he exploited Puck's temporary shift of attention away from him.

"—My brain…is…trembling."

His lips twisted darkly, and a moment later, Petelgeuse's shadow exploded. Simultaneously, Subaru's body was cast aside as a total of seven arms bore upon Puck, floating in the sky.

With Puck's power, dealing with the gently advancing evil hands was child's play. But Puck made no reaction to the advance of the hands—because he didn't see them.

"Puck—!"

When Subaru tried to raise his voice to warn of the danger, the voice and eyes Puck turned toward him made his blood run cold.

"Be quiet, Subaru. I will deal with you la… Ngh?"

But before the spirit finished speaking, the black hands trapped his tiny body, which vanished from Subaru's view.

"Ahh…"

Puck's body was so small that a normal adult's hand was more than large enough to conceal it from view. There was no way anyone could have seen it through seven hands. And each of those black hands were so overwhelmingly powerful that they could rip a human body apart with ease.

"Carelessness! Negligence! In other words, Sloth! You should have eliminated me immediately! You possessed such power, yet you neglected its proper use! And this is the result! This! Thisss! Thisthisthisthiiiisssss!!"

The Unseen Hands that only Subaru could detect enveloped

Puck's body and crushed it. Before Petelgeuse, who danced with mad delight, the Great Spirit was cruelly erased—

"Don't make me laugh."

In the next moment, Subaru saw the converging black limbs being blown apart.

"That's all? You're four hundred years too young to be invoking the Witch. If you really want to kill me—"

The frozen trees, unable to bear their own weight, shattered into shards of ice with one flick of his tail.

The corpses of the Witch Cult followers who had become ice sculptures were smashed to smithereens. The front paws responsible for this made the ground under them into an absolute-zero zone of death. Its softest breath rivaled a raging blizzard, and within that white mist, its eyes were like dazzling, glittering gold—eyes that mercilessly towered over a world of death.

"Then stretch half of Satella's Thousand Shadows, toward me."

It was a four-legged, feline beast with gray fur, boasting such size that it stood above the forest.

It was the Beast of the End that had destroyed the mansion and brought death to Subaru in a prior world.

—It was indeed a grand manifestation of the End.

"—"

The intensity of the cold went up another level, and it hurt to even keep his eyes open to watch the world go white. Subaru endured the pain as he looked up at the beast, agape.

"What...?"

A shaking voice echoed from a tiny corner of that world of ultimate cold.

"What is it you are telling me to bring?!"

This time, Petelgeuse's scream brought a vertical cut to his parched lips, from which a trace of blood trickled—but in the blink of an eye, this, too, froze over, bringing an end to the bleeding and pain.

Subaru feared that closing his eyes amid the blowing cold meant he would never open them again. He took in Petelgeuse's final cry and looked up at the beast once more.

"Puck, is that you...?"

"I suppose it would be a little mean to say, 'Isn't it obvious?'"

The gray-colored beast's titanic mouth moved in reply to Subaru's broken question. Each word came with a gale, but it was the enormous beast's sarcasm that confirmed Subaru's suspicions.

With that answer, Subaru came to accept the fact that in the previous world, and the world before that, Subaru had died at the end because—

While Subaru was compelled to stay silent, Petelgeuse glared at Puck and murmured, "Im...possible..."

The madman thrust his intact hand into his mouth, crushing his fingers one by one, and they oozed blood. It was as if that pain was what tethered his perpetual madness to the world.

"This is impossible; it cannot be! A mere! Spirit! A lowly spirit! Cannot possess such power! If that was possible, I—!"

"—Echidna."

"—"

Petelgeuse's movements stopped as bloody froth trickled from the corner of his lips, his eyes wide open.

Puck had whispered a word that had interrupted Petelgeuse's denial. The color of Petelgeuse's face had changed the instant he heard what was apparently a name.

"As a man of the Cult, you understand what that name means, don't you?"

"Filthy...!!"

Petelgeuse's reaction to it was nothing short of dramatic. Along with the sound of something hard, blood gushed from his mouth. It came from his molars. He was so angry, he'd bitten down on his teeth hard enough to break them.

"It is repugnant to even speak that name! Ahh, you poor, lazy fool, ignorant of fear! You dare speak the name of a fallen witch, a witch other than Satella, before me...!"

Petelgeuse's eyes had gone from bloodshot to scarlet-dyed; maybe the arteries had burst open. Tears of blood flowed from the corners. The madman turned his bitten and torn fingertips toward Puck.

"My faith! My love! That is nothing less than an insult to everything I offer to Her!"

"—A human living mere decades has no business arguing time with a spirit."

Just like that, Petelgeuse ceased his mad writhing. No—this was not something he had done consciously. He had frozen from the feet up, and that had made him stop.

As Subaru lay on his side, his vision blurry and white, he saw his mortal enemy brought to the verge of death.

Petelgeuse, too, knew that his freezing meant his death was not long in the offing. However, to the very end, his madness was directed not toward his own impending death but at Puck, towering before him.

"The depth of one's faith has nothing to do with time! You are a lazy beast, born with eternal time, yet exhausting most of it in idleness! Do not compare me with a fool such as you! Ahh! Ahh, ahh! My brain is treeeeeeeeeeeembling!"

Even knowing his own end was near, Petelgeuse's madness never wavered. To Subaru, who knew no phenomenon more absolute or terrifying than death, Petelgeuse's behavior was truly deviant.

Seeing him profess his faith at the moment before his demise was proof that he was a truly corrupt being.

"Death is not punishment enough for you—that's why I hate your kind."

"The trial has been fulfilled! No matter what happens to this filthy body, so long as my feelings reach the Witch I revere, She shall grant Her favor... Ahh, it will be so good to see Her again!"

Spreading both hands before the sky above, Petelgeuse let out a cackle.

The snow blew with greater intensity, dyeing his gaunt body white. Subaru wasn't sure whether his voice or his movements gently slowed first.

Yet even then, Petelgeuse's laughter did not cease.

He was one with his buoyant madness until his laughter finally ceased and, with it, his life.

"—Quit while you were ahead, didn't you?"

The gray beast murmured as it thrust down its front paw, smashing the Petelgeuse ice sculpture into dust.

Even as Subaru watched the madman's life expire, his shattered fragments carried away by the wind, no strong emotions stirred within him. He had hated the man so; he had so wished to kill him. Petelgeuse was where it had all started; Subaru had believed that killing him would make everything turn out all right.

But was that truly the result?

Though he had witnessed the death of his hated foe, Subaru had only hollow emptiness inside him. The defeat of Petelgeuse meant clearing away the threat posed by the Witch Cult. But Rem, who ought to have been there sharing his joy, had been erased from the world; Emilia, who should have been quietly waiting for him to bring good news upon his return, had died at Subaru's own hands.

The accumulated weight of both their deaths had made Subaru desire his own demise, but in the end, he could not even manage that, and a different avenger had claimed retribution—

Subaru had nothing left. He'd done everything over and, as a result, achieved nothing.

"—Now, then."

Subaru felt his own powerlessness beaten into him as the beast quietly looked down upon him. He was reminded anew that the giant beast was Puck; the enormity of that truth made his body quake. He was reminded of how, previously, he'd watched with detached bemusement when the Knights and the Council of Elders at the royal palace had acted so terrified of fighting Puck when they heard his alias.

"Let's talk, shall we?"

—Now, he was painfully aware of just what they had felt back then.

The cold was making it hard to think. Already, the pain tearing across his whole body had vanished. Subaru heard the gentle footsteps of his own death drawing near. And just as his body slackened from the sweet premonition that the end was nigh—

"Oh, this won't do. You're bleeding out too much—I'll put a stop to that."

"—Dwah!!"

He felt like he was being roasted alive, waking up his fading senses.

With merciless pain blocking his throat, Subaru saw that each wound on his body was audibly freezing over. White steam rose as sharp ice connected, stitched, and tethered his wounds, even the ones inside his body.

Through this act of treatment, abandoning all consideration for the human body, Subaru's flesh was violently healed. Blood vessels exploded within his eyes, dyeing his vision scarlet.

It was more than an *ow, ow, ow*. The hell that had erupted within his body transcended even pain.

"Subaru, you have committed three sins."

Subaru reeled, howling with a voiceless scream. The giant beast continued to speak as if nothing had happened. Though he had become enormous in size, his mouth lined with endless sharp fangs, and the tone of his voice had changed, the cadence was as gentle as always.

That terrified him all the more.

"First, you broke your promise with Lia. It seems you do not truly understand just how weighty a promise formed between two people is to a spirit mage. I suppose you truly do not know how much your rashly breaking that promise hurt Lia."

His mind rejected an understanding of what Puck was saying. No—his mind was dominated by pain. His internal organs were frozen, and his broken bones were connected to one another by ice gouging obstructed flesh. The crimson ice over his open wounds had been ripped away, the areas affected frozen to the core, violently stopping the bleeding. The freezing had spread farther. The pain had spread farther. Death was spreading. *It hurts, hurtshurtshurtshurtshurtshurtshurtshurtshurtshurtshurts...*

"Second, you ignored Lia's wishes and came back. Do you even know how much that drove her into a corner and made her suffer, when she didn't want to see you again? Not only did you break your promise, you had to trample on Lia's heart as you pleased."

With Subaru on the white ground, limbs spread wide, Puck drew his face close and blew with his icy breath. Subaru's flowing tears became needles stabbing his eyeballs. His brain convulsed from the intense agony.

"And third, you let Lia die."

It was like having his very soul filed down. The extreme pain made Subaru forget how to breathe. Amid that agony, like having every nerve in his body immersed in magma, Subaru cursed his own shallowness.

He'd thought that pain was a lesser thing than death. He was wrong. He was wrong about everything. "Pain," "Death," "Fear"—these smashed the heart of the weakling named Subaru Natsuki in equal measure.

The soul of Subaru Natsuki had been backed into a corner with nowhere to run.

As Subaru's sluggish mind began to appreciate that terrifying truth, Puck stated to him, "—In accordance with the pact, I'll be destroying the world now."

Puck's eyes had contained anger. Only at that juncture did a new emotion begin to come to the fore.

"I will bury everything under ice and snow, as my parting gift to Lia."

"…That won't…"

"It has nothing to do with making her happy or not. No matter what the pact, I will not break what has been agreed upon."

Puck's eyes narrowed as he responded to Subaru's incoherent voice.

"But that act will end unfulfilled, I imagine. Even if I spread this world of ice to cover every land, like the forest where Lia and I dwelled…the Sword Saint will stand before me. That is a battle I will not win."

Puck seemed to lament the disparity in strength when he brought up a certain red-haired hero's other name.

Subaru couldn't believe he was hearing those words.

Puck, wielding such overpowering might, had bluntly stated that he had no chance of defeating the Sword Saint.

And if Puck knew he'd be struck down in the process, why would he sacrifice himself in such a battle?

"Wh-why...?"

"—Lia was the entire reason for my existence."

Puck responded to Subaru's inquiry.

The wind grew even colder, stabbing Subaru's flesh, filling up his eyes, freezing his blood— The end was nigh.

"It is meaningless for me to remain in a world without her. Now that I've lost her, I will not allow the world to move on. For me, everything ended when that girl died."

When Puck finished speaking, the wind's intensity suddenly spiked.

"How long will it take for a person to die if he's slowly, gradually frozen from the tips of his extremities on up? Have you ever wondered that, Subaru?"

"—"

"I'll take that as a yes. I want you to learn the answer."

Slowly, slowly, the chill consumed more and more of his flesh.

His wounds and internal organs were already frozen, so they were exempt as the rest of Subaru's flesh expired from the fingertips up.

If pain could truly drive a person mad, his sanity would have been shattered long before.

He wanted his mind to be ripped apart, smashed to bits, scattered in all directions. For if not...

"—Mist is coming. It seems you've lured quite a nasty one."

He couldn't hear. Someone was saying something, but he couldn't hear.

"Gluttony's... Ahh, nowadays they call it the White Whale, don't they? Calling it over, letting Lia die, losing your own life... You truly are incorrigible, do you know that?"

He couldn't hear. He couldn't hear. But even though he shouldn't have heard it, he heard the voice.

He heard laughter from somewhere. A mocking voice.

Cackle, cackle.

He knew that laughter. The voice of the man he hated to the point of death.

Where is it coming from? With the end near, his consciousness sought an answer to that question.

Then he realized it.

The incessant cackling was coming from his own throat.

Ecstasy began to rule his brain, drowning out his pain.

He took his first steps into a spreading world of madness. The way it warped everything around him felt…good.

The laughter wouldn't stop.

His own laughter was mocking him—the one who had let Rem die, who had killed Emilia, and who was dying like a dog himself.

Ah yes. He was truly…how would you put it…

"—Subaru, you're lazy."

With a sharp sound, he blacked out.

It probably was not only his consciousness, and his life, that had been severed.

—It was something more, something that had been barely holding him together, that audibly came apart in that moment.

Snap.

CHAPTER 5

FROM ZERO

1

Amid the white world, everything vanished.

He couldn't tell if his flesh had dissolved, if it had been smashed to pieces, or if it would remain as an ice sculpture for all eternity. No matter how terrible the end of the body he had left behind, it was all the same to him now.

There was only one thing he understood with clarity.

Over the course of repeating, repeating, repeating, he'd seen things end cruelly, with the situation growing worse with each repetition, and now, having destroyed with his own hands that which he most wanted to protect, he finally realized it.

—No one expected anything of Subaru Natsuki. Not even him.

No matter how many times he experienced it, he'd never get used to the feeling of the senses he had lost suddenly come rushing back.

He no longer felt frozen to the core, or even cold at all, and he could tell that white world into which he had sunk deeper and deeper was gone.

In the blink of an eye, all his dulled senses became clear, and every last thing was just as it had once been.

Blood flowed through the limbs that had known so much pain. The agony of his nerves being immersed in ice was no more. The cold stabbing his skin had been peeled away, replaced by dazzling rays that could give him a sunburn.

"—"

"—!"

"—aa."

Sounds from hustle and bustle to the left and right intermingled as his dead sense of hearing returned with a vengeance.

Blocking out the meaningless noise, Subaru checked the condition of his body. His frozen limbs, his injured spine, and his internal organs that had been turned to sherbet were all functioning without any problems.

Everything was back as it should be. Subaru felt relief that the body lost to him was under his control again. And what brought Subaru more tranquility than anything was...

"Why are you staring into space like that, Subaru?"

Behind the counter, Rem tilted her head slightly, gazing at him with concern.

He had been abandoned by everything and everyone, had an implacable sense of powerlessness drilled into him, had despaired at the loss and disappointment at what his own actions had wrought, and after dying like a helpless dog, he had returned.

"—Rem."

"Yes, it is me, your Rem... What might be the matter?"

Rem responded to the call of his voice, slipping away from behind the counter and heading out of the shop. Subaru was rooted to the spot as Rem walked right in front of him, reaching out with her hand and touching him on the cheek. Her brows knit in worry, revealing a tinge of gloom on her noble face.

"I am sorry for not noticing. The crowd has worn you out, yes? I am a failure as a maid to have forgotten my most important duty of all."

"Tired. Yeah, that's right… I am."

As Rem's hand rested on his cheek, he slowly lifted up his hand, pressing it down upon hers. The touch between them made Rem raise her eyebrows in surprise, but Subaru's haggard voice and expression left her at a loss for words.

Rem looked like she was trying to say something, but Subaru didn't even look at her; instead, he felt Rem's firm, solid presence against his hand—as if clinging to that warmth to keep it from running away.

"I guess all that…falling and getting worn down…was exhausting…"

Yet in spite of all that, the Rem he had surely lost was right there with him at that very moment, so…

"Subaru?"

Subaru resolved that, if nothing else, he would never let go of the girl right before his eyes.

2

He ran rapidly through the crowd, heading down a gently descending slope. He scowled from the dust kicked up by a passing dragon carriage, but Subaru's gaze was aimed straight in front of him.

He knew where he was going. His running feet were sure.

When he thought back, Subaru had harbored nothing but uncertainty during those repeated days: uncertainty about what he should be like, about what lay in Emilia's heart, about whether his existence held any purpose, about whether he could bring out the best of all possible futures, all amid a vortex of madness. He was an unsure man lost in an uncertain, foreign world.

But Subaru, unable to make a single manly step in one direction throughout, advanced with clarity of purpose he had never before known.

Finally, he'd come to understand.

Now that he'd arrived at that answer, the repeated days had not been in vain.

Backed into a mental and physical corner, Subaru truly realized for the first time what he could do, what he must do.

"—ru!"

His uncertainty lifted, his gaze was trained squarely on his objective, his legs powerfully thudding along the earth. His body was light. Relieved of the pressure on his heart, Subaru wasn't afraid of anything anymore.

"Please, Subaru, listen to me!"

Pulling his arm forward, he could see the main street at the end of the downward slope. Even in the royal capital, it boasted the greatest width, continuing all the way to the main gate through the stout walls that surrounded the capital.

Everyone entering or leaving the royal capital had to pass through that gate. With the announcement of the royal selection, the main street was even busier with people coming and going; at that very moment, it was bustling with the numerous people along it.

He cut past the shadow of a building. Abruptly, sun rays slid into his field of vision. Subaru used a hand to shield his eyes from the bright light as he raised his face up, looking at the symbols carved into the gate that read, LUGUNICA, THE ROYAL CAPITAL.

One more step, and she and Subaru would be—

"Subaru!"

Having brought him all that way, his feet stopped when he felt a sharp tug on his arm. The unanticipated resistance made Subaru look back. As Rem stood still, her eyes wavered with bewilderment.

When Rem freed her hand from his grasp, she seemed to shrink as she pleaded with him.

"What's wrong? What has happened? If you do not explain, I..."

Hearing those words, Subaru accepted that it was right for Rem to harbor misgivings. In her eyes, Subaru's transformation had to look sudden, even unthinkable. It was natural for her to be angry with him for dragging her by the arm all that way without an explanation.

"Ahh, my bad. I was in a bit of a hurry. I have a lot of things to think about. Sorry for cutting corners on explaining."

"It troubles me, you know. Even I understand you have many

things on your mind, Subaru, but you must speak to me about them… Though I do not mind you being assertive."

Rem put both hands to her very slightly reddened cheeks as she let out a sigh of relief. Perhaps she had sensed from the tone of Subaru's voice that he had regained his composure and concluded that she'd made too much of his odd behavior over the last little while.

I see. Observing Rem's relief, Subaru thought his own lack of consideration was even more pathetic. No doubt Rem, who only knew the Subaru of before, thought that his transformation in the seconds after Return by Death was nothing short of dramatic. The experiences of several days changed Subaru in the span of a single second.

Furthermore, on that day, in his own way, Subaru was busy trying to avert his eyes from the gloom in his own heart. He'd put on a disgraceful show at the royal selection conference, had been beaten half to death by Julius at the parade grounds, had created a fatal chasm between himself and Emilia and, having been left behind in the royal capital, had lost the purpose for his existence.

He'd been idly spending his time at the Crusch residence, sinking deeper into the doldrums as he asked himself what he could do, what he needed to do, without finding any answers. It couldn't be called anything short of ridiculous. Subaru very much thought that now.

From Rem's point of view, that uncertainty in Subaru had vanished in a literal blink of an eye. If you couldn't call that a thunderclap out of the blue, what could you call it?

"Sorry for making you worry. I'm all right now. I feel like you've had to see me all pathetic and bent out of shape, but I understand finally."

"No, to me, time spent thinking about you is time well spent… You understand finally?"

Subaru was speaking with unclouded eyes. There was a liveliness to Rem's voice as she replied. She couldn't hide her reserved delight at being able to converse with Subaru like that again.

Then Subaru smiled shyly and nodded at the question Rem raised.

"I really do feel more than a little sorry for the trouble I caused everyone running around and worrying like that, but I finally know how to put everything in order. Well, no, now that I think about it, I saw it from the start, and people mentioned it to me, too… I'm just bad at giving up."

"I think that is a marvelous thing about you, Subaru…"

Subaru smiled weakly at Rem's soft-spoken reply. Then he looked up at the sky. Its height and breadth gently made his chest feel lighter.

The world had probably been looking down at Subaru in frustration all along. But with this, that oppressive time would finally come to an end.

The answer had been under his nose all along.

No matter where Subaru headed, no matter what challenges he recklessly faced, no matter how much he ran around doing stupid things, she'd followed him without a word of complaint.

Yes—

"Rem, I've decided."

She stood close enough for him to reach out and touch as he looked straight into her eyes.

Her short blue hair fluttered in the wind. Her pale, clear blue eyes held only Subaru within them. Her petite figure was clad in a modified black-themed apron dress. The overly serious way she carried herself projected her nobility and steadfastness. The vivid floral hair ornament delicately added to the loveliness of her small, refined visage.

"Yes, Subaru."

Her pink lips formed a small smile. She narrowed her eyes, the benevolence in them piercing right through Subaru. The soft echo of her voice, full of affection, enchanted him; she seemed to be hanging on to his every word.

"First, we'll rent a dragon carriage. With the capital in such an uproar, hiring one seems to be rough, but we'll play dirty if we have to. No intro from Anastasia, so it's best to keep this on the up-and-up if possible."

They needed a fast land dragon with plenty of endurance; if it was friendly on top of that, great.

They'd need to keep running. They needed to travel light, to keep running without pause, day and night.

"A dragon carriage, you say...?" Rem cocked her head slightly and echoed Subaru.

From the confusion welling in her eyes, Subaru's rush to the conclusion meant his explanation had told her little. But he pretended not to notice Rem's natural misgivings and pointed at the huge front gate.

"We'll have to kill some time while we pick out a dragon carriage, so we should go buy some food during the downtime. Ah, I'm no good with old-style rations, though. Plain water's better than those things."

He'd actually eaten simple rations and preserved foods on field trips and the like back in his old world. The hateful memory had made Subaru brand both as "no good."

"Ah, wait, maybe there's some nice magical power to preserve food here...? We managed to make mayonnaise, so maybe we can experiment and find something good..."

"Er, Subaru?"

"Mm, ah, sorry. My thoughts started running in a weird direction. What's wrong?"

Realizing he'd gone off on a tangent, Subaru righted himself and smiled kindly as he looked at Rem. That smile made Rem go briefly silent. Then she lifted her head, seemingly trying to set aside her doubts.

"Er, I'm sorry. I am a poor guesser, so I do not understand what you are trying to do, Subaru. Er, what are...?"

"Ahh! Right, my bad! Sorry, I didn't realize at all! Er, just now I was completely caught up trying to make plans for stuff we've gotta do. So embarrassing!"

Subaru slapped his knee, grinning in recognition of his mistake.

"It took a whole lot of experiences for me to realize a few things, but the answer was obvious a good while ago."

A wry smile, a truly wry smile, appeared.

He'd tasted bitterness. He'd chewed on his regrets. He'd shed tears over the absurdity and irrationality of it all. He'd been toyed with by a cruel fate. He'd been smeared with the blood of others, dying an absurd number of times.

All of it had led to a single answer, one he now keenly understood.

"Rem."

Calling her name, Subaru slowly stretched a hand toward her. Rem watched his hand, waiting for his next words. Responding to Rem's unspoken request, he put the feelings welling within him into words—

"Let's run away together. As far as we can."

His defeat at Fate's hands was loud and clear.

3

"...Huh?"

Rem, unable to grasp the meaning of the words spoken to her, let out only a faint gasp from her throat. Subaru, unsurprised at Rem's reaction, shook his head and said, "We'll leave the royal capital and head west...that, or north. I've heard that we can't get into the empire down south, so it's one of those two... I'm not good with cold, so personally, I vote for west."

"Er, um, excuse..."

"It'll be a long journey with no clear end, and I don't think we'll have an easy time just 'cause it's a good chance to start over. Besides, in the first place, if we rent a dragon carriage, I can't see us ever getting a chance to hand it back. What should we do about that, huh...? Maybe buy a dragon carriage instead of renting one?"

He'd left procuring dragon carriages to Rem. Subaru didn't know if they had some rental car–like system in place. He didn't even know where you'd buy one. He figured there had to be some means so that you couldn't just grab one and run, but—

"P-please wait!"

Subaru was in the middle of that thought when Rem urged him to pause. She kept her palms pointed toward Subaru as a rare expression of nervousness came over her.

"Er...what do you mean by 'run'? Subaru, from the way you are speaking right now, you sound as if you are trying to go to a different nation, one that is not Lugunica..."

Rem's gaze wandered as if she half doubted her own words. Then her expression changed to an *Ah!* look as she clapped her hands together.

"Since it is you we are talking about, you have another incredible idea, don't you? Something that will aid Lady Emilia and Master Roswaal..."

"Nothin' of the sort, Rem."

"Eh...?"

Rem seemed to be clinging to the best possible interpretation of the true intent behind Subaru's words. But right in front of the girl who believed this of him, Subaru decisively repudiated that thought.

"I told you, we'll run away. Even if I stay in the royal capital, I can't do anything. But if I return to the mansion, that won't change the fact that I can't do anything—I understand that now."

His powerlessness, his emptiness, the irrationality of the world—these weighed heavily on Subaru. No matter how hard he tried to deny it, the absurd would never leave him. But how light his heart had become, now that he had accepted it.

Now, Subaru was free of the troubles he had endured, almost as if they had never existed.

"So run away with me, Rem. Every last person's told me that I can't stay here. I didn't want to accept it, so I kept on desperately denying it, but...ah, that's right. I'm weak. No one's ever told me, 'I need you.'"

He thought he'd been...too full of himself.

He'd thought wrong. He'd been mistaken. He'd gotten carried away.

Having arrived in another world and, through the power to rewind fate and just the tiniest bit of good fortune, he felt like he'd saved people on two separate occasions, but he'd been wrong.

He didn't even possess the power or feelings deserving of being saved by others.

"That's not...!"

"No one's said it. And I have been told, loud and clear…over and over."

No one needs the likes of you.

The first time around, Subaru had ignored Emilia's wishes and rushed out of the Crusch residence. He didn't listen to Rem's attempt to stop him, courting a massive tragedy as a result.

The second time around, he'd been unable to change one iota of the result, everyone had died again, and through fleeing from reality, he'd caused Rem to lose her life; again, no one was saved.

The third time around brought about the most despicable of all outcomes. He'd gotten even innocent merchants on the roadside involved, offered Rem up to the White Whale, and had robbed Emilia of her life with his own hands. Puck had slaughtered the Witch Cult, but if, after Subaru's death, Puck had indeed destroyed the world as he had proclaimed, the damage was surely greater than any time that had come before.

What about the time unrelated to the power of Return by Death that could not be rewound? When the candidates had assembled at the royal palace, Subaru had dragged down Emilia in epic fashion. Merely by standing at her side, let alone speaking his impertinent words, he'd tarnished her reputation, and his "duel" to save face had resulted only in even greater humiliation. As a result, he and Emilia had had a falling out, and he had hurt her heart with his emotional arguments, which had been little more than outbursts of anger.

"…Kha-ha-ha!"

He laughed drily at the realization. Now that he thought back, it was a masterpiece. When he calmly reflected on his own actions, it was painfully clear that he'd been a pestilence.

He wanted to lend Emilia his strength?

There had to be people only he could save?

There was no doubt everyone was done for if he wasn't there?

What thoughtlessness. What arrogance. Yes, what hubris.

Subaru's actions had only worsened Emilia's standing. Even so, he'd betrayed her enormously generous heart, and his foolish undertakings had only dragged Rem with him to her death.

Incredible. Just incredible. No doubt everyone knew that would be the result. That was why everyone had told Subaru, *You need to behave, don't do anything, your strength isn't required, don't butt in, just go away.*

Those around him who had told him so knew a great deal about the future. They were very different from Subaru, who ought to have known that he could do nothing, that he understood nothing, that he was able to comprehend nothing.

Maybe they were the ones really doing things over?

"If they aren't, I'm the only one…screwing up like this."

It was pathetic.

There was no one lowlier, more unsalvageable, or more miserable than he.

What did you call a man who resigned himself to being laughed at by others and acted so as to make others laugh? You called him a clown. Subaru, who wasn't even aware of the customers pointing at him and laughing, was unworthy of the title.

—He was just a simple, irredeemable fool.

"So I've decided to go away. That's best. I know that's best. If someone like me tries to do something, it'll just add one more corpse… and if I'm not lucky, a lot more than one."

Corpses. Corpses. Corpses. Corpses. Corpses.

Strangers. Acquaintances. People precious to him. Important people. People who believed in him. People he wanted to think believed in him— Endless corpses.

He'd had it.

Why did all those things have to happen to him? He'd suffered so much; didn't he deserve some reward? Even Subaru knew that the idea that hard work was always rewarded, that any wish with a clear objective could come true so long as you gave it your all, was nothing but a pipe dream. But despite that, was it so wrong to have but one tiny wish—to avoid the worst of all worlds?

Subaru had been wrong. That was why the results continued to betray his expectations.

"Let's run away, Rem. You, me…we can't stay here in this country."

Subaru had resolved to leave it all behind, flip the bird at everything, and run.

And having decided to put so many things behind him as he fled, he wanted to take only one with him—Rem, the girl standing before him.

He couldn't bring himself to abandon everything in its entirety.

He was afraid of being alone. He was terrified of solitude.

Even in that vast world, that world of incomprehensible darkness, knowing that having nothing so that he would lose nothing was the right answer, Subaru couldn't put aside his fear of being all by himself.

As the days repeated themselves, Rem had been the only one who'd stayed with Subaru. She'd been right at his side, watching his disgraceful displays, unsightly words and deeds, and off-the-wall way of living.

Subaru thought that made her worthy of one final gamble.

—Each of the three times, Subaru had let Rem die.

To keep her from dying, he couldn't return to the mansion. Even when he had arrived at the mansion, she had heroically offered up her life along the way, in the end. Nor could he say with certainty that he could save her by keeping her at the royal capital. Even if they were spending their time in peace and quiet here, if Ram conveyed news of the crisis at the mansion, Rem would probably rush out of the city.

If it came to that, Subaru wouldn't be able to stop her. And she would meet the same fate. He'd lose her again, and Subaru could clearly see how empty he would be without her. If he seriously wanted to save her, he had to get her out of the kingdom.

"You are saying all this so suddenly, I do not know what to do..."

Rem shook her head a little in the face of Subaru's forceful plea. It wasn't a gesture of rejection. Her expression projected the uncertainty that reigned inside her.

Rem couldn't simply accept at face value what Subaru had suddenly said. He had cited far too few facts to make an informed decision.

Subaru understood the irrationality of it, but even so, he could speak no further of the circumstances. He no longer knew how much information he could divulge with the Witch's evil hands looming.

He felt like he'd brush against the Witch's curse no matter what he talked about. No matter what he did, he felt like it would lead to more sacrifices to the irrationalities of Fate. And if that came to pass, it wouldn't be Subaru who would be sacrificed but people precious to him.

"—"

—It was a stalemate. He was hemmed in on all sides. Fate had shut off every avenue of escape. Therefore, Subaru had no means left to him but that plea.

He was earnestly appealing to Rem's conscience, knowing that it was underhanded in every possible way, knowing that he was using the feelings for Subaru that Rem harbored in her heart.

"There's no time. I'm sorry this is so sudden. Really, really I am. I'm sorry from the bottom of my heart... But please choose."

"Choose..."

"Me or everything except for me... Please choose."

Subaru hated the situation he'd put her in, saying all that and making her suddenly choose based on the little information he'd provided her. But it was also a fact that giving her time to calmly think it over worked against him. He couldn't dismiss the notion that he was using the pressure of her predicament for his own benefit.

Only in this situation, giving Rem little time to decide whether to leave Subaru there or not as he pled right before her eyes, did he have a shot at winning this.

Or if not "winning," then fulfilling a cherished desire more like hope—the selfish hope that Rem, at least, would forgive him for running away.

"Let's get a dragon carriage and head west. Let's leave Lugunica and go all the way west of...Kararagi, was it? Let's buy a little house and live there, just the two of us."

Rapid-fire, Subaru began sketching his vision of the future. It was an ordinary, tranquil future, one surely divorced from irrationality and cruelty.

"It means using the traveling funds, so I feel bad for Roswaal, but we can just borrow what we need and send the rest back. I'm gonna work hard to help set us up from the start, too… I've never worked at a proper job before, but it'll probably be all right."

He was a delinquent who had dropped out of high school with only a middle school graduation under his belt. His work experience in this world consisted of nothing but a stint as an apprentice servant. Furthermore, though he didn't like saying it, his current work as a subordinate was little better than that of a child helping out with the chores.

It'd probably be hard doing a real job, but he'd find work, come hell or high water. Compared to pain, suffering, and death, it'd be a walk in the park.

The more Subaru thought about it, the more his future opened up. Thinking back to how he'd aimed for a single future, spending day after day courting the worst calamities no matter how hard he tried, it was a happy thing indeed.

"Even if it's tough, if you're there, I know I'll try hard. Even if I'm tired, just the thought of you waiting for me with a smile when I come home…!"

Even if every last person he left behind blamed him for running away, he figured he could take it if Rem was at his side.

So please, I'm begging you, like I've never begged for anything before—
"Please choose me…!"

Subaru offered his hand to petition her, almost like he was trying to drag a yes out of her.

"If you pick me, I'll give you everything I have. Every part of my life will be yours. I'll spend my life for you. I'll live only for you…so please."

Even with Rem standing right in front of him, he couldn't look at her face. He didn't have the courage to see what kind of expression she was making. Courage didn't suit him, not in the tiniest bit.

If he did, surely everything would have worked out differently. Cowardly, underhanded, and pathetic as he was, he had nothing left.

"Run away with me… Live with me, please…!"

At least let me keep you from dying, he earnestly pled from the bottom of his heart.

Putting all his feelings into his parched voice, Subaru felt his heart beat quickly, his breathing grow ragged. Exhaustion from the fierce mental pummeling Subaru had received struck him with fatigue, as if he'd sprinted with all his strength.

Rem made no reply.

The sounds of the crowd were distant now. It never entered his mind to wonder what other people might think of two people having a conversation like this in public.

Rem was everything to him. To Subaru, in that moment, her existence was everything to him.

Unable to endure the silence, Subaru opened his firmly closed eyes to peek at Rem's expression as she stood before him, all the while seized by the fear that it might reveal her answer.

"—"

In silence, Rem pursed her lips, not realizing he was looking at her. Her expression struggled to remain neutral, but her brow and the corners of her eyes were faintly strained in a way she would not normally permit.

Subaru could tell that a vortex of uncertainty, bewilderment, and hesitation swirled within her. The various things Subaru had just said were greatly, powerfully, fiercely shaking her heart.

The long battle felt like an eternity. A sense of unease burned Subaru's back. But finally, that time came to an end.

"—Subaru."

Gently, she called his name with a voice that was full of affection.

The instant Subaru heard the tone, the echo of her voice, he was certain his hopes had been answered.

Rem had accepted Subaru. She'd forgiven Subaru for being weak. She'd embraced the human being called Subaru Natsuki and everything that came with him.

A flood of emotions welled within him. He felt like he'd finally been rewarded.

Then Subaru lifted his face—

"I cannot run away with you, Subaru."
With a very sad face, Rem dashed his hopes.

"After all…"
"—"
"When we talk about the future, we need to smile, don't we?"

With an expression resembling a tearful smile, Rem spoke the words that had once come from Subaru's own mouth.

4

He'd gambled, and he'd lost.

When Rem threw his own words back at him with a tearful smile, Subaru's inner self was exhausted, overwhelmed by a feeling that he'd thrown everything into one match and lost.

Subaru had trusted—no, hoped—that Rem, with her strong dependence on him, just might say yes. That maybe, just maybe, even as he cast everything aside, she might choose him.

It was a fleeting dream, a conceited thought. He should have understood that from the start. If his inability to find any worth in himself was the whole reason he'd chosen to run away, what business did he have expecting that?

"Right now…I might not be smiling, but…I mean, if we actually did it I'm sure I'd be smiling… Yeah, that's right. So, ah…"

Even though the matter had already been settled, unconvincing arguments poured out of Subaru's mouth in an attempt to smooth things over.

He couldn't think of an effective rebuttal to Rem's words. But if he didn't say something, his desires were over then and there. He might still have a chance to change her mind as long as they kept talking—though that might have been an exercise in wishful thinking.

As Subaru clung to that hope, Rem watched him, a faint smile coming over her as she murmured, "…I have…thought of it as well."

She raised her shapely face up ever so slightly.

"After arriving in Kararagi, first we would rent a room at an inn. Though a house is the foundation for building a life, we could not be reckless with the money at our disposal. First, we would need a stable income."

Rem lifted a finger up as she added to the image of the future Subaru had proposed earlier.

"Fortunately, I received a proper education due to Master Roswaal's good judgment. Even in Kararagi, I believe that finding employment would be a simple matter for me. As for Subaru...you would probably need to settle for physical labor, but perhaps you could work in close proximity to me."

With a little giggle, Rem made light of Subaru's inability to do anything. It was no doubt an accurate assessment of Subaru's worth, as he was still largely ignorant of the culture and technology in that world.

"Once our income is stable, we would look for a slightly better place to stay. During that time, you would need to study properly for future employment... It would take about a year before you could do real work, maybe. You can become independent even faster, but only through your own efforts, Subaru."

With that, Rem laid out an unexpectedly brutal studying regimen.

When she had instructed him in Ram's place, her method of teaching was gentle, but her criticisms were merciless. He might have grumbled along the way, but he was rather fond of her strictness.

"With both of us working, we could save some money... Perhaps enough to eventually buy a house. Maybe a store of some sort would be better. Kararagi is a land overflowing with commerce, so there will surely be a way to profit from your eccentric ideas, Subaru."

With an amused clap of her hands, Rem laid out a future that sounded too good to be true.

Subaru, too, felt like he could clearly picture the scene playing out in Rem's head. As usual, Subaru would cause her lots of trouble, and she would indulge him. Of course he would feel responsible for that, so he'd end up working hard with plenty of sweat rolling off his brow for sure.

That would be nice.

An honest living, for her sake and hers alone—how happy a life would that be?

"As our work progresses…ah, this is embarrassing, but maybe… children? As half-demon and half-human, they would most likely be very rambunctious. Boy or girl, twins or triplets, they are sure to be very cute children, too."

Rem's cheeks reddened as she shyly let her thoughts run a little further ahead. She counted on her fingers one by one, and just as the number reached a terrifying ten, she continued.

"It would not be all fun, and I do not think it would all go as well as I imagine. Perhaps we would have no sons and only daughters, and you might not be able to feel proud of your family."

"…Rem."

"But, ah, even when the children get big enough to be mean to you, I will always be on your side, Subaru. We would be famous with the locals as the always happily married couple and slowly spend our days together, growing old together…"

"…Rem!"

"Subaru, I am sorry to say this, but if possible, I would ask you to please let me pass away before you. I would like to lie upon a bed with you holding my hand, surrounded by our children and grand-children, while I say, 'I was happy,' and you all would send me off—"

He couldn't hold up his head.

The future Rem was portraying with her words was quietly, gently wounding Subaru's heart.

"That would be a…happy, happy way to end my life."

"If you've…!"

Listening to the bittersweet future Rem had refused was like having an irrepressible itch deep inside his chest that made him want to scratch himself raw. By the time Subaru finished listening, there was nothing left filling his heart but a pathetic, indescribable storm of emotion.

His throat trembled. Something heavy sank deep inside his lungs. His head hurt.

He shook his head to try and ignore the relentless heat filling the depths of his eyes.

"If you've…thought it through…!"

Then she could run away with Subaru as far as their feet could take them—

"Subaru, if you could smile while wishing for that future…I truly believe I could be happy after a life like that."

But filled with a sadness that exceeded even Subaru's, the smiling girl did not answer his plea.

Dumbfounded, Subaru stared at that small, painful smile when he finally understood. No matter how much he clung to hope, he could not get Rem to change her mind. He had truly, utterly lost the gamble, and he had no recourse.

"—"

A sense of fatigue assailed him, as if he were carrying something very heavy on his shoulders. He was so disheartened that he could collapse on the spot. Subaru barely managed to avoid doing so, covering his face with his hands as he despaired.

Rem had refused to go with him.

That meant he was out of ways to save her.

If he stayed by her side to protect her, all that awaited her upon their return to the mansion was a cruel future—an unchangeable tragedy and Fate's pitiless dead end.

Then perhaps it would be best to leave Rem behind and run away by himself…?

If he did so, he could not escape loneliness, but he could at least flee from the despair in front of him. Of course, the fate of the people in and around the mansion would not change whether or not he was present. Subaru would simply be covering his eyes and ears, pretending not to know, spared from seeing reality for himself.

In that moment, Subaru was so desperate for something to cling to that this paltry salvation would do. But even if he accepted that himself, would there be any salvation at all? Whether Subaru was challenging his foes, fleeing into madness, or putting everything on the line, Fate had not cut him the slightest slack. What, then, could he do—?

"Subaru, that you thought of running away with me…that you

thought of living your life with me...thrills me to the bottom of my heart. But it will not do."

Even having spurned the hand Subaru had offered, Rem's cheeks were still flush from the feelings swirling within her. She herself knew that they could flee, flee, flee and, eventually, make that fantasy a reality. She craved it. She'd stated firmly that the tale was a happy one—and yet, Rem had rejected it, because—

"I mean, if we did run away right now...I am certain that I would be leaving behind the Subaru I love most."

"—"

What was Rem saying? He didn't get it.

Trembling, Subaru lifted up his face and looked at her with blank eyes. Rem was giving him a small, sad smile, but even so, her eyes projected her firm sentiments. Subaru felt overwhelmed by her gaze as she continued.

"Subaru. Please tell me what has happened."

He shook his head. He could not. If he did that, Rem would die.

"If you cannot talk about it, then please trust me. I will manage somehow."

He shook his head. He could not. If he left it at that, Rem would die.

"...But at the very least, can we go back now? If you settle down and think about it more calmly, you might be able to find a different answer."

He shook his head. He could not. If he waited, everyone would die.

"I've...worried already. I've thought already. I've suffered already... That's why I gave up."

No one believed Subaru.

No one expected anything from him.

If he told anyone he'd do something, they'd spoon-feed him his own foolishness.

He'd ignored that, brushed it off, seen his own many stupidities, and thus arrived at his current state. To Subaru, that time, that wear and tear on his heart, was—

"—It is easy to give up. However."

Suddenly, Rem voiced a rebuttal to Subaru's words of weakness.

* * *

—It is easy to give up.

The instant the words entered his ears, a jolt of comprehension rushed through Subaru's whole body. It was as if a bolt of lightning had struck the crown of his head. Something he couldn't put into words exploded inside his chest, and every pore of his body felt like he'd been set on fire.

"It's easy...to give up...?"

"Subaru?"

"Don't...tell me that...!"

Subaru clenched his teeth, rasping with resentment at a perplexed Rem.

It's easy to give up? That's a bad joke. You think it's a simple thing to abandon your goal and run away empty-handed? Like hell it is...!

"There's no way it's easy to give up...!!"

Subaru's throat trembled from the unbearably dark emotions exploding within him.

Surprised by Subaru's angry outburst, Rem seemed to shrink. Even pedestrians traveling along the royal capital's main street were wondering what was up as they shifted their eyes to the enraged Subaru.

Heedless of the offended gazes, Subaru glared only at Rem, standing before him.

"I didn't do anything, I didn't think of anything, I abandoned everything without a care, threw it all away just like that, and gave up—is that what you think?!"

The decision was killing him. He'd cried tears of blood and yelled enough to rip his throat apart, and still he had gained nothing. Knowing that, he had made his decision.

Giving up on everything. That was the only conclusion he could put into words, but just how many sacrifices had to be made for him to reach that conclusion? He wouldn't let anyone diminish that.

"Giving up wasn't easy at all...! Thinking you can fight, that you can manage somehow, that's way easier...! But I couldn't manage somehow! I had no choice! All the paths were blocked except for giving up…!"

Fate was mocking Subaru, for every path available to him ended in a dead end. No matter how much he fought, how much he stood tall, plotted, schemed, begged, or even ran away—

It was no longer possible for him to have it all.

Even the people he wanted to save had slapped his hand away. He was supposed to keep trying, then? Who could tell Subaru that it was too soon to give up? If someone had been through the same experience, the same suffering, the same hell, would that person be able to say such a thing?

"If I could do anything…I'd…I'd…!"

He truly wanted to do something.

To help people, to save people, to keep them from being stolen away.

But he couldn't. The world wouldn't let him.

Everything during those repeated days had come back around to bite him again.

That's why Subaru had—

"Subaru."

As Subaru hung his head, drained of emotion, his voice petering out, Rem called to him.

Subaru's ears were ringing heavily. The pathetic revelation of his unsightly true feelings left him unable to even look her in the face.

And to that miserable, unsalvageable, hopeless man who had challenged Fate and lost, she said, "It is easy to give up."

"—"

"However…"

Rem repeated once more the phrase that had sent Subaru into a rage just before.

Sensing something almost incomprehensible in her words, Subaru lifted his face, dumbfounded.

Why won't she understand?

Why, after all this, couldn't she comprehend Subaru's anguish?

The gloom, the dissatisfaction, the wounds on what seemed like every corner inside his heart—

"—It does not suit you, Subaru."

It all vanished as Rem stared directly into Subaru's black eyes and spoke.

Rem stated those words as if she truly believed them, as if they represented some kind of absolute truth.

"I do not understand what painful thoughts, what knowledge is making you suffer, Subaru. I believe I cannot belittle it by saying that I understand."

"—"

"But even so, there is one thing that even I recognize."

"—"

"And that is, you are not someone who can give up on things before they're done, Subaru."

To the man lost in sorrow before her, who'd cast away everything, who had said he was giving up but a moment before, Rem said such a thing without shame, without fear, without hesitation.

"I know this."

"—"

"When it is a future you want, you smile when you talk about it, Subaru."

To the man who had spoken to her of running away to a world that was no doubt warm, peaceful, and tranquil, with guilt and regret on his face, Rem spoke plainly, without any disappointment.

"I know this."

"—"

"I know that you are a man who does not give up on the future, Subaru."

This, Rem declared to a young man hanging his head, seemingly gritting his teeth.

There was only sincerity in her eyes. They conveyed nothing but trust to him.

Subaru was overwhelmed by that powerful, intense light.

After all, Rem was wrong about him. So wrong, this was a veritable farce.

Her statements valued the human being called *Subaru* far too highly.

He didn't know how proud and noble the Subaru in her eyes must have been. But the real Subaru was nothing so fine a person as that.

Spouting weakness, crushed from adversity, lamenting his own smallness and pathetic misery, defeated and beaten so hard that he was running away—that was Subaru Natsuki.

"You're wro... I'm not that kind of person... I'm..."

"I am not mistaken. Lady Emilia, Sister, Master Roswaal, Miss Beatrice, and everyone else... I know you have not given up on them, Subaru."

She refuted him in a strong tone.

But she was wrong. He'd thrown away all of them.

"I gave up. I gave up! I can't take them with me...my hands are too small, everything falls out of them, then I have nothing left...!"

"No, that is not so. Subaru, you are—"

Just how far, how far, would Rem go in denying that Subaru had given up?

Why, after he had suffered such humiliation, did she so deny that he was in the wrong? Just what did she see in Subaru?

It was so disturbing that he couldn't take it anymore.

—Just what is it you're trying to say?

"—What! Do you! Think you know about me?!"

He vented the flames smoldering inside his chest in an incandescent rage. Subaru shouted angrily, slamming a fist into the wall right beside him. With a hard sound, his knuckles broke; when he waved his fist around, blood splattered onto the wall.

"This is all I am! I have high hopes even though I'm powerless; I have all these dreams even though I'm dumb; I keep trying even though I can't do anything...!"

Everyone had at least one thing they could do right. And everyone pushed that one thing as far as they could to find a place suited to them.

—But Subaru Natsuki didn't even have that.

The lofty heights he yearned for were far above his station.

"I…! I hate myself!!"

Faced with the truth that he'd smiled frivolously in an attempt to hide, making light of things as he kept running from them, never facing them seriously—for the first time, Subaru admitted what he really felt.

More than anyone, Subaru Natsuki hated himself.

"I'm always nothing but talk! I'm full of myself even though I can't do anything! I'm worse than useless, but I'm still a world-class complainer! Who the hell do I think I am?! How dare I live such a shameful life this long?! Right?!"

Because he was unable to raise himself higher, he'd tried to bring others down. Because he wouldn't admit he was inferior to others, he tried to find fault in everyone else to protect his banal, paper-thin pride.

"I'm empty. I've got nothing inside me. Of course I am… Yeah, it's obvious. There's no question! Until I came here, until I met all of you, do you know what I was doing?!"

Before he'd fallen into another world.

What was he doing in his former world except living out his idle, boring, ordinary, unchanging days one at a time—?

"—I…wasn't doing anything."

He'd wallowed in idleness, slumbered in indolence, spent his days far removed from studying and effort. It wasn't that he'd given up on himself but rather, he'd held on to the convenient idea that if the time came, he could just roll up his sleeves and do it.

"I didn't do anything… I didn't do one little thing! With all that time to do it! With all that freedom! I should have done lots of stuff, but I didn't do any of it! And this is the result! The result is the man I am now!"

If he'd properly used the time he had, even Subaru would surely have achieved something. But in reality, he had grandly squandered and wasted the time allotted to him, and as a result, he had gained nothing, and nothing had come from it.

That was why, now that he actually wanted from the bottom of his heart to accomplish something, he lacked the strength, intelligence, and skill to achieve any of it.

"I'm powerless, talentless, and all of it, all of it, is because of my rotten personality...! I want to achieve something when I haven't done anything before—conceited doesn't even begin to describe it... I was lazy and imposed on other people; I wasted my whole life away; I killed you."

He was unsalvageable. He was hopeless.

Even if he'd redone it all from birth, he'd probably go down the exact same path, waste his time in the exact same way, arrive there with the same feelings, and experience the same regrets. His rotten personality wouldn't change. A shallow human nature was the only one suited to the human being called Subaru Natsuki. That fact would never change.

"That's right, my personality hasn't... I thought I could live here, but not a single thing's changed about me. That old man saw right through me, didn't he?"

When he'd remained in the royal capital, Wilhelm had instructed him in the sword at the Crusch residence. Watching Subaru be knocked down time and time again, all beat up while challenging him over and over, the old man had nonetheless seen through it all.

During those days of training, the old man had spoken of those who wield the sword, but he had shaken his head and said, "There is little point lecturing someone about what it takes to become stronger when he has already abandoned the choice to do so."

At the time, Subaru hadn't understood what Wilhelm was saying, so he'd denied the old man's words—even though he knew deep down exactly what they meant.

"It's not like I really thought I'd get stronger or I'd be able to do anything... I just went through the motions...I was just a poser trying to justify myself..."

Emilia had abandoned him after he'd put on a more miserable display than any other at the royal selection site. Unable to bear being viewed as such by those around him, he tried to protect himself by adopting the mantle of a "hard worker" where those gazes could see. His behavior was the simple product of his search for a suitable excuse.

I'm changing myself. He should have known that the thought was itself proof that nothing had changed.

"I wanted to say, I couldn't help it! I wanted other people to say it couldn't be helped! That's all it was! That's the only reason I pretended to put myself on the line like that! Even when you were helping me study, I was just putting on a show to cover up the embarrassment! I'm a small, underhanded, filthy guy down to the bone, always worrying about what other people think of me, and none of that's ever changed…!"

His bluffs had been stripped away, and the hubris underneath had crumbled.

Once his thin shell was shattered, his vainglorious heart, not wanting to be thought of badly by others, and his ego, asserting that he wasn't wrong, poured out.

"…Even I knew. I understood all of it was my fault, really."

If he could yell that it was somebody else's fault, that there was some reason for it, it was easier. He wouldn't need to look at who he truly was. If he kept his facade intact, he'd never have to look at what was on the inside.

He wouldn't have to look at his ugly self. He wouldn't have others see it.

Though he was weak, selfish, and all talk, he wished to be loved nonetheless.

"I'm the worst… I—I hate me."

Subaru was short of breath after venting all the gloomy darkness tearing him up inside.

He'd let himself have it with all the filthy, corrupt things in him since coming to that other world—no, those dark things had been in him long before in his old world.

His nature as a human made even him want to puke.

Even though he'd spewed it all out, the deep feelings in his chest only soured further. Weren't you supposed to feel a little better after you vented something pent up inside?

On top of not feeling the slightest bit better, he realized with crystal clarity just how foolish he was. The shame seething inside him made him want to die then and there. And his weakness in exposing so much filth, thinking of nothing beyond his own concerns, was the stupidest thing of all.

With Rem standing right there, still believing in him, Subaru had tried to sully and stain the beautiful picture in front of her sparkling eyes, exposing it as a fraud. And now, after all that, he was more concerned with his own standing than with her.

That was it in a nutshell.

Truly accepting and recognizing the corrupt, flawed parts of himself that he hated didn't mean things were going to instantly improve. If anything, the depth and darkness of the chasm within him underlined just how incorrigible he was, robbing him even of his will to live.

The true character of Subaru Natsuki did not merit pity.

As Subaru sank to the lowest depths of his filthy ego, still, the blue-haired girl—

"I know this."

"—"

"I know that Subaru is someone with the courage to reach out, even with impenetrable darkness all around him."

—Even then, Rem would not forsake him.

5

Her absolute love, her inviolate trust, chafed upon Subaru like nothing before.

Having berated himself so much, having divulged so much of the ugliness in his heart, having confessed that he was a complete fraud, an unsalvageable piece of garbage—

—Why did she look at Subaru with such affectionate eyes?

"I love it when you stroke my head, Subaru. I feel connected to you when your hand passes through my hair."

With Subaru fallen into silence, Rem began to express something unexpected in a soft, quiet voice.

"I love your voice, Subaru. I feel my heart getting warmer from every single word. I love your eyes, Subaru. They're usually quite sharp, but I like how they become soft when you're being kind to someone."

Subaru said nothing as Rem continued, showering him with her words.

"I love your fingers, Subaru. They're very pretty for a boy's, but when they hold my hand, I always think to myself, 'They really are a boy's fingers.' They are slender and strong. I love how you walk, Subaru. When someone is beside you, you always check once in a while to make sure you really are side by side. I love that you walk that way."

His heart was screaming.

While Rem wove those words, Subaru's chest cried out.

"…Stop it."

"I love your face when you sleep, Subaru. You're as defenseless as a baby. Your eyelashes are just a little bit long. Your cheeks are so gentle when I touch them, and even if I touch your lips to tease you, you don't notice… I love it so much that it makes my chest hurt."

"Why…?"

Why was she still talking?

Why was she still able to toss out such compliments at Subaru, the useless fool that he was?

"You said that you hated yourself, Subaru, so I wanted you to know that you have so much good in you."

"None of that is real…!"

Rem was looking at a convenient illusion.

The real Subaru wasn't that kind of person. The real him was filthier than that. His genuine self was ugly, the exact opposite of the one she viewed so favorably.

"You just don't understand! I know more about myself than anyone else!"

"You only know about you, Subaru! How much do you know about the Subaru I see?!"

Reflexively, Subaru raised his voice, but Rem's shout was even louder than his own.

Subaru was shocked. It was the first time she'd raised her voice since they'd arrived here.

The shock made his breath catch in his throat. At long last, he realized that Rem's eyes, dutifully maintaining their neutral expression, had large teardrops welling in them.

Of course hearing Subaru's confession had hurt her.

Of course listening to his extreme masochism had brought pain to her kind heart.

Yet even so, she believed in Subaru.

Rem knew all the horrible things within him that he had told her about, and she believed in Subaru despite them.

"Why do you...? So much... I'm weak, puny... I'm running away...! Even now, I'm running away just like I did before, so why...?"

Why do you believe in a pathetic, unreliable guy drowning in his weakness like me...? If I can't believe in myself, how can you...?

"—Because you're my hero."

When those words of unconditional, infinite trust hit him, Subaru's heart quietly trembled.

No matter what awful conditions piled atop one another, no matter what flaws he might have, that one sentence was infused with the hope that he would come running and chase evil away.

And far too late, finally Subaru realized it.

He was wrong. He'd thought wrong. He had been so, so wrong.

He'd thought that she, Rem, was the only one who'd allow Subaru to fall as far as he needed to, that no matter how weak, pathetic, and humiliated he was, she'd forgive him—and he'd made a mistake.

It had been an error, a lethal degree of foolishness.

—Rem was the one, the only one, who would never allow Subaru to give in.

Everyone had told Subaru that he didn't have to do anything, that he should just behave himself. They had said that they expected nothing from him and that his actions were futile.

—But it was Rem who would not permit Subaru to be weak.

She was the only one who'd kept saying, *Stand up. Don't give up. Save everyone.*

No one expected anything from Subaru. But she had refused to abandon him, even when he had abandoned himself; nor would she accept his giving up.

Such was the "spell" that Subaru Natsuki had cast upon her.

"In that gloomy forest, a world where I had lost myself, a world where I could only lash out without thinking, you came and saved me."

"—"

"When I woke and was unable to move, when Sister was exhausted from having used too much magic, you stood up and faced the demon beasts as a decoy so that we could escape."

"—"

"You had no chance of winning, and your life was truly in danger, but even so, you survived…and when you returned to my arms, you were warm."

"—"

"When you woke up, you smiled and said the words I most wanted to hear, at the time I most wanted to hear them, and you were the person I most wanted to hear them from."

One by one, she enumerated the "spell" that Subaru had cast upon her.

Those spells had bound her deeply kind heart with the chains called trust, and these firmly bound her until that very moment.

"On that fiery night when I lost everything except Sister, time stopped for me, never to move again."

Rem gazed squarely at Subaru as she spoke of a fragment of her terrible past.

Her gaze was infused with intimacy that had not wavered to even the slightest degree.

"My heart had stopped, frozen in time, but you softly melted it and gently made it move again. Do you know how much you saved me in that instant, on that morning? You can't possibly know how happy I was, Subaru."

"That's why," said Rem, placing a hand on her chest as she continued.

"—I believe in you. No matter how much you might suffer, no matter how much things seem to be going against you, even if no one else in the whole world believes in you, even if you cannot believe in yourself—I believe in you, Subaru."

As Rem spoke, she took a step forward, closing the distance.

They were close enough to touch. Subaru, hanging his head, did not move as Rem reached out with both arms, wrapping them around his neck.

Even though there was very little strength in the pull, the unresisting Subaru could not avoid her embrace.

Though Subaru was taller, Rem held his head to her chest, and he heard her voice from directly above as she said, "The Subaru who saved me is a real hero."

From the slippery sensation on his forehead, he knew she had brushed it with her lips.

Heat spread from where she'd touched him. Incomprehensible emotions welled up deep inside Subaru's chest.

Blood flowed through his unmoving limbs. The static filling his skull began to clear—

"No matter how hard I tried, I couldn't save anyone."
"I'm here. The Rem you saved is right here, Subaru."

"I'm empty. There's nothing inside me. No one'll listen to me."
"I'm here. If they are Subaru's words, I want to hear whatever they might be."

"No one expects anything from me. No one trusts me... I...hate myself."

*　　*　　*

"I love you, Subaru."

The hand that touched his cheek was hot. Her eyes, gazing at Subaru from up close, were moist.

That look, everything about her, made him accept that she was truly sincere.

"You're…fine with a guy like me…?"

He'd tried over and over, redone over and over, and he had nothing to show for it.

Everyone died. His hand never reached them. He'd let everyone die. His thoughts were inadequate. He was empty, powerless, dumb, late to act, a blockhead dragged around by his desire to protect someone.

Was he really good enough for her?

"I'm fine with you, Subaru."

"—"

"I don't want it to be anyone else."

If he, who could not believe in himself, had someone who had faith in him…could Subaru Natsuki fight?

—He didn't have to give up on fighting Fate?

"If you really are that empty, if you have nothing, if you cannot forgive yourself—let's start over, here and now."

"Begin wh…?"

"Just like how you made time move again for me, we can make the time that stopped for you move again, right now."

He had taken his regret and shame at his past of achieving nothing, his days of doing nothing, his hours spent in waste and idleness, and tried to give up.

Rem smiled at this Subaru, stating:

"Let us start over from here, from step one… No, from zero!"

"—"

"If you find it difficult to walk alone, I shall support you. Let us divide the load and support each other as we walk. You said that to me on that morning, yes?"

So let's laugh, hug each other, and talk about tomorrow, he had said.

Leaning on each other, supporting each other as they walked, he had said.

"Please show me the best in you, Subaru."

He'd shown her nothing but the worst in him for the longest while. After all, it was Subaru himself who had cast the indelible "spell" upon her.

It was his duty to take responsibility and see it through.

"...Rem."

"Yes?"

When he called her name, she quietly responded.

He lifted his face. He looked straight ahead. He gazed into Rem's eyes.

Softly, gently, they awaited the reply from Subaru's lips.

So he wanted to be the Subaru Natsuki she loved so much.

"—I...like Emilia."

"—Yes."

Seemingly knowing all along, Rem smiled and nodded at Subaru's confession.

He knew full well how cruel he was being to that smile, that gentleness, as he continued, "I want to see Emilia's smile. I want to be in her future as a help to her. Even if she told me I'm in the way, not to come back... I want to be by her side."

Now that he'd accepted Rem's feelings, he again voiced the feeling that remained unchanged inside him. But the way he felt it was different from before.

"The idea that she'd put up with anything from me just because I liked her...was pretty arrogant, huh?"

"—"

"Even if she doesn't get it right now, that's fine. Right now, I want to save Emilia. If there's a future of pain and suffering coming for her, I want to bring her to a future where everyone can smile."

So he offered his hand to Rem, right at his side, and asked, "Will you...help me?"

He knew it was an underhanded way to respond to the feelings she had offered to him. He knew he was using her emotions. But it was that Subaru, the Subaru who would not give up on the future of those precious to him, whom she loved.

"I can't do anything by myself. I come up short in everything. I don't have the confidence to just walk straight ahead. I'm so weak, fragile, and puny, so… Will you lend me a hand? Help keep me on the straight and narrow when I take a wrong turn?"

"You are a terrible person, Subaru. Right after you dump a girl, you ask such a thing?"

"Hey, it's pretty tough for me to ask someone who turned down a once-in-a-lifetime proposal of mine, you know?"

Rem was unable to hold back a little sigh at Subaru's weak chuckle.

They smiled at each other for a while. Then Rem straightened up, elegantly grasped the hem of her skirt, and in a display of perfect courtesy, she said, "If this will bring a future where Subaru, my hero, can smile, then I humbly accept."

"Yeah, you just watch. You'll have a front-row seat."

Rem took the hand Subaru had offered as they exchanged their vows. She let out a small "Ah" as Subaru drew her close, burying her petite body in his chest. He was grateful that there existed a girl so soft, so warm, and who liked him so much.

"—The man you fell in love with is gonna be the coolest hero there ever was!"

It was hot within her breast.

As Subaru embraced Rem, she buried her face in his chest, hiding her expression.

Her breathing was hot. Her forehead and cheeks were hot as she rubbed them against him.

But the tears flowing from her eyes were probably the hottest of all.

—Even then, Subaru could not like himself. He still hated himself.

But a girl had told Subaru she liked him.

If there was a girl who could like him, just as he was…

*   *   *

—Emilia was watching. Rem was watching. He could not yield.

"—"

The tale of Subaru Natsuki would begin anew.
His life in another world would start over.

—From zero.

CHAPTER 6
THE CARD THAT'S BEEN DEALT

1

The room was silent but filled with a strained sense of tension.

Feeling that tension on his skin, Subaru moistened his parched lips with his tongue, grateful that arrangements for the first step of the scenario were in place.

To Subaru, each and every face now present was absolutely indispensable. After all, he had no strength of his own. Lacking ability and manpower, all he could do by himself was to die in vain as he had done to that point.

"Now I can finally understand why you have gathered us here and delayed my supper."

Crusch Karsten, sitting on the sofa with her hands crossed atop her knees, broke the silence, murmuring with a look of understanding on her gallant face.

"Reawwy? To be honest, Ferri still has some doubts, *meow*. I mean, how does such a clumsy boy get that look in his eyes all of a sudden?"

With an expression as casual as his tone, Ferris kept his guard up as he gazed at Subaru. He was brimming with a willingness to defend his lord from any danger.

"—"

In contrast to Ferris, Wilhelm kept his silence as he sat to Crusch's left. Wearing his sword on his hip, the aged swordsman closed his eyes, with only his refined martial spirit hovering about him. There was no trace remaining of the warmth with which he had greeted them upon their return from the lower city. Now, he was wholly immersed in his role as a man wielding his sword for his master, Crusch, rather than for himself.

Subaru was meeting Crusch and her retainers in the reception room of her residence, a place of which Subaru had few good memories. Twice in the past, he had endured bitter hardships there.

He was meeting with Crusch, Ferris, and Wilhelm. That much was the same as before. But there was something different this time.

"It feels somewhat uncomfortable to be back so soon after my first visit. I fully expect that Mr. Natsuki will say something to sweep away such misgivings."

The blond man of delicate features, defined by his comical beard, commented with a chuckle. This was Russel Fellow, a representative of the Merchant's Guild who possessed great influence in the royal capital.

Subaru lightheartedly slumped a little at Russel's apparent diversion.

"Rem's calling one more person over right now, so please wait just a little longer. It isn't guaranteed my guest is coming but…it's a good bet."

"I await a prompt arrival. Incidentally, may I inquire as to your evidence for this 'good bet'?"

Russel didn't even blink in the face of Subaru's presumptuous statement. Subaru's lips twisted as he faced off against a real merchant with a head, mouth, and tongue superior to his own.

"It's a simple story. The person I invited is sensitive to the smell of money, or so I heard them say personally. If that's true, there's no doubt. That was true for you as well, wasn't it, Russel?"

"My, my, you certainly have me there."

Russel put a hand to his forehead, seemingly indicating that Subaru had scored a point on him. Of course, even Subaru wasn't blithe enough to take the gesture at face value.

He was well aware of the danger posed by the narrow tightrope he planned to walk. The rope was just about set to be tied on both ends.

The crossing was yet to come.

Subaru would do it, supported by the power of borrowed courage.

A few minutes later, the door opened and a lone girl—Rem—appeared.

"I am sorry to have kept you all waiting."

"That's okay!"

Subaru brought up his right thumb with a wink as she walked to his side and leaned her face close to his ear.

"She said that she would be slightly delayed but that she would definitely come."

"—That so. All right, good work, Rem."

With that, preparations for Subaru's tightrope performance were complete.

Before arriving at the negotiating table, he'd prepared the argument he would use to move the deal in the direction he desired. Subaru's memories and experiences in this new world had led him to a single answer.

"Apparently, the last participant will arrive slightly late, but all the actors will be on the stage. No point waiting any further—should we start?"

Subaru's statement brought a change in the air and various reactions from others in the room. Crusch made a thin smile; Ferris strongly pursed his lips. Wilhelm maintained his silence, his expression unchanging even then. Russel slowly sank into his chair.

Seeing their reactions, Subaru took a deep breath and calmed his emotions.

He could feel his own heart pounding rapidly. His blood circulated throughout his body. The deep anxiety simultaneously residing in his head made everything before his eyes seem to dim.

But Rem, right beside Subaru, gently touched his sleeve in an effort to put him at ease.

"Subaru."

She wasn't holding his hand, nor was she asserting her own existence. That little act of consideration was very Rem-like. The sense of relief enveloping him was as if ten thousand cavalry were riding to his aid.

Rem was watching. He could not disappoint.

"—Okie."

Subaru hid his fears behind an impetuous smile and challenged the first wall.

He needed to thread the eye of a needle, both to get to a Happy End and to take one step closer to becoming a hero—for the sake of the girl who believed in him, the girl who'd told him she liked him.

Just as Subaru lifted his spirits and faced forward, Crusch raised a finger and spoke.

"Subaru Natsuki, there is something I wish to confirm—I would hear, from your own lips, the purpose of this gathering."

As she sat, she raised a hand and rested her chin against it as her sagacious gaze landed on Subaru. Even though she knew full well the answer to her question, her posture showed no sign of softness that would allow Subaru to say so.

Now that he had failed time and time again, he understood.

—The game was on before he had even spoken a single word.

"Of course, what I want is—"

So Subaru made a grandiose gesture, smiling powerfully to keep himself from being cowed by Crusch's rapier-like gaze and repeating his earlier failures.

"A negotiation so that the Emilia camp and the Crusch camp can become allies on equal terms."

He thus began to challenge the first of many obstacles standing in his way.

2

The exchange with Rem along Main Street had made Subaru decide to restart in a true sense.

This was his sincere answer to Rem, who'd told Subaru she believed in him even after he'd bared everything inside his heart. Thanks to that, he gained a clear awareness of what he had to do.

"There's way too many walls I have to climb over to get there, huh...?"

The sheer number of the obstacles standing in their way didn't change the fact that they were one move away from checkmate.

Subaru scratched his head as if he was trying to put his thoughts in order.

"But I've still gotta do something. Will you help me, Rem?"

"Yes. If that is what you desire, Subaru..."

Rem readily nodded.

Even after Subaru opened up to her, the same trust hovered in Rem's eyes as before. They lit two fires inside Subaru: courage and a sense of duty.

Subaru no longer held any thought of hiding from Rem his own humiliation and panic at having his hands tied. After all, he'd half bawled his eyes out while venting every complex he had. Rem, too, had revealed truths that had raged within her; in a true sense, Subaru and Rem were now friends for life.

And because Subaru had set his heart on something, his head remained remarkably clear.

"First, let's double-check the time we have left. If we head back now, that'll be just under an hour...and then..."

As previously established, the time limit until the Witch Cult caused upheaval in the Mathers domain was five days—or rather, to be precise, they had a grace period of only four and a half days. He also needed to consider the sealing of the highway during that time. In reality, he had only two days to prepare.

"And those two days are full of unavoidable problems to deal with."

The number and nature of the barred gates they had to bust through put previous sets of loops to shame. Clearing any of them alone was hopeless. A fist large enough to smash through the lot of them was required.

The first problem was, naturally, the Witch Cult. If they didn't stop the fanatics under Petelgeuse's command, there was no way to save anyone at the mansion, let alone the residents of the village.

The second was, though the killer and means had been varied, Rem's certain death.

Even if Rem went with Subaru, fate would invariably lead her to her death. The first time, she'd died far from where he could see. And he had been despondent when she was lost to him before his very eyes the second and third times. It was no exaggeration that the shock was what had driven Subaru down the path of giving up entirely.

The third problem was that Emilia's death would trigger an indiscriminate rampage by Puck, the Great Spirit.

Thinking back, Subaru deemed the possibility that Puck had been the cause of his death on all three loops to be very high. When he considered his icy demises from the first time around through the third, he was almost certain of it.

All those walls were formidable, but all three had to be grappled with, or else the future world Subaru Natsuki wanted to live in would be lost. That would mean betraying the image of the hero who Rem believed in.

"—Whole bunch of 'em."

Subaru murmured under his breath, underlining the depth of the problem.

Rem, watching Subaru as he sank into thought, made no reply to his murmur, nor had Subaru been looking for one. Subaru knew that she was simply waiting for the words that had to follow.

She was waiting for the best judgment of how she might contribute greatest to the hero she loved the most. That was the present Rem's reason for existing and her ultimate means of expressing her love.

With Rem silently watching him, Subaru used his limited time to search his memories for any clue, any way to break out of the trap of limited time.

—His head tied itself into knots. His mind was on fire. Neither his flesh, nor his abilities, could live up to those current ideals.

—*Think. Remember.*

To not let his death that third time be in vain, to not let the will of the girl he'd let die that third time be lost in vain, Subaru's mind assembled everything that had happened during that third, finished world into one heavy pile.

The people he'd met. The conversations he'd had. Partings. Encounters. Anger, madness, sadness, despair, recovery.

And—

"There's a…possibility?"

Suddenly, something little more than a single option rose up in the back of his mind. Each of the threads was weak, so fragile that tying them together threatened to make them collectively snap. They seemed far too unreliable to rest his hopes upon.

—But he was all in. It was worth a shot.

"Rem. We need to talk. I have a few things I wanna ask you."

"Yes?"

Subaru sought Rem's cooperation in drafting the plan that he'd only just thought of in his head.

"Now that Emilia's participating in the royal selection, it looks like the Witch Cult is gonna move. If they go after Emilia, there'll no doubt be harm to the mansion and the village. I wanna stop that."

"The Witch Cult…"

A grave look came over Rem's eyes the instant she heard the words. But as Rem nodded at Subaru's words, her self-control held those emotions in check.

"Master Roswaal also has concerns that the Witch Cult might make a move. Though I do not know the details, I believe that he has studied the matter and drawn up countermeasures."

"But that's not gonna be enough."

In fact, Subaru didn't really know what countermeasures he'd taken against the Witch Cult. He didn't know if they hadn't been executed or if they had just proven ineffective. Either way, whatever preexisting preparations Roswaal had set weren't up to the task, and he knew that hell would come to pass without fail.

Now that Subaru knew that future, he had to secure the power to protect the lives at the mansion and the village without relying on Roswaal.

"I'm pretty sure the Witch Cult is gonna come in a quick, decisive battle. Rem, what does the mansion have to fight with?"

"…This is a difficult thing to tell you, but the possibility Master Roswaal is absent from the mansion is quite high. He had planned to visit an important associate within his domain upon his return from the royal capital."

Based on Rem's prevaricating reply, the situation was the same as last time. Roswaal wasn't there. The only people at the mansion at present were Emilia, Ram, and Beatrice. Only three people, and one of them was Beatrice. He was deeply suspicious that the uncooperative girl would willingly engage the Witch Cult in battle.

That made Subaru recall the exchange between Beatrice and him the last time around, if only a brief one. He remembered that he'd asked Beatrice to kill him. He remembered Beatrice's face, turning eyes toward him like that of a child whose hopes had been betrayed—

"Right now…I've gotta set that aside."

Subaru somehow brushed off the girl's tearful gaze and faced Rem once more.

"So that leaves two people to fight. Even if you and I go back there, we'd just be two drops against a bucket."

"As the majority of the main residence's fighting strength rests with Master Roswaal's personal abilities, I cannot deny it. If Frederica was still with us, it might be a different story, but…"

Rem lowered her gaze as she ruefully invoked the name of a former coworker at the mansion. Subaru patted her shoulder in consolation as he mentally filled the gaps in his own understanding.

There was no point speaking any further of the mansion's available combat strength. Therefore, the next issue was the main one.

"Rem."

Subaru sat up straight and stared at Rem. Then, as Rem, detecting that the atmosphere had changed, lifted her face and looked at him, he said, "Please tell me what Roswaal ordered you to stay in the royal capital to do."

"—"

Subaru thought her expression was dubious, or perhaps surprised that he had gone for an unguarded opening.

However, Rem's reaction thoroughly defied Subaru's expectations.

"—Yes. As you wish, Subaru."

Rem nodded to Subaru as a small smile came over her, as if she was happy from the bottom of her heart. A single tear rolled down from the corner of her eye.

3

"An alliance...you say."

He was now in the reception room at the Crusch residence.

Crusch murmured with all eyes falling upon Subaru as he answered her question concerning the goal of the meeting.

She lowered her head, falling into thought briefly before shifting her gaze from Subaru to Rem. Rem quietly deduced the meaning of her probing gaze and slowly shook her head.

"In accordance with Master Roswaal's instructions, I have proposed nothing—this is something Subaru arrived at by himself."

"I do not doubt your loyalty. However...I see..."

The face Crusch made seemed to indicate that she understood, even if she did not exactly accept it.

"Then should I take this to mean the right to engage in these negotiations has...shifted from Rem to you, Subaru Natsuki?"

"Yeah, that's what it amounts to. Roswaal was a real jerk with how roundabout he set this up, though."

With an exaggerated sigh, Subaru expressed his personal thoughts as his clown-faced employer floated into the back of his mind.

Secret orders concerning the royal capital had been kept from Subaru, handed down to Rem alone. Roswaal had strictly instructed Rem not to reveal the details to Subaru so long as he did not realize that fact for himself.

"It's not like it wasn't bothering me a little from the start. In the first place, it's plain as day that our side is short on manpower. So he'd leave Rem in the capital without a set plan? Rem, the one from the mansion who'd be most missed? There's no way. I really should've realized that earlier."

Of course, the cover story was that Roswaal couldn't take responsibility for healing and repaying the man who'd saved his own domain from crisis without at least a single person to look after him.

"But I don't think that eccentric would let go of Rem for a humanitarian reason like that. When you think, 'There's gotta be something else going on'…"

Crusch recrossed her legs, picking up where Subaru left off to state her conclusion.

"So he naturally settled on her as the one who had the best opportunity for an audience with my house…"

"Besides, I heard that Rem and Crusch were having secret meetings every night. I hate myself for being an idiot and not considering what the discussions were about, though."

He couldn't even manage a laugh for how he'd been unable to see beyond himself that whole time. After all, even though Rem had actually dropped plenty of hints to convey Roswaal's secret intentions, it had taken him until the fourth time to look back and realize it.

"So every night you've been meeting about forming an alliance. I heard from Rem all about what my side's offering for the terms of the deal."

"The deal chiefly concerns magic crystals in the Great Elior Forest and the mining rights thereof."

Just like that, Crusch exposed what Subaru's words had only hinted at, seeing that there was nothing to hide. The instant the words reached the ears of the lone merchant present, his eyes glimmered.

"My, my, that is quite a fascinating tale."

Russel, who had maintained his silence to that point, positively glowed. He sounded pleased now that the details finally concerned him in some way.

"When one considers how magical stone craftsmanship has advanced by leaps and bounds in recent years, magic crystal mining rights hold ever-increasing value. That goes all the more for virgin territory."

Subaru could not conceal his surprise that the merchant had bit on the hook harder than expected. When he'd first heard about the mining rights from Rem, the fact that Crusch had held out so far convinced Subaru that it wasn't all that attractive an offer.

"Does it really have enough value to put you in such a good mood, Russel?"

"But of course. Magical stone craftsmanship thrives in the markets of Kararagi, and magic crystal craftsmen of my own nation have polished their talents over many years. Recently, their products can be seen here and there, even gracing the hands of the general public. These days, the more magic crystals the better. Until now, we have relied upon trade with Gusteko to the north for most of our supply, so I am overjoyed to learn of the existence of a rich local vein."

Russel held up a finger and spoke with a buoyant tone as he answered.

"A magic crystal is composed of mana; it is pure crystallized magic. Their attributes are greatly influenced by the land of their origin and the skill of the craftsman who wrought them. In turn, the hand of a skilled craftsman can be applied to a variety of magic crystal crafts. If not mishandled, their intensity is excellent, lasting reliably for a period of several years. Surely it goes without saying that they make for very attractive merchandise."

In contrast to Russel, listing all the good points adding to the value of magic crystals, Crusch went on to coolly enumerate the parts that diminished their value.

"However, the craftsmen able to work magic stones are few in number. Once a magic stone has been wrought, it is unprofitable to redo the work. At present, many mines have been placed under the kingdom's management, with the majority of magic crystals being distributed for public works. Though you say some reach the general public, it represents only a fraction."

Undaunted, Russel carried on.

"There are no untouched mining sites that are not immediately snapped up the moment they are found. There is a rich history of succeeding generations of the marquis of Mathers tapping undiscovered veins to build a fortune. And we have the knight of Lady

Emilia, a candidate in the royal selection, to vouch for it. It is a trust-worthy bet."

Russel spoke in a fervent tone, slyly glancing at Subaru all the while. He had quite a rotten personality to know of Subaru's humili-ation at the royal palace and still declare his word to be proof of any-thing. Nor did Subaru forget that dressing up the issue of mining rights in such a frivolous manner was meant to hold him in check. Russel was driving home for Subaru that this could not be unheard.

Not that Subaru had the slightest intention of backing out to begin with.

"Yeah, I don't mind if you trust that. I don't think we're villains enough to bluff at the first people we team up with over the course of a long royal selection."

Subaru could rest easy because Roswaal had been the one to pro-pose selling the mining rights.

Russel seemed to recoil deliberately in response to Subaru's answer.

"I see. You would appear to have truly embraced the role of negoti-ator. I apologize for my rudeness in speaking as if I was testing you."

"Nah, it's fine. After all, I plan on using all the stuff you just said for all it's worth over the rest of the conversation."

Subaru hadn't expected Russel to rate him highly to begin with. He'd correctly surmised that his ability would come into question and his measure would be taken then and there. He'd prepared a topic offering an easy avenue of attack, avoiding an assault on a far more pernicious front before broaching the main issue. He could not conceal his relief that the bait had been taken as intended.

He put on meaninglessly grandiose airs of amiability to conceal the tension in his cheeks.

"Having said that, since he's apologized, I expect you to overlook one or two rude things I might say."

"So you seated Russel Fellow at the same table in hopes of this? You are an unexpectedly crafty man yourself."

As Subaru flippantly commented, Crusch smiled slightly and voiced her appraisal to end the exchange. The fact that she hadn't ended the discussion seemed to indicate she hadn't given him a failing grade.

Even as he felt a cold sweat at having climbed over the first gate, Subaru maintained his friendly smile as he looked at Crusch.

"Well, I also wanted an adviser, since this is talking about profits, but…calling Russel here has to do with the main topic coming next."

"Really now? The main topic?"

Subaru continued, and the atmosphere inside the room grew tense once more.

Crusch, who had merely been humoring the conversation to that point, rectified her seating and quietly closed her eyes for a time. After that, she slowly opened her amber eyes; their gaze pierced Subaru like an arrow.

Before its power, sufficient to bring to mind a cold, blowing wind, Subaru did not falter. The tightening of his mind served only to make him straighten his back and put his feelings in order as he faced her.

"Subaru Natsuki, I formally acknowledge you as the proxy of Marquis Roswaal, and also as an envoy from Emilia, and whatever details you and I negotiate will also hold true between Emilia and me."

All it took for her to overwhelm people was for her to face them head-on.

Crusch was not intentionally attempting to bowl Subaru over at that moment. All she'd done was switch mental gears from Crusch, the private individual, to Crusch Karsten, the public persona. Such was the power and presence of the current duke of Karsten.

—This was what the valiant woman closest to the Kingdom of Lugunica's throne really looked like.

Subaru felt goose bumps rise as exclamation points danced inside his head. As he quietly shuddered, Crusch extended a hand to him, firing the opening salvo to announce the start of the negotiations.

"I believe you have already heard, but I shall state it regardless. Rem and I were negotiating the sale of mining rights, but I have not accepted the offer. Though I imagine you already knew this?"

"...Yeah."

On the one hand was Rem, visibly lamenting her own insufficient strength; on the other hand was Subaru, pathetically unable to look past himself to even notice what had caused her such anguish. Subaru would take those two laments and regrets and put them to good use to avoid future distress—and so that all his previous failures would not be in vain.

"I wanna make sure of something myself. So the offer just isn't good enough as it stands? Each camp lays off the other, mining rights for the Great Elior Forest are sold to you, and you work out the fine details of what to do with the magic crystals themselves later?"

"The draft proposal came from Rem's side. I suppose I should say, as to be expected of Marquis Roswaal. On top of securing profit for his own camp, he offers just enough advantage so that my house might accept it. Normally, it is an offer one would never refuse. Such a proposal makes me want to have a written agreement prepared immediately, but..."

Subaru couldn't speak in any informed manner about the arithmetic behind the deal. If he did clumsily say something, it could wind up being taken as, *Okay, take all the mining rights, then!*

"In this case, what would follow such negotiations is the problem. Do you understand?"

"It's not simply that...you don't trust Roswaal?"

Subaru was of the opinion that if Roswaal's conduct was being questioned, he could rectify that by behaving with absolute propriety henceforth, but that wasn't Crusch's problem with it.

"Making a deal with Emilia would mean an agreement with a rival royal selection candidate... Furthermore, one slandered as a half-demon. If one considers the consequences, caution is inevitable."

Subaru was unexpectedly discouraged to hear Crusch quietly speak such words. The image he had of Crusch was of someone so steadfast, the words *majestic* and *sincere* suited her. She had been the living incarnation of those things when stating her convictions at the royal selection conference. It was precisely because he had heard her address that made her acting as if she cared about rumors seem so odd—

"Don't tell me this is merely a justification for saying no?"

"—"

"Subawu? Ferri thinks that is really, really not the sort of thing you should say during an important negotiation?"

Ferris had held his silence since the start of negotiations, but Subaru's careless remark brought anger to his smile. A vein on his forehead was bulging as Subaru quickly covered his mouth and lowered his head.

"Goodness, this puts me in a bit of a bind."

As he did so, Crusch, watching the exchange, loosened the corners of her lips very slightly.

"It is I who is embarrassed to have my justification exposed so bluntly. I shall learn from this. The opportunity does not often arise."

With convoluted logic, she overlooked Subaru's present rudeness. That said, being saved by the awkwardness of his opponent's position put him in a precarious place.

"So that is an excuse for… Then you don't really think that forming an alliance with Emilia is a terrible thing in and of itself?"

"Subaru Natsuki, I shall correct one misconception."

Crusch raised a finger, pointing it toward Subaru.

"A person's worth is decided by how her soul lives and how it shines. A person's true nature is absolutely not determined by the circumstances of one's birth and where someone was raised."

Of course, even Crusch understood that they had an indirect influence. She did not lack the power of imagination to deduce how the senseless cruelties inflicted by Emilia's environment, simply because she was a half-elf, had strengthened her in the process.

"Her words at the royal selection site were not false. It is because I am certain of her pride and resolve that I acknowledge Emilia as a rival."

"Well, that's convoluted. In other words?"

"Forgive me. I have a fondness for theatrics."

Crusch pursed her lips slightly, seemingly fully aware of just how grandiose her own statement was. A moment later, her expression tightened.

"I am not refusing an alliance with Emilia because she is a half-elf. From my perspective, Emilia, who is in no way politically opposed to me, is not someone I need to go out of my way to antagonize. I would even be willing to ally with her."

"Meaning that…"

"Do not be so hasty to reply, Subaru Natsuki. It is no exaggeration to say that what you utter, and how your words are interpreted, will determine the course of these events."

Crusch chided Subaru for assuming her reply was favorable as she threw the ball into his court once more. In other words, now that Subaru held the right to negotiate, she wanted to see what cards were in his hand.

"Mining rights for the Great Elior Forest would be highly advantageous for my side. On the other hand, it is a fact that there is no need for me to rush to get ahead in the royal selection. The period of time is three years. Too much haste to stir things up would sow the seeds for troubles down the road."

"So you're saying the advantages and disadvantages of forming an alliance with Emilia don't match up?"

"Not precisely. At present, the advantages and disadvantages cancel each other out. By my house's thinking, we require convincing, a push for us to take that one final step."

Crusch seemed personally in favor of the idea of forming an alliance. On the other hand, a noble house was apparently too large to be swayed purely by Crusch's private opinion on the matter.

Hence, she sought "something" from Subaru—something that would silence the voices around her urging her not to stir things up.

"__"

When Subaru tried to speak, he was a little surprised at how his own throat seemed to be blocked. The tension and anxiety welling up in his chest blocked his throat just as he was on the verge of stepping forward.

From here on would be completely ad-libbed in a way he had never before experienced.

He hadn't checked it with anyone. It was possible he was reading this wrong.

But Crusch would probably bite.

—Yes. Subaru believed in his own idea.

"To form an alliance, we're offering mining rights...and information."

"—Information?"

When she heard the word, Crusch stroked her own long hair as she prompted him to continue.

She hadn't decided yet. Now came the hard part.

"Yeah, that's right. I'm offering a certain piece of information with it."

"Then I would hear it. Will these words from your lips stir us to action?"

Naturally, Subaru's entire body trembled from anxiety and tension.

But a slight warm sensation to his elbow drove all that away, for Rem's fingers, touching Subaru's arm, were the spark that lit the borrowed courage within him.

Subaru inhaled. In a single breath, he said:

"—The card I'm playing...is the time and place where the White Whale will show up."

AFTERWORD

Thank you very much! This is Volume 6. This is Tappei Nagatsuki. This is also Mouse-Colored Cat.

This time around, let me say words of thanks before anything else. Namely, I am truly grateful that you have stuck with this work, *Re:ZERO -Starting Life in Another World-*, all this time.

Arriving at the contents of this sixth volume of a work originally serialized on the web was one of the milestones I set when I started. When I reached this point during the web serialization, I had a sense of achievement then, too. I am purely grateful, and honored, to be able to relive that sense of achievement by getting it in print. Truly, thank you very much.

I wonder how the contents of this volume were for all of you who have stuck around for the tale to this point. Even in the web version, the parts I put most of my efforts into as an author were the parts that garnered the largest reactions. At the time, the author and the readers of the web comic shared that sense of achievement. If many of you reading this book come off feeling the same way, there is no greater accomplishment.

When people commented on the web version, they said things like, "This is strong stuff, you've gotta end it here (^_^)," but don't worry, he really does recover and go on the counterattack. Along with the main character, I will strive so that everyone sticking around during these greatly frustrating developments will be able to appreciate them.

Now then, as is customary, here are the last of the thanks and apologies.

To Mr. I the editor, you've been a huge help for this entire series. Since the content of this sixth volume was, I believe, the biggest trigger for your calling me up to begin with, thank you very much for helping me reach this point.

For Otsuka-sensei the illustrator, forgive me for the especially large number of guidelines for the illustrations in this volume. There were a lot of them, starting with the no-spoilers cover illustration. In particular, I was really worried about the last illustration, so thank you, thank you, thank you. Also, the two cover illustrations, for the normal edition and the special edition, are just over-the-top cute. The special edition version was even more amazing. Are you a god?!

And for Kusano-sensei the designer, thank you very much for having given this a thumbs-up. I can't get enough of those cover illustrations, and I am extremely, deeply grateful to have the *Re:ZERO* series showing off its best. Please take good care of me from here on out.

Also, the *Re:ZERO* comic versions are going fantastic! Daichi Matsuse-sensei is handling Arc 1 in *Monthly Comic Alive*, and Makoto Fuugetsu-sensei is handling Arc 2 in *Monthly Big Gangan*. I'm sorry for pushing you to publish in parallel with this sixth LN volume, so thank you very much. Matsuse-sensei will also be taking care of Arc 3 later. Best regards.

As always, to all the other people whose cooperation made this work possible, including everyone at the MF Bunko J editorial department, sales managers, copy editors, bookstore salespeople, truly, thank you very much.

I am even more grateful from the bottom of my heart for all the warm messages and fan letters all of you readers are sending me. Thank you very much for having read this volume.

Well, let us meet again next volume. Expect both author and main character to put up a good fight.

February 2015
Tappei Nagatsuki
(Who got the date wrong for the first
signing event of the year)

Afterword

Until now, I have been a Ram loyalist, but in this volume, Rem brought me to my knees. Rem-lin,

M-M-M-M-MARRY ME PLEASE!

Shinichirou Otsuka

Subaru

"Sooo, this is the traditional next volume preview corner we have every book. In this volume, you saw loud clear that Rem and I have a partnership for life. Let's give this our best shot."

"Yes, leave it to me. If it is for your sake, I will do my best as much as needed."

"Hey, this is still the main story so don't glom too much! They asked us to do this, but it's a little embarrassi〟

"Tee-hee, you are wonderful even when trying to cover up your blushes, Subaru. Now, the introductions. Th are many notifications this time around, aren't there?"

"Y-yeah. Right! First, the comic versions in *Monthly Comic Alive* and *Monthly Big Gangan* are selling like h cakes! The *Alive* version's Volume 2 and the *Gangan* version's Volume 1 went on sale at the same time as the l〟 novel Volume 6 here! They're both filled with their own special stuff, so go check 'em out!"

"*Alive* is also publishing a *Re:ZERO* novel short story every month. A second short story compilatio〟 planned to go on sale in June. They show off Subaru working hard at the mansion quite a bit, so I am very ha〟 about it."

Rem

"It's a little weird having people happy to see me shown off that much, but anyway, a second edition means a ?ond go at that! The Ministop joint project is back! *Re:ZERO* is back at a convenience store near you!"

"Are they going to sell Subaru body pillows, too? I'd buy a hundred of them."

"Er, you can check the *Re:ZERO* public website and Twitter for the details, but there's probably no body pillow ?me, okay?! But there will be a pile of ultra-fan goods that'll put the last campaign to shame!"

"Is that so, there will not be a body pillow... That is a pity, but I am consoled somewhat to see a rubber strap is ?ning with the *Monthly Comic Alive* special edition."

"Using that as the lead-in to smoothly introduce something else... You're a scary girl, Rem!"

"It has been decided that Daichi Matsuse-sensei will be handling Arc 3 in *Monthly Comic Alive*. There will be ?en *tankobans* in all. I really won't be able to take my eyes off you, Subaru."

"It's not just me in them. Expect good stuff out of everybody! Well, there you have it, see ya next volume!"

"You are wonderful even when you blush and run away, Subaru."